Once upon a time, Romy dreamed of living in one of the fairy tales in her head. But she grew up in Durban, South Africa – not exactly the sort of place where fairy tale princesses grow up. It took the help of a great many fairy godmothers, the slaying of a few dragons, and not nearly enough pretty glass shoes, for Romy to eventually became the princess she'd always dreamed of being.

As a 2016 finalist for the Romance Writers of America® RITA Award, and as Chairperson of ROSA (Romance writers Organisation of South Africa), all of Romy's dreams have come true. She is not only a multi-published author, but as a writing coach and teacher, she now helps make other writers' dreams come true too.

Though Romy's heart lies in Europe, she doesn't cope well with the cold, so she lives in sunny South Africa, in the City of Gold, Johannesburg, where she is mom to two little princesses and a pet dragon (okay, he's a bearded dragon, but that counts!)

She writes contemporary fairy tale romances and short 1920s historical romances.

romysommer.com

Also by Romy Sommer

Waking Up in Vegas
The Trouble with Mojitos
To Catch a Star
Not a Fairy Tale
Last of the Summer Vines

My Best Friend's Royal Wedding

Romy Sommer

One More Chapter
a division of HarperCollins*Publishers*
The News Building
1 London Bridge Street
London SE1 9GF

www.harpercollins.co.uk

This paperback edition 2020

First published in Great Britain in ebook format by
HarperCollins*Publishers* 2020

A catalogue record for this book
is available from the British Library

ISBN: 9780008353582

Set in Birka by Palimpsest Book Production Ltd, Falkirk
Stirlingshire

Printed and bound in Great Britain by
CPI Group (UK) Ltd, Croydon CR0 4YY

Dedicated to the ladies of Coffee Club, who keep me sane and motivated, and who give me an excuse to drink both coffee and champagne (not that anyone ever needs an excuse for either!)

Prologue

Khara

"You're off the floor tonight." My boss grabs at my elbow as I slide behind the bar. "They need you upstairs in the private dining room. One of their waitresses didn't show."

"Why me? Surely they could use one of the regular restaurant servers?" I set the tray of dirty glasses down beside the sink and face him. "I just serve drinks."

"Taking food orders isn't much different from taking drinks orders, and you're our most experienced waitress."

I roll my eyes. 'Most experienced' means nothing more than 'the loser who's been serving drinks since the moment she was legally allowed to, and still hasn't got out.'

"Big tippers?" I ask.

Frank shrugs. "You never can tell with the kind of guests who book the private rooms. They like to throw their money around, but when it comes to remembering the hired help ...? You might get lucky, you might not."

I really don't want to do this. I'm comfortable here on the casino floor, where I know the score and the tips are good. My friend Phoenix would have been a much better choice, but she's off back-packing around Europe at the moment. I squeeze my eyes shut for a second at the thought of Europe, a place that has always seemed magical but impossibly unreal. The odds of me ever doing something so impetuous are so low no bookie would risk taking that bet.

Frank tries again. "Khara, you said you wanted to move onward and upward. Maybe this will lead to a permanent promotion." He grips my arm, his expression serious. "You know I don't want to lose you, but you're better than this." He nods toward the casino floor, toward the constant ding-ding-ding of slot machines, the never-ending night, and I hear what he doesn't say: Don't end up like me.

"Fine. But can I get a moment to change first?" I glance down at my black tank top bearing the casino's logo, where an over-enthusiastic gambler slopped beer on me earlier.

"Sure, just remember to keep it classy. Then get your skinny ass upstairs quick as you can. Wouldn't want to keep Their Highnesses waiting."

I laugh. Frank is one of the reasons I haven't already quit this job. Only in his world would my ass be considered skinny.

In the cramped staff locker room, I strip off my top and hot pants and stuff them into my locker. There is one sure-fire way to earn tips in a casino, and dressing classy isn't it. Luckily, I always keep a dress in the locker in case of emergencies – like an unexpected hot date. With its above-the-knee skirt and plunging neckline, the little black skater dress might not be quite the look management has in mind for its restaurant servers, but it's classier than the other options I have stashed in there, and yet still guaranteed to get me noticed. And getting noticed is the best way to earn tips.

I hurry up the back stairs to the restaurant. While the casino floor is where the everyday tourists and slot machine addicts hang out, the upstairs restaurant is where the people with money go. It was decorated by a famous interior designer, and has a Mediterranean cuisine menu curated by a Michelin-starred chef, but to me it just looks dark and pretentious. Its only saving grace is the view over the hotel's lush gardens. The Bellagio has its fountains, the Luxor has its pyramid, and we have our water gardens. In the seven years I've worked here, I've walked through those gardens exactly once.

The three private function rooms are separated from the restaurant by a long corridor. The restaurant manager sends me to the largest of the rooms where two burly men, who look ominously like bodyguards, flank the door. I'm scared for a moment that they're going to frisk me, then one nods curtly and holds the door open for me. The guests are already seated. The head waiter gives me a disapproving once-over, thrusts an opened bottle of expensive Champagne into my hands, and gives me a not-so-subtle shove in my lower back to get moving.

Two things are immediately obvious. The first is that the guests aren't much older than me, and the second is that they clearly started their party elsewhere, because they're already pretty buzzed.

I top up their Champagne glasses, then head to the kitchen to fetch the starter platters. The first course is served on delicate white porcelain plates. Bacon-wrapped scallops, crab cakes, and jumbo shrimp. My mouth waters.

As I serve, I get the opportunity to observe the guests. Four men, three women and, judging by their accents, none of them are American. No wonder Frank called them 'Their Highnesses'. Perhaps they are. They all sound like Prince Harry. Which one of them is the reason for the bodyguards at the door?

The men are in smart evening suits, the women wear cocktail dresses. I can't tell designer from knock-off, but I'm pretty sure *their* dresses don't come from Target.

The next course is lobster bisque with Caesar salad. My stomach rumbles and I hope no one else hears it. I haven't eaten since that burger at Wendy's before the start of my shift nearly eight hours ago. This is why I prefer serving drinks on the casino floor: less temptation.

"I don't think I'm going to make it to the end of the meal," I complain to the sous-chef as I watch him flip prime steaks in the kitchen. "Those smell so good!"

He wipes the sweat from his brow and grins. He has the warmest brown eyes imaginable, and the broad-shouldered build of an athlete – a swimmer or a wrestler maybe. "You wouldn't say that if you were the one grilling them all night. What time do you get off?"

"Whenever that lot do." I nod toward the dining room.

"Want to go grab something to eat at Tacos El Gordo afterward?"

I grin back. "It's a date. I'm Khara."

"Raúl." He holds out his hand, then ruefully yanks it back before I can shake it. His hand is spattered with basting sauce.

With an extra sway in my hips, I push through the swing doors, balancing the tray of prime sirloin, lobster linguine, and sea bass. The food no longer looks quite as enticing. I can make it through this evening. Tacos shared with an attractive man with a sense of humor beats the fanciest dishes in the world any day.

Half my tray is empty when I feel a hand grasp my thigh. "Hey, gorgeous," a voice slurs.

I'm not unused to being groped by customers. I should have known better than to assume these people, with their money and looks and rank, would be any different from the drunken tourists on the casino floor. I turn, icy glare in place, to look at the man whose hand is now sliding higher, under the hem of my skirt, getting way too familiar.

What else can I do? I glance at the head waiter, wondering if I'll be fired if I make a scene. Serving on the casino floor is so much easier. There, I could slap the hand away and give a sharp retort, and no one would bat an eye. Not to mention that Security would be all over a drunk and difficult gambler in a heartbeat. But here ...?

The man's blond hair flops down over his forehead, almost into his pale blue eyes. He might have been attractive, if not for the receding chin and boyish looks. I prefer real men. The kind that work with their hands.

His too-soft hand is still sliding higher, almost at the edge of my panties now. I think I've just discovered the reason why none of the restaurant waitresses wanted to work this room tonight.

"Please remove your hand. Sir." The last is an afterthought, and more for the benefit of the head waiter, who turns to eye me suspiciously, than for the pale man looking at me as if I'm nothing more than another prime steak.

"Do you know who I am?" He says it with charm and a sloppy smile that almost takes the arrogance out of his words. Almost.

"Cut it out, Nick. The waitress isn't on the menu." This from the dark-haired man at the end of the table. "I'm hungry and you're holding up my food." He sounds bored.

Blondie lets me go, and I scoot around the table to distribute the rest of the plates. When I reach the dark-haired man, he leans toward me, voice low. "I apologize for my cousin. He's had a bit too much to drink."

"No shit," I reply, keeping my voice equally low. I set down his plate, the Chilean sea bass, and turn to leave, but one of the women waves for me to stop.

"What is this? I can't eat carbs." Her voice has taken on a haughty tone, completely different from the giggly, effervescent way she spoke to her friends.

"You ordered the lobster linguine." I keep my voice soft, polite, though it's an effort.

"Yes, I ordered lobster. Not pasta."

The dark-haired man laughs, a soft sound, quickly stifled. I glare at him, wishing I could do the same.

"I'll ask the kitchen to prepare a new dish for you," I say, forcing a smile for the woman and removing her plate.

"What's wrong?" Raúl asks as I slam down the tray beside him.

"Damn entitled rich folks, that's all." I draw in a deep breath, and let it out very slowly and carefully. I need their money. I have to be able to smile when I walk back in there.

"Can you whip up something with lobster, but no linguine? She can't eat carbs."

"No worries." He smiles and takes the plate from me, carrying it over to the chef.

I lean up against the wall, out of everyone's way. The familiar sound of real people doing real work soothes my temper. *These* are my kind of people.

When the meal is done and I go in to clear away the dirty dishes, the porcelain plates are still half-piled with food. Our restaurant isn't exactly famous for its large portions, and yet the young women have barely touched their food – including the specially prepared lobster.

The wastage is enough to make me want to throw the food in their faces. Instead, I keep on smiling and stack the dishes on my tray.

The head waiter circles the table once more, clearing away the empty Champagne bottles, and opening the next. Haven't they already had more than enough to drink?

The dark-haired man looks up from studying the dessert menu. His gaze snags on me, slowly kindling. It's a look that gets under my skin, prickly and hot with a hint of amusement, and I don't like it at all. He is by far the best-looking man in this group. His dark hair is artfully tousled, his green-gray eyes are piercing, and his chin is definitely not weak. He exudes confidence and charm, but I'm immune. I've met enough of his type.

At any given moment, there are dozens of men like him in Vegas. Bachelor parties and frat boy weekends and conference groups. All with money to burn and the same attitude of entitlement. Most of them barely give me a second look, since I'm just the hired help, but those that do notice, like this one, are even worse. They seem to think that because I wear a short skirt and an apron, I'm as easily available as the drinks.

"Anyone for dessert?" I ask brightly.

The three women, all blonde, all skinny, and indistinguishable from one another, shake their heads in unison, and I hear Frank's voice in my head. *Nothing but bone – nothing to hold onto.* I suppress a grin, but not quickly enough.

The dark-haired man raises an enquiring eyebrow at me; that amused look is in his eyes again, almost as if he read my thoughts. Then, "I'll have the New York cheesecake." He holds out the menu to me, but when I reach to take it he doesn't let it go, teasing me. Or more likely taunting me, like a typical playground bully.

The woman to his right pouts. "But I want to go down to the casino."

"And you will, Flora. As soon as I've had my dessert. Or you could go downstairs in the meantime and I'll join you there later, once I've had dessert."

Flora's pout deepens. "But it'll be no fun without you."

Having observed them all evening, I completely get where she's coming from. This dark-haired man is the one who has kept the dinner conversation flowing, deftly handled his cousin's moods, made everyone laugh, and flirted with the ladies. He's also the least drunk in the party. Without him, they make a deadly dull group.

Nick the Obnoxious' eyes narrow as he looks from his cousin to me. "I know what your idea of dessert is."

The dark-haired man merely laughs, then flashes a flirty

smile at Flora. "Don't listen to him, Flora, darling. You know I love you and only you."

I stifle another laugh, cover it with a cough. Maybe for this week. I'd bet all my worldly goods this man says the same thing to many, many women. And because he has money, I'll also bet these brainless model types are just queuing up to be next.

When I return to the dining room with his dessert, the room is empty except for the dark-haired man. Since the burly bodyguards disappeared along with the rest of the group, I assume he's not the VVIP.

He takes his time, sipping the last of his Champagne, and twirling the stem of his glass. Now that the others have gone, he looks bored.

The head waiter brings the bill, and he signs it with a flourish. The tip is generous, and I breathe out a sigh of relief. Since no cash or cards change hands, they must be guests in the hotel. Not that I care.

Silently, I clear away his dessert plate and empty Champagne flute. It's just the two of us in the room again, and I can feel his gaze burning me up. It strokes down my legs, making me feel naked. Hot, bothered, and naked.

Nervous, awkward, I nearly tip my tray and have to grab for the glass.

He laughs.

I glare.

With the bill already paid, I have nothing to lose. "Don't you have someplace better to be?"

"When you've seen one casino, you've seen them all."

Talk about preaching to the converted. I've worked in this one long enough that I'd be happy never to step foot inside another casino. And as soon as I graduate – *if* I ever graduate – I plan to get a job somewhere that has windows that let in real daylight.

"Throwing your money away at the tables is supposed to be thrilling," I say. Not that I'd know. I have better things to do with my money than throw it away, but I'm desperate for him to leave. Raúl's shift in the kitchen has already ended.

But the dark-haired foreigner merely shrugs again, and this time the movement looks weary, as if he's not bored but tired. If being the heart and soul of this little party is so much effort, why does he bother?

"There's more to Vegas than casinos. You could always try the Stratosphere Tower, or the Zombie Burlesque show," I offer.

His cool green-gray eyes kindle again, wiping away that weary look. "What time do you get off work?"

Seriously? I narrow my eyes at him, but say nothing.

"You can show me what lies beyond the Strip. I can pay."

My back stiffens. I may be almost permanently broke, but I am not for sale. "I already have a date," I say stiffly.

He shrugs as if he doesn't believe me. "In case you change your mind ..." He smirks as he lays a room card down on the table, no longer even bothering to pretend he's looking for a tour guide.

Anger ripples through me, white-hot. "The waitress is Not. On. The. Menu."

Then I turn and walk out, my hands shaking so hard the glass wobbles dangerously on the tray.

Chapter 1
Adam

One year later ...

As we crown the rise that separates the estate from the outside world, I see an ominous black car pull up beside the stable block and groan aloud. The sleek stretch limo with its dark-tinted windows can't mean anything good. My horse, sensing home and her nosebag of hay, picks up her pace, but I'm less keen. Whoever is being driven in that vehicle, it's certainly not anyone I want to see. Has my father sent someone from the office to check why I'm skiving off work again? I wonder if I should turn around and keep riding until the unwelcome visitor is gone. Riding is my one escape, my only chance to be alone, away from the stifling confines of family and work and expectations, and I resent this intrusion.

But Bonney is growing tired and needs a rub down and a rest. Unwillingly, I keep her on course. I slow her to a walk, though, reluctant to find out what this visitor wants from me. Because there is no doubt that it's me that he – or she – wants, and I am so tired of everyone wanting things from me that I can't give.

By the time I reach the red-brick stables, a relic of the Victorian era, a groom has already come running to take the reins. I dismount, just as the uniformed chauffeur leaning up against the vehicle moves to open the limo door. The visitor who steps out is tall and slim, grey-haired and wearing rimless glasses. I don't recognise him, so maybe he hasn't been sent to drag me back to the city for some mindlessly boring meeting I forgot.

"Adam Hatton?" the man asks.

I nod, otherwise ignoring him as I give Bonney the apple slices out my pocket and a pat, before relinquishing her to the hovering groom.

"My name is János Alsóvári."

The name doesn't ring any bells, but it's enough to tell me where the visitor is from. Or rather who. "My uncle sent you?" I ask, stripping off my riding gloves and finally turning to face him. And that can only mean one thing: my cousin Nick has got himself into some kind of trouble again. His escapades are growing tiresome. He's over thirty, for heaven's sake, and well past the age when all-night parties at Mahiki, losing a small fortune gambling, or getting photographed with drunk and/or naked women should have lost its appeal. When is he ever going to grow up?

"What has Nick done now?" I ask, unable to hold back a sigh.

The visitor clears his throat. "It is my unfortunate duty to inform you that Prince Nicholas died this morning."

I freeze in the process of removing my second glove. Maybe I heard him wrong?

But the man's face tells me I didn't misunderstand his words. He looks the way I feel. Tired.

"What happened?" I manage at last.

"He wrapped his roadster around a tree in the early hours."

"He was drunk?"

"Of course." The man's expression remains neutral, but his lips press together, betraying his disapproval.

"Was anyone else injured?"

János shakes his head and I breathe out a sigh of relief. At least Nick didn't take anyone with him. Where were his bodyguards? I rub a hand across my face, trying to process the news. I shouldn't be surprised. The way Nick lived, hard, fast and completely without regard for anyone or anything, an early death was almost inevitable. Still, it feels as if a sledgehammer has slammed into my chest.

Nick. I saw him at the polo club just last weekend. And we're supposed to play a match on Sunday. I know I shouldn't be thinking of something like that right now, but I can't help but wonder who we'll get to replace him at such short notice. Rik's halfway around the world in the Caribbean with his new bride, and these days Max is too busy being a prince. Everyone else I know who's any good is already in a team.

"Your uncle requests a meeting with you. He is at the townhouse in London."

I'd almost forgotten the visitor was still here. "I'll be there as soon as I can."

János' lips press together again. "Now."

"I'm hardly dressed for a meeting." I glance down at my jeans and muddied riding boots.

"His Royal Highness requests your presence. Your attire is of no consequence."

I shrug, and allow the man to bundle me into the limo. The chauffeur takes his seat up front. The dark glass is up between the front and back, leaving János and me alone in the back. The car pulls away, following the curve of the drive through a copse of trees and past the neo-classical mansion that's been the Hatton family country seat for just two generations. My mobile phone and wallet are upstairs, still in the jacket of the three-piece suit I wore to work this morning, but I suppose I'll hardly need them where we're going.

"What does my uncle want with me?" I ask János. Though in my head the question is phrased a little less politely. After all, there's nothing more I can do for Nick now. Unless Uncle Lajos is already planning the funeral, and wants me to get involved. But my uncle has never done anything in haste, which is why this whole mad rush seems bizarre.

Or does he hold me responsible for Nick's death? He hasn't held me responsible for Nick's behaviour before, even though I've felt responsible.

János doesn't answer. I want to ask how he found me. I lied and told my secretary I was meeting a client when I left the office early this morning. The groom is the only one who even knew I'd come home to my parents' house. Lucky guess, or does my uncle have some sort of scary intelligence network at his disposal? Since I know I wouldn't get an answer to that question, I don't bother asking.

I lean my head back against the plush leather seat, and close my eyes. János makes a call, speaking in the dialect of my mother's homeland, a language I've never really got the hang of, but even I can tell it sounds like damage control. My thoughts drift, not really settling on any one thing. I think of how proud Nick was of that damned car, and how he always drove too fast. Has my mother heard the news yet? She wasn't home when I arrived earlier. And my sister Jemmy? She's away on a business trip in New York, so most likely not. I hope they don't hear of Nick's death through the media. Though it's unlikely they'll grieve much. Nick burned a lot of bridges with the family these last few years.

János' voice drones on in the background as he makes phone call after phone call. Since I barely understand half of what he's saying, I don't bother to listen in.

The drive from Hertfordshire into the heart of Belgravia takes over an hour, but I only open my eyes again when the car slows for the congestion of London's narrow streets. Beyond the air-conditioned bubble of the car, the city seems to shimmer with the summer heat. I left London just a few hours ago to escape its humidity and the press of tourists. I really didn't plan to be back so soon. I rub a hand over my eyes. The weariness that is my constant companion these days weighs even heavier on my shoulders than usual. Perhaps because now it's more than just weariness. There's guilt mixed in there too. I roll out the tension in my neck, but it doesn't help.

The limo pulls to a stop outside the elegant Georgian townhouse that has been the embassy and London bolthole of the Erdély royal family since 1938, when my great-grandfather brought the family here to escape the Austrian *Anschluss*.

Apparently it was considered an act of cowardice, and his people never forgave him, but I personally am rather grateful. My grandfather, just in his early twenties when the war started, was an outspoken critic of the Nazis and he would almost certainly have been killed if he'd stayed, and then I wouldn't have been born. Suffocating as my life has become lately, I'm rather attached to it.

Uniformed guards swing open the gates and the car rolls forward, up the short drive to the imposing front entrance. There are no photographers at the gate so clearly the news hasn't broken yet. It won't take long, I'm sure. When a young playboy prince dies, it's headline news, even if he was hereditary prince of a country most people have never even heard of. That, at least, is a small silver lining to Nick's death – by tomorrow, there'll be quite a few people Googling Erdély to see where the hell it is. The tiny principality sandwiched at the junction of Austria, Hungary and Slovenia is about to get famous for all the wrong reasons.

Another uniformed guard opens the limo door, and yet another holds open the front door for us. János stands back, waiting for me to enter first, so I step over the threshold into the cool, marble-floored entrance hall. I find the hall just as intimidating now as I did as a kid when we visited my grandfather here.

"His Royal Highness is in the library," the footman at the door says over my shoulder to János. His use of English is no doubt for my benefit.

The library is a double-volumed room at the back of the house, overlooking the neat lawn where Nick and I used to play cricket. We hit a cricket ball through one of its high, stained-glass windows a lifetime ago. There's no sign of the damage now.

My uncle, looking considerably greyer than the last time we met, stands before the window, staring out at the garden as if he isn't really seeing it. He cradles a whiskey tumbler in his hands, though it isn't yet noon and he's never been a big drinker. Unlike his son.

I step further into the room and János shuts the door behind me, leaving us alone. I can't remember when last I met my uncle alone, if ever.

"I am so sorry," I say. The words feel inadequate, but what else does one say to a man who has just lost his only child? "How is my aunt?"

Uncle Lajos turns slowly to face me. His eyes, so similar to mine I've been told, are grave. "She is sleeping. We had to make her take a strong sedative."

I nod. Aunt Sonja adored her son, blindly.

Lajos sets down the tumbler. "We spoiled him. We let him do as he pleased."

Since a response clearly isn't expected of me, I wait for him to get to the point.

"Nicholas was my heir," the older man says needlessly. "Erdély will need a new crown prince."

It seems callous to be thinking of who is next in line, but I'd be lying if I didn't admit that thought hadn't already crossed my mind during the long drive here. "Mátyás is next in line," I answer promptly. Though my other cousin is five years younger than me, his mother was the elder sister.

"Your cousin Mátyás is cut from the same cloth as my own son. Too indulged and too self-absorbed. Erdély cannot afford any more public embarrassment."

He looks at me intently, as if trying to look deep inside me. I choke on an intake of breath as realisation dawns. "You called me here to make me your heir? But Mátyás ..."

Lajos shakes his head. "Our laws state that the *Fürst* of Erdély may choose his own successor, as long as his choice is a blood relative."

I feel like a fish trying to breathe out of water. "I don't even understand the language!" And I most certainly don't want this! I don't even want the job I already have. I have no idea what I want.

"You'll learn it soon enough." Lajos' voice is calm but brittle.

Under any other circumstances, I would have thought my uncle was having me on. After all, grief makes people do crazy things, doesn't it?

I'm just as indulged, just as selfish, as my cousins. Okay, so I dialled down the partying a little this last year, but I'm still not exactly princely material. I haven't achieved anything of value with my life, and I'm hardly likely to start now. I'm not sure I even have the energy to try.

Lajos stands taller, looking very much what he is – the ruler of a nation. "You have a job in your father's firm, and I hear that you are even good at it. You achieved a first in your MBA so you clearly have brains. You're one of the few people Nicholas ever listened to, and you're the least likely of my nephews to drink himself into an early grave."

For a moment, grief etches lines into his face before he

regains control of his expression. I take just a little longer to recover from the sudden slash of pain in the vicinity of my heart. Nick's isn't the first violent death I've known. It's not the first I feel part-way responsible for either. But I can't think of that now. "If you can choose your successor, then my sister would be a far better choice," I manage at last.

"Jemima is an admirable young woman, and undoubtedly would make a far better ruler than either you or Mátyás, but the law is clear: only a male may inherit."

"That's positively archaic."

"If you feel strongly about it, then when you are *Fürst* you may attempt to change the laws. I have had other battles to fight."

I'm well aware what those battles have been. There have been calls for Erdély to scrap its royal family since my great-grandfather's day, and Lajos has had a hell of a job convincing the people his title is still worth something. It's only been since his accession a couple of decades back that women have been granted the right to vote, and gay marriage was only legalised mere years ago. Lajos was instrumental in passing both pieces of legislation. The tiny principality hasn't been in any hurry to join the twenty-first century. Yet another reason I want nothing to do with the place. I like my twenty-first century comforts.

"I haven't been to Erdély in years! I don't even remember the place," I protest, aware I'm scrabbling for excuses.

"Again, that is something that is easily rectified." My uncle reaches for the whiskey tumbler and takes a long sip. His hand shakes, betraying unexpected emotion. "I will not force you to accept this role. Mátyás will no doubt be delighted to accept, should you decline." His lips purse together, just as János' did earlier. Is that an Erdélian thing? "But I will ask that you at least consider my request. By law, when Nicholas' funeral is over, I must announce my successor. We can delay the funeral by one month, but no longer. You have until then to let me know your choice."

One month to decide my entire future? If it were that easy, sometime over this last year I would have figured out what the hell I want to do with my life. And my uncle isn't offering me a job I can walk away from if it doesn't work out. There'll be no trial period if I accept.

I'm pretty sure I know already what my answer will be, and it's a very easy decision. *No, thank you.* I may be bored with my current life, but I'm still rather attached to doing what I want, when I want to seriously consider one day carrying the burden of an entire country on my shoulders, for ever and ever until death us do part.

But I can't tell him that now, not here or like this, and certainly not until I've figured out how to politely decline his offer.

So I shrug. "Sure. I'll think about it."

The drive back to Hertfordshire seems to take even longer. Perhaps because it's now Friday afternoon and the mad commuter rush out to the suburbs has begun. At least I have the back of the car to myself, and the chauffeur still has the dark glass up. I need time alone to process everything. Nick being dead. That other, long ago death that sometimes still knocks the wind out of me when I remember. And my uncle's offer.

I've spent a lot of time this past year trying to picture my future, and not one of those scenarios featured me being a prince. And certainly not a future ruler. Not that it bothered Nick much. He hardly ever visited Erdély because he said it was boring (by which I presume he meant there wasn't any good gambling), and he'd never shown the least interest in being responsible for anything, but if I say yes to Lajos' crazy offer there's no way I'll be treated with the same leniency. I'll need to step up, and that's the one thing I am really not good at doing.

But if I say no, what will I do with the next fifty plus years of my life? I went to work in the family business after uni because I'm good with numbers and have a natural flair for talking clients into trusting me with their money, but it's pretty obvious to anyone who really knows me that my heart isn't in it. If I'm still there in another five years, I think I'll need a straitjacket.

If I were a better person, I guess I'd do something useful with my life, like build houses for the homeless in South America, or bring clean drinking water to villages in Africa. But I like the comforts of home far too much. I even briefly toyed with the idea of doing what my best friend Rik does these days: sail the Caribbean. But I gave him my yacht as a wedding gift, and couldn't be bothered going shopping for another one.

And yes, I am fully aware how self-indulgent and entitled that sounds. Poor little rich boy. Has enough money to do anything he wants, but nothing appeals. Maybe being a crown prince would be a lark … But I don't even know what the job entails. I'm an investment broker, for heaven's sake. I could ask Max, Rik's brother. He's archduke of another of those tiny European principalities no one has ever heard of. But at least Westerwald has vineyards. And a city.

And thinking of Max I groan out loud. I was really looking forward to his bachelor party next week – but how will it look now if I go partying with the Archduke of Westerwald when I'm supposed to be in mourning for Nick? Though Nick would be the first person to tell me that life is for the living and to go to the damn party.

Even though I have my own loft apartment in the city, Hartham Manor still feels like home. It's more than four times the size of the Belgravia townhouse I just visited, but with its mellow red brick façade and wildflower-filled gardens it feels far more welcoming. While my maternal great-grandfather ran away from his country in its time of need, my paternal great-grandfather was an East End nobody who, with nothing more than his own gumption, made himself into a somebody. He bought this stately home in his quest to move up the ranks of England's strictly hierarchical society. Even with his big dreams of joining the aristocracy, I don't think he imagined for even a moment that his grandson – my father – would be a respected member of the old boy network, or that he'd marry a princess. I stifle a laugh, wondering if his great-grandson will one day inherit a nation. That would have made the old man proud.

The title of *Fürst* of Erdély might be obscure, but for those who care about these sorts of things it's a very ancient and noble title. Back in the Middle Ages, the title of *Fürst* – Imperial Prince – was given to princes who had the power to elect the next Holy Roman Emperor. Once upon a time, my mother's ancestors literally had the power to influence European history. I may not have been to that backwater country since I was a kid, but my mother drummed Erdélian history into both me and Jemima before we were barely old enough to walk. Other kids got *Jack and Jill* and *Humpty Dumpty*, and we got medieval politics.

When I stride into the drawing room my mother is waiting for me, and I can tell from her face that she's heard the news.

Krisztyna Eszterháza de Erdély Hatton doesn't look like what you'd expect of a princess. There are no twinsets and pearls in her wardrobe. She's short and plump and maternal, prefers jeans and riding boots to ballgowns, and tends to smell more like the horses she breeds than Chanel. I have absolutely no clue what drew her and my vain, Savile Row-suit-wearing father together but, whatever it was, it clearly works. They're headed for their fortieth anniversary.

Her over-excited beagle starts to yap and dance in circles as I approach. My mother rises and holds out her hands. "You've been out riding?"

I squeeze her hands, then, out of habit, bend to scratch the dog's head while she pours tea for us both from the fresh pot that is steaming gently on its silver tray – though I could do with something a great deal stronger. "I was. Until Uncle Lajos sent for me."

She frowns as she settles back in her favourite armchair and accepts the teacup I hold out to her. "János just called with the news. Sonja must be devastated! I tried to call her, but her secretary said she was sleeping."

"They sedated her."

"Miklós was always so headstrong." She always insisted on calling Nick by the name on his birth certificate, even though he hated it and even his parents called him by his Anglicised name. "And he wasn't fit to be crown prince. He had no interest in Erdély's culture or traditions, let alone current policy. But what will my brother do now? Mátyás is a money-grubbing leach who'll probably sell everything of value in the country to the highest bidder. But if there isn't an heir, then Erdély defaults back to the crown of Hungary."

"Which hasn't existed since Hungary came under Austrian rule in the fifteen-hundreds," I point out, rather pleased with myself for having remembered that, and equally keen to divert her from this line of thinking.

"Exactly! What will become of us?"

I shake my head. She's lived in the UK her entire adult life and yet still thinks of herself as Erdélian. Besides, does it really matter what happens to some tiny, backward country halfway across Europe? It could become a province of Hungary for all I care. Not that I'd say that out loud anywhere my mother can hear.

She sips her tea, then looks at me sharply. "Why did Lajos want to see you?"

Damn. I really hoped she wouldn't ask, and she knows me too well to let me get away with a lie. I clear my throat. "He offered me the opportunity to be his successor." Not that it's much of an opportunity. More like a life sentence.

My mother's eyes shine. "Yes. That would be an excellent solution. My sister won't like it, of course, and Mátyás will be spitting mad, but that would be the sensible thing to do."

Sensible for who? Certainly not for me! And I am no different from my cousins. I am vain and selfish enough to put my own interests ahead of Erdély's, and I'm not going to pretend any different, not even to spare my mother's feelings. But I choke back my retort and instead I say, "He has asked me to think about it, and to give him an answer by the time of Nick's funeral."

Her gaze sharpens on me and she frowns again as she senses my lack of enthusiasm. "Promise me that you will at least give his offer serious consideration."

Shit. I really don't want to make that promise. "I promise," I say.

Chapter 2

Khara

"I want you to be my bridesmaid."

"Am I experiencing déjà-vu, or is this for real?" I'm stretched out on a towel beside the local public pool, my textbook open in front of me. Though it's a weekday and the place is pretty empty, there's a kids' swimming class on the go and the kids are screaming and laughing. I have to cover my other ear so I can hear my friend's reply.

"For real. Big white dress, cathedral, the whole nine yards."

I have to pinch myself. My friend Phoenix is married to a prince. About to marry a prince. I'm one of only three people other than the happy couple who know that they married in secret a year ago and this big royal wedding is just for show. It's a long story – the kind that can only happen right here in Vegas.

"Let me get this straight: you want me – a waitress who still lives with her mother in a double wide – to be your bridesmaid at a *royal* wedding?"

Phoenix's chuckle doesn't sound at all princess-like. "Of course I want you to share this moment with me. You were there for me first time round, and you should be there this time round. The only difference is that this time you'll need a passport."

Yeah, sure. As if a royal wedding is going to be anything like the quickie Vegas chapel wedding Phoenix and Max had first time round. For one thing, I don't think any cathedral will allow glitter guns.

Luckily, the crackle of the long distance call (or is it my cheap, bottom-of-the-range cell phone?) masks the fact that my laughter is really hysteria. I am so not the kind of girl who should be a bridesmaid at a royal wedding. I've never been outside the state of Nevada, let alone out the country. I don't even own a passport.

"It's all taken care of," Phoenix says. "We have an embassy in DC. They'll help you get a passport, visa and sort your travel arrangements. The invitation's for you and your brother, since you were both there to witness our first wedding. And his girlfriend, of course."

"Calvin won't come. The baby's due around then, and he won't travel without Aliya. But he'll be so thrilled to be invited." Certainly more thrilled than I feel right now. Nope, the emotion I'm feeling is terror.

"Just you then. Come spend the rest of the summer, until school starts. You'll love it here! Westerwald is unlike anything you can imagine."

She's told me a lot about the little fairy tale kingdom tucked in between France and Germany, a place of castles and vineyards and rivers, and I've dreamed of one day seeing it for myself. I just didn't think 'one day' would come so soon. Or ever.

"I can't take all that time off work," I protest. "Frank's a sweetheart, but he'll never be able to hold my job open that long." And I can't afford to lose this job. I still have a final semester's tuition to pay for, and every day I spend in Westerwald will be a day I won't be earning.

"You won't need to work. We'll take care of everything while you're here, and I promise you won't need to worry about your tuition when you get back home."

My back stiffens. "I won't take your charity."

On the other end of the line, Phoenix huffs out an exasperated breath. "Don't be an idiot. This isn't charity. This is me, needing your help to get through what is going to be the biggest and most nerve-racking month of my life. I *need* you here, and I'll do anything to make that happen. Please, Khara. For me?"

Even though I only knew her a few months before she met Max and traveled to Europe, Phoenix is the closest friend I've ever had. I'd jump through a ring of fire for her.

"How many other bridesmaids will there be?" I ask. If it's a royal wedding, surely there'll be a big entourage. Maybe I won't stand out so much if I can hide in a crowd.

But when was I ever that lucky? "It's a European-style wedding," she says. "One bridesmaid, one best man, a couple of flower girls. We want to keep it simple and classy."

Classy. I choke on that word. My idea of class is paper napkins. "This really isn't a good idea. Isn't there a duchess or something you could ask?"

"You can't seriously turn down an all-expenses-paid trip to Europe and free board in a palace, now, can you?" Phoenix continues. "Consider it an educational experience."

I press my eyes shut. Her invitation is tempting. So tempting. But ... whoever heard of a royal bridesmaid with blue hair?

"Think of it this way: one whole month away from your mother," she says.

And that right there is all the argument I need. "Okay. But I'm still paying my own tuition."

Love is a lie we tell ourselves. It's really nothing more than chemistry. That tremor we feel when we meet someone's gaze and think 'This is it'? Yup, that's just hormones. What it really means is that we're looking at a guy and thinking 'Yeah, I'd like to do him' – and then, to make ourselves feel less slutty, we tell ourselves we're in love.

But I've never been one to lie to myself. So in this moment I'm looking at the best man and thinking 'Yeah, I'd like to do him.'

You can call me slutty if you like. I don't care. At least I'm honest.

He hasn't seen me yet, which is just as well, since I wasn't expecting company and I'm not wearing any make-up. What I *am* wearing is a ratty old Vegas 51s sweatshirt and tracksuit pants. It might be summer, but Europe is chilly compared to Nevada, and this palace's heating system must be at least two hundred years old. The creaks and groans of the pipes at least make me feel a little less like I'm inside a Disney fairy tale.

Unlike all the other girls I grew up with, I never wanted to live a fairy tale life. I never dreamed of fame and fortune; all I ever wanted was to belong right where I am. I believe in honest hard work, not glass slippers and fairy godmothers. Besides, I've seen what chasing unrealistic dreams does to people. No, my dream isn't to live in some draughty palace with a prince, but rather a three-bedroom bungalow in the suburbs with its own yard and a garage, with an honest, steady, dependable man. And don't tell me men like that don't exist, because they do. Men like my stepfather and my brother. And like Max.

The two men on the level below me move to sit in armchairs close to the empty fireplace – high-backed leather armchairs, the kind I've only ever seen in the movies. Behind them is a glassed-in wall of old-fashioned books, all in matching sets, which look as if they're just for show.

I'm up in the gallery, a carpeted walkway above their heads which circles the enormous high-ceilinged library. Phoenix suggested I look here for entertainment if the jet lag kept me awake and since my body has no idea what time it is and clearly doesn't want to sleep, here I am. And she was right – these books hidden from public view are definitely more my kind of books. They look just like the shelves in my favorite second-hand bookshop.

Neither of the men has looked up and noticed I'm here, and I plan to keep it that way. I crouch down behind the wooden railing and edge over a little so I can see them better. The back of Max's armchair is turned to me so all I can see of him is his fair hair catching the low yellow light. That same light falls directly onto the man seated in the armchair across from him. The best man.

He looks vaguely familiar, like a TV actor you know you've

seen before but can't quite place. Thick dark hair that I'm sure would be curly if he let it grow longer, strong cheekbones, and a pointed chin sporting two days' worth of scruff. He's wearing a black leather jacket that makes him look like a biker rather than a stockbroker, or whatever it is Phoenix told me he does. She spent much of the drive between the airport and the palace telling me about him, but I have to admit that as soon as I realized he was one of those spoiled trust-fund types I tuned out. I am so done with entitled men and their groping hands. Looking at him now, though, I wish I'd paid a little more attention. After all, I'm young and single and a girl has needs.

"Have you made a decision yet?" Max asks.

His best man shrugs, slinging one leg casually over the other. "What's there to decide? I don't want the responsibility. My life would have to change, and I rather like things exactly as they are right now – easy, commitment-free, and no one else to think about except myself."

And just like that he stops being sexy. I don't care how good he looks in a leather jacket – or out of it. Any man who shirks his responsibilities so he can keep having fun isn't worth a dime in my book.

"How did your family take the news?" Max asks.

The best man looks down, as if he's concentrating hard on swirling the golden liquid around in his tumbler. "I haven't told them yet." Then he glances up at Max. "I was kind of hoping I could lie low here with you in Westerwald until after the wedding."

And a coward to boot. Seriously not a sexy look on any man.

He leans forward, his elbow on his knee. "But I'll also understand if you no longer want me as your best man. With all the media speculation since Nick's death, it might detract attention from your wedding. Wouldn't one of your brothers be better for the job?"

"Hmm, talk about Hobson's Choice: my mother's bastard or my father's bastard? Either way, the press would be savage. Thanks for the offer, but you're still my safest bet."

I grin. Yup, Westerwald's royal family takes dysfunctional to a whole other level. Makes mine look almost normal.

"Who would have thought I'd ever be considered a safe choice?" The best man sprawls back in his armchair, oozing the kind of self-assurance I only wish I had.

Max laughs. "Yeah, well, I asked the Duke of Cambridge but he was busy, so you'll have to do."

"Any hot bridesmaids to sweeten the deal? That's supposed to be a perk of being best man, isn't it?"

I shrink back into the shadows. This is definitely not a conversation I want to be caught eavesdropping on.

"Only one bridesmaid, and yes, she's hot, but she's not your type."

I make myself even smaller, which is about the size I feel. No, I don't suppose a girl like me would in any way be considered the right type for a man like him.

"One is all I need," the best man says. "And I don't have a type." Even from here, I can see he's smirking. The expression makes him look even more familiar, as if I've seen that expression before.

Max chuckles. "Good luck with that. Khara will have your

balls and eat them for breakfast. And I hate to be the one to break the news to you, but you do have a type: easy."

I'm not sure whether to be flattered that my best friend's husband doesn't think I'm easy, or insulted that he thinks I'm a ball-breaker.

"The women I date only look easy because no woman can resist my charm." The best man takes a sip from his tumbler and smiles. Forget self-confidence. What he's oozing is arrogance. And right now the only thing I want to do to him is smack that smirk right off his face. The white-hot anger that rises up in me reminds me where I've seen him before, of that other time when he made me feel small and insignificant, as if I was nothing more than an object, something that could easily be his for the taking. He has even less chance with me now than he did a year ago.

Slowly, I unclench my fists. I really don't want to hear any more of this conversation. I'll have to do without a book to read tonight. As silently as I can, I creep away toward the narrow door in the wall of books that will lead me out into the upstairs corridor. I leave the door open behind me. I don't want to give away my presence with squeaking hinges.

I may be leaving without the bedtime read I came looking for, but I'm still glad I came looking. I wasn't expecting this wedding to be a picnic, but at least now I've been forewarned of one danger.

Chapter 3

Khara

When I wake I have to pinch myself. I still can't believe the last few days weren't just a dream. The three flights I had to take to get here were thrilling and scary in equal measure, but those emotions were nothing compared to the joy of seeing Phoenix when I got off that last plane. I admit, there were tears. She hasn't changed a bit, still that same warm, friendly person I knew when we worked together in the casino bar, not a princessy air or grace in sight. Then there was the luxury car ride through a town that looks like something out of a picture book, even if the sky was gray and overcast and threatening to rain. This palace is something else too! Phoenix gave me a tour that made my head spin – breathtaking state rooms, the royal family's private apartments, guest rooms that look like they belong in the pages of a Condé Nast magazine, and an entire wing of offices.

"Sometimes it feels more like living in an office building, with people coming and going all the time, and official government meetings," Phoenix told me. "Our real home is the castle in Waldburg where we usually spend weekends. You'll get to spend some time there after the wedding." She said it so casually, like everyone has a medieval castle as a weekend holiday home.

We had to skip a tour of the gardens (yeah, there's more than one!) as it started to rain, but that's just as well since my head was already about to explode.

And then this room! I really have stepped into a fairy tale. Any moment now I expect a fairy godmother to appear and offer me a magical ballgown. My guest room is massive, big enough to fit two sofas, a writing desk, a dresser, an antique cabinet which I discovered last night conceals a flat-screen TV, and enough floor space left over for me to waltz in, if I knew how to waltz.

The bed isn't one of those fairy tale canopied ones with drapes, but it's still super-impressive: solid, with wooden bedposts topped with giant carved acorns. Compared to the single bed which is all I can fit into my room back home, it's big enough to throw a party in, and feels like sleeping on a cloud. I really must remember to ask Phoenix what thread count these bedsheets are.

I stretch, looking around the room, absorbing every detail just in case this *is* a dream and I wake up back in the same bedroom I've slept in the last thirty years. The walls are papered with a simple pattern of broad stripes in pale green and cream. No paintings or decoration, but on the ledge above the white-painted fireplace are two porcelain figurines of dancing couples. I slide out of bed and cross the cool, patterned parquet floor to the windows, pulling back the floral drapes that feel like silk under my fingers. The windows on this side of the palace are bigger, Phoenix explained last night, because they overlook the royal family's private garden, so this wing has more privacy than all the others.

There's a window seat and everything, so I settle on it, resting my chin on my knees as I look out at the colorful flowerbeds below. The private garden is four times the size of the yard I dream of having one day, and it's surrounded by a red brick wall that must be at least ten feet high. Beyond the wall is a park with trees, and then the roofs of the town, catching and reflecting the slanting morning sunlight. I itch to go exploring. This is Europe, full of history and culture and architecture that Vegas, with all its attempts to copy it, could never hope to achieve.

I would have loved to study history and art in college, but they're just not practical for a career unless you plan to be an underpaid teacher, so I'm studying accountancy and finance. With those majors I at least have a shot of getting an office job with a steady paycheck, regular hours, and windows. You might think that's not particularly ambitious, but trust me, for some of us that's ambitious enough.

But here, for the next few weeks, I plan to indulge in all the art and history I can. For one month I will live the fairy tale.

My cell phone alarm buzzes, startling me out of my contemplation of the view. It's time to get dressed and go downstairs – and just like that the bubble pops and I'm no longer in fairyland. I'm in the harsh reality of a world I'm completely unprepared for and not at all ready to face.

***

Remember how I said I'd jump through a ring of fire for Phoenix? Well, that's exactly how it feels when I come down for breakfast.

"Jeans and tee shirts are fine," Phoenix assured me over dinner in their apartment last night, but when a servant finally points me in the direction of the breakfast room I baulk in the doorway. I'm almost blinded by the silverware. And there are more porcelain plates and crystal glasses on the dining table than I've washed in my entire life. Did I mention that before I was old enough to serve drinks, my previous job was washing plates in a restaurant kitchen?

The room is big enough to fit a highly polished wooden dining table that could seat at least twenty. But it's not just the size of the room that's impressive. The walls are painted plain ivory-white and when I look up I realize that the ceiling is painted like the Sistine Chapel. At least, what I imagine the Sistine Chapel looks like, since I've only ever seen pictures during a long-ago art class. Blue sky, clouds, and frolicking gods and goddesses.

I hover in the doorway until Phoenix turns her head and spots me. So does everyone else in the room, and there's rather a lot of them. They all look like they're dressed for a *Vogue* fashion shoot. Phoenix is the only other person in the room wearing jeans.

"Did you sleep well?" she asks, her ready smile lighting up her face as I walk in.

"Not really. I guess it's going to take my body clock another day to adjust."

"You'll feel better once you've eaten. Breakfast's on the

sideboard." I have no clue what a sideboard is, but she waves toward a buffet at the far end of the room, where a heavily pregnant woman is dishing up scrambled eggs and bacon onto an empty plate.

"Hi, I'm Rebekah," the woman says, smiling at me in welcome as I tentatively approach the buffet. "I'm Claus' wife." She nods at the fair-haired man seated beside Max at the head of the table. I was introduced to Claus yesterday. He's Max's Steward – whatever that means – and one of the main organizers of the royal wedding. Both men greet me, then their blond heads bend together again to pore over paperwork.

I've heard about Rebekah from Phoenix. She was Phoenix's boss when she first arrived in Westerwald, and they're still good friends. I can see why. Rebekah has a kind, open face, smiling eyes, and a scattering of freckles across her nose, which make her look younger than she probably is.

Taking my cue from her, I head to the side table and pick up a plate then serve myself from the buffet. The chafing dishes look tarnished enough to be real silver, and the range of choice is almost as good as the casino's breakfast buffet. This is certainly a world away from my usual bowl of cornflakes eaten at the faux-granite counter in my mom's tiny kitchenette.

Once I've dished up, I take my plate to the table, choosing the seat next to Phoenix. I set my plate down, sit, and then stare bewildered at the array of cutlery before me. I've only ever eaten with one knife and one fork. This place setting has four of each. Does it matter which one I use? Oh God, of course it does.

And there are real cloth napkins.

How the hell did I think I could do this? I can't even get through breakfast without making it obvious I'm nothing more than a hick from Hicksville.

Trailer park trash.

If anyone dares say that to my face I'll claw their eyes out with my bare hands. Even if it is true. Not that trailer parks are as bad as their reputation. I've lived in one my entire life and let me tell you, it's a whole lot better place to grow up than many other places I've seen. But I also know on which rung of the social ladder it places me, and it sure isn't the one I've woken up on today.

Phoenix has already finished her meal and further down the table Max's private secretary, the press secretary, and the Master of the Household are so engrossed in conversation that they've barely touched their food. I was introduced to them all yesterday, but in the haze of jet lag from my first ever airplane flight I forgot their names as quickly as I was told them.

I'm still contemplating the cutlery when it's as if a breeze stirs the air in the room and I feel rather than hear someone enter behind me. I know straight away who it is, and have to force myself not to turn around to look. My back stiffens.

The best man drops a light kiss on Phoenix's cheek. "Hello, gorgeous!"

"Hello, charmer." She smiles warmly back at him, and I'll admit to being more than a little surprised. Phoenix is usually a really good judge of character.

Then he turns his attention on me, and for a moment I

freeze. He gives me the once-over and smiles. I remember that smile. Full of heat and stripping me naked, as it did back in that private room at the casino. Will he recognize me? But of course he doesn't. Not even a flicker of recognition. And why would he? Men like him don't remember the hired help. I'm probably one of a thousand servers who've waited on him in the last year, one of a thousand women he no doubt invited to his bed without even asking for a name. And I didn't have this rather distinctive turquoise ombre on my hair a year ago. His gaze takes in the striking effect of my hair, and his smile turns to a cheeky grin. "You must be the bridesmaid."

"Khara," I correct, not smiling back.

He doesn't seem to notice my frosty attitude. "I'm Adam Hatton. It's a pleasure to meet you." The way he says the word *pleasure* makes my skin prickle. And not in an entirely bad way, though I'd never give him the satisfaction of knowing that.

Out of the corner of my eye, I see Phoenix sit straighter like a bloodhound, or a shark scenting blood in the water.

When Rebekah joins us I am so grateful for the interruption I could hug her. Adam circles the table to give her a quick kiss too. "You're looking good. Positively glowing."

She beams up at him and I roll my eyes. Then he steals a slice of crispy bacon off her plate and with another jaunty smile heads to the buffet to serve himself. I let out a breath I wasn't aware I was holding.

Rebekah sits across from us, lowering herself into the seat as if her pregnant belly weighs a ton. She has my sympathy. I suffered through a couple of pregnancies with my neighbor Carly before she followed her latest husband to Ohio.

As relaxed and comfortable as if she were eating in her own home, Rebekah unfolds her napkin and spreads it across her lap. I copy her. Note to self: don't tuck the napkin in your shirt like a bib.

Then she picks up one of the forks beside her plate, and I do the same.

I manage a few mouthfuls before Adam is back, sliding into the empty seat to my left, not-so-accidentally brushing his thigh against mine, and for a moment an honest-to-goodness thrill shudders through me before I shift away. But he pays me no attention as he goes straight for the correct fork. Rich people make it look so easy. For the record, it's not, when you have no clue what you're doing and you're terrified of screwing up and making your best friend look bad.

This may well be the best breakfast I've ever eaten, but it tastes like cardboard in my mouth since I'm so busy concentrating on what to do, how to sit, how to hold my fork, while at the same time trying to completely ignore the man sitting right beside me. Which isn't easy. He smells heavenly. I mean, I have never met a man who smells like this before. If I had to give it a name, I'd say he smelled like pure male hotness. Not the sweat of manual labor, or kitchen grease, or the scent of after-shave, but a clean, crisp, heady, manly smell that makes me want to squeeze my thighs together.

Please, please don't let Phoenix notice that my hormones are having a field day.

Thank heavens she has other concerns. She leans on the dining table, cupping her chin in one hand while she studies the typed schedule she holds in the other. "This morning I have a meeting with the Department of Internal Affairs to discuss the final housing and security arrangements for the visiting dignitaries, then in the afternoon we have your dress fitting to fit you with your outfits for the wedding, then—"

"Outfits?" I interrupt. "As in plural? Surely I only need one bridesmaid dress?"

She shakes her head. "Church weddings aren't legally binding here, due to the whole separation of church and state thing, so we have a civil wedding the day before the big church wedding. You'll need a separate outfit for that. Then you'll need a dress for the gala dinner that night, and another for the ball after the church wedding."

I swallow, choking on a piece of scrambled egg. Adam thumps me on my back, which doesn't help.

"And to think the ..." This time I pretend to choke because I was about to say 'And to think the last time you got married you wanted to do it in jeans'. I was the one who had to convince her to wear a dress that time. But I don't know if anyone else at this table knows they're already married, so I drown the words with a gulp of water from Phoenix's glass.

On the plus side, my coughing fit attracts the attention of a maid in a navy and white uniform who brings a pot of coffee to our end of the table, and I'm no longer the focus of everyone's attention. She fills all our cups, blushing when Adam thanks her.

Phoenix looks back at her schedule. "This evening we're hosting a dinner party." She flicks to the next page. "Then tomorrow we have your photo sitting—"

"My what?"

"The palace will be making the official announcement of the bridal party in the papers the day after, so we need to get you some official portraits that can go out to the press. Unless you already have a picture you'd like to send out to the papers?"

I swallow the lump in my throat, drowning it down with a gulp of hot, black coffee. She knows very well I don't. I hate having my picture taken.

This is my last chance to back out then, before my name and my life go public. Before Phoenix becomes a laughing stock for choosing me as her bridesmaid. "Can't Rebekah be your bridesmaid instead?"

The others laugh.

"Can you imagine me waddling down the aisle?" Rebekah asks. "Besides, I don't think they make bridesmaid dresses in tent size."

You'd be surprised. The first time Carly married she was already heavily pregnant.

I change the subject away from weddings and me being on public display not just once, which I've sort of come to terms with, but a gazillion times over the next few weeks. "I was wondering – what thread count are your sheets?"

Beside me, Adam makes a noise as if he's suppressing a laugh, and Rebekah's eyes go wide. My face flames. I said something wrong, didn't I?

Phoenix doesn't bat an eyelid, though. "I have no idea. But I'll ask the housekeeper and get back to you."

I need another subject change. Stat. "Can we ask your secretary to schedule some time in your diary so you can give me a grand tour of this town?"

Phoenix frowns at her schedule. "Things aren't usually this crazy. It's just all the wedding arrangements ... But we've got a girls' day scheduled for Thursday. I was thinking of a spa day, but I guess we could do some sightseeing instead."

I was joking about having to book time in her diary, but Thursday ... "That's two whole days away!"

I'm not usually this needy, I promise. It's just that days off are rare in my life, and even when I do get a day off I spend it running errands, or doing chores, or studying, and I have no idea what I'm going to do to keep busy while the only person I know in this town is in meetings ...

I swallow down my panic and manage a smile. "Then maybe I can go out exploring on my own." I say it bravely, though I don't feel very brave. Do the people in Westerwald even speak English?

Phoenix eyes me skeptically. She knows I'm not big on adventure, and wandering around a strange place on my own will most definitely be the biggest adventure of my life.

"It's not much fun getting lost in a foreign city." Her expression is wistful, though. After her impetuous secret marriage to Max last summer, she ran out on him to backpack around Europe on her own. Or he ran out on her – the jury's still out on that one. It's kind of like the whole Ross and Rachel 'they were on a break' thing.

But that's Phoenix, not me. She thrives on adventure, while stepping outside my comfort zone is my idea of hell on earth. It's one of the reasons I still live with my mother, even though she drives me batshit crazy.

"I'm sure we can find someone on the palace staff who

can take you out and show you the sights," Phoenix says, but she sounds doubtful.

"I'll take her."

I jump at the sound of Adam's voice, far too close to my ear for comfort. He's talking to Phoenix, but the purr in his voice suggests his words aren't meant for her.

Phoenix claps her hands. "That's a great idea. You can go out this morning and see a bit of the city while I'm in my meeting."

I open my mouth to argue, then shut it again. Firstly, because I know from past experience that she'll win any argument we have and secondly, because she's paying for my whole damned trip. What kind of ungrateful friend would I be to insist someone else give me a guided tour, when every member of staff is no doubt frantically preparing for the royal wedding?

"Thank you – that would be lovely." I even manage a smile. But getting lost alone in a foreign city no longer seems like the most dangerous way to spend the day.

Chapter 4

Adam

When I come down the back stairs from the guest wing, Khara is already waiting at the private entrance, seated on an uncomfortable-looking antique bench just inside the door. She's still dressed as she was at breakfast, in jeans that fit her like a glove and a cropped tank top that leaves her midriff bare. I've seen plenty of bare female flesh in my life, but somehow that tantalising glimpse of tanned skin gets my pulse racing with a thrill I haven't felt in a long while. It's good to feel alive again.

She's holding a book open in her lap, but paying no attention to it as she chats to the footman stationed at the door. As I cross the vestibule to join her, she turns her head and frowns. Not the usual reaction I get from women when they see me, which is frustrating and challenging in equal measure.

"Please get someone to bring my car round from the garage." I hold out my car keys to the footman.

Khara hops off the bench. "There's no need for that. We can walk." She waves her Frommer's guide at me. "The guidebook says all the major attractions are within a few miles' radius of the palace."

"Exactly – we could be walking a few *miles*." Most women I know, with the possible exception of my sister, who is exceptional in everything she does, object to walking any distance further than the block between Harrods and Harvey Nichols.

But then Khara's scuffed sneakers are more suited to walking than the high heels most women I know wear. Not that she needs heels. Even in flat shoes she only has to tilt her head a little to look up at me.

"Okay, let's go then," I say, offering her my arm. She looks at it as if it's poisoned, so I shrug and let her precede me through the door.

It turns out that, unlike Khara's sneakers, my leather brogues aren't made for walking. By the time we've toured Neustadt's historic town centre, visiting the baroque cathedral, the city hall, the opera house, and the national museum, my feet are killing me, and it's taking all my effort not to let her see me wince. While acting like a wimp is most certainly not part of my seduction plan, the need to pretend I'm fine is seriously hampering my ability to flirt. Or maybe I'm just rusty. It's been a long, long time since I've had to work this hard to get a woman's attention. Usually a grin and a flutter of eyelashes does it. Or a flash of my credit card.

As we traipse through one historical building after another, I initiate Stage One in my seduction repertoire: laying the groundwork. This first stage is about getting the woman to feel comfortable enough to relax and be open to more. Standing close, but not too close that she'll feel threatened, opening doors for her, paying her an honest compliment, appearing interested in everything she says, making eye contact.

Those last two are harder than usual. Khara barely says a word, and seems to find her Frommer's guide way more fascinating than me. She doesn't stop moving, as if she's determined to work her way through the entire guidebook in one morning – which might actually be possible, since it's the shortest guidebook ever printed. Westerwald is not a very big nation and its capital, Neustadt, would fit into Greater London five times over. Though Westerwald is still triple the size of Erdély – I checked on Google. I doubt that Frommer's have ever bothered to print a guidebook for Erdély.

Khara shows genuine interest in everything she sees, and it's almost as if she's trying to absorb everything, store it up in her memory, with a single-minded focus that excludes everything else – including me. But I can't help wondering if there's something more to her over-enthusiastic sightseeing – could it be an attempt to avoid me?

Which must mean I'm already having an effect on her. So maybe it's time to step up to Stage Two: touch. A light hand on the bare skin of her lower back, a brush of an arm, moving in a little closer to whisper in her ear.

But every time I step closer, she steps away. Every time I touch her, she shrugs me off.

The last time a woman shut me down like this even though she was clearly attracted ... I screw up my face, trying to recapture that memory, but that evening was a bit of a blur, and over-shadowed by me taking a fist in the face for Nick in a brawl over a bad poker hand. Didn't Max tell me that Phoenix and Khara met in Vegas? Maybe it's just Vegas women who are my Achilles heel.

I'm a heartbeat away from giving up, deciding that maybe she doesn't want my advances and I'm just being a dick, but then I catch her swift intake of breath as I brush against her. Sure, it could be a sign of discomfort, but then I spot her blush as she turns away. A woman doesn't blush if she wants nothing to do with you.

I can work with that. I can turn 'interested but won't admit it' into 'I want you right now, any way I can get you.'

Though maybe not right now. "When I offered to play tour guide, I envisioned a Champagne cruise along the river where we could see the sights without actually having to visit any of them," I groan as we step out of the dark interior of the smaller Church of St Boniface into blinding sunlight. I'm also not sure who the tour guide is here. Turns out Frommer's has an extensive section on the church's eighteenth century frescoes while I didn't even know this church existed.

Khara smiles, perhaps for the first time all morning, but it looks too saccharine-sweet to be real. "Feel free to go back to the palace. It looks like I'll be able to manage this town on my own. It seems everyone here speaks English after all."

"I know all the best bars in this city, and most of the nightclubs," I offer, injecting as much humour into my smile as my aching feet will allow.

She rolls her eyes. "I didn't travel halfway around the world to see the inside of yet another bar. Aren't you even the slightest bit interested in history or art?"

Would she be more interested if I told her my ancestors used to make history, and were patrons to some of Europe's most famous artists and composers? I'm not really willing to find out because I suspect I might know the answer, and my ego has already been bruised enough by her lack of interest.

"I promised Phoenix I'd show you around the city, so that's what I'm going to do." Even if it kills me, which, if my feet are anything to go by, might just be possible.

"And you always keep your promises?" Khara scoffs, a look in her eyes that seems to pierce right into me.

Her words are a lance, striking me in the open wound that Nick's death reopened. I promised my mother I'd consider her brother's offer, and instead I'm doing everything I can to avoid thinking about it. I promised Nick I would keep him out of trouble. I promised my best friend Charlie that I'd always be there for him. I failed them all.

I lift my chin. "I need a drink," I say, though my jaw is clenched so tight I'm surprised I manage to get the words out. "The Landmark Café has got to be in that damned guidebook."

She looks at me as if I'm a bug she wants to squish, then reopens the guidebook. "Yes, here it is. It's part of the Beaux-Arts Guildhall, which houses the tapestry museum."

I draw the line at tapestries. "Great, you can look at tapestries and I'll drink." It's close enough to midday for drinking to be acceptable.

I've barely had a few sips of one of the Landmark Café's electric-blue signature cocktails when Khara rejoins me, looking disgruntled. "The tapestry museum's closed," she announces, sliding into the seat across from me.

"Thank God for that." I reach across the table and tug the guidebook out of her hand. "Because now we're going to see this city *my* way."

"As long as there are no bars," she warns.

"Sweetheart, we're sitting in Neustadt's most famous bar right now."

She glares at me, clearly not liking that epithet, then looks around as if seeing the place for the first time. "There's so much light!"

The Landmark Café is housed in a glass box overhanging the river that bisects the city. At night, this place buzzes with loud music, neon light, and Neustadt's young and trendy, but it's not one of those bars that looks seedy in daylight, and there is rather a lot of daylight in here. Sunlight reflects off the silver surface of the river, throwing dancing patterns against the glass ceiling. I lean forward, dropping my voice seductively. "The Guildhall was built in the eighteenth century, over the foundations of an earlier, older Guildhall. This conservatory is said to have been a precursor to London's Crystal Palace." I straighten up. "Is that what you want to hear?"

She licks her lips and for a second her expression of indifference cracks, proving she's not as unaffected as she appears and that I was – sadly – right that the way to this woman's heart is through ancient history. I grin, and just like that her disinterested expression is back.

"Since this bar is also famous for its lunch menu, we'll grab a bite here before we carry on our tour." I wave for the waiter. And that'll give my feet a chance to recover before we make the long walk to the bridal boutique for her dress fitting.

The waiter brings our menus, which are printed in French, German and the local Westerwald dialect. Khara studies the menu, and I can almost feel her anxiety mounting across the table.

"Shall I order?" I ask.

She nods and hands back the menu to the waiter, giving him an unconsciously flirty smile, the kind I've been trying to get out of her all morning. I barely glance at my own menu before I place the order. In perfect French. Okay, I'm showing off a little. But a man's got to use every weapon in his arsenal.

I still don't earn a smile.

"So tell me how you met Phoenix," I prompt as soon as the waiter heads to the kitchen.

Khara shrugs, looking out of the tall windows towards the river. "We worked together for a while when she lived in Vegas."

Phoenix worked in a casino bar, as I recall. Which makes Khara a barmaid too. No wonder bars don't feature high on her list of must-see places. If anyone told me I had to spend my holiday visiting corporate offices I'd probably also not be very impressed.

"And you? How do you know Max?" She looks at me then, her gaze meeting mine, and I think it must be the first time she's looked directly at me because I notice now that her eyes are a really dark blue, almost indigo, and it's as if I've had a hit of a particularly powerful drug, the sudden unexpected whammy of attraction sending a rush to both my brain and my groin.

She's not a classic beauty but her face has character, with perfectly shaped eyebrows and a sultry Cupid's bow mouth. Her make-up is on the too-heavy side, the smoky eyeliner making her almond-shaped eyes look even bigger. Her blue-tinged hair is frizzy, making her look like a mermaid – wild and exotic. I find myself leaning forward like an eager schoolboy.

Since it's never a good idea to let a woman know you're too interested, I force myself to sprawl back, crossing my arms over my chest.

And speaking of chests ... My gaze flits down hers. Her arms are also crossed over her chest, pushing up her breasts to give me an excellent view of her cleavage, since her tank top leaves very little to the imagination. It's so skimpy her bra straps are visible.

Her eyes narrow when my gaze lingers too long, and she rapidly uncrosses her arms. Not that it makes much difference. I'm still picturing those breasts cupped in my hands.

She asked me something, didn't she? I focus back on the conversation and clear my throat, more than a little pissed at myself. Since when do I get enthralled by a woman's eyes – or chest – for heaven's sake?

"I was at university with Rik, Max's brother, and we all played together on the same polo team for a few years, before Max moved to the States," I answer, finally piecing together her question.

"Polo's the one in the water, isn't it?"

I grin. "No, it's the one with the horses."

Her eyes are wide again. "Isn't it dangerous?"

I shrug. "Not if you know what you're doing."

She shudders.

"You don't like horses?"

"I have no idea. I've never seen one in real life."

I have to close my mouth. There isn't a single person in my circle who hasn't grown up around horses. Everyone I know owns either racehorses, thoroughbreds for everyday riding, or polo ponies – and sometimes all three. I received my first Arabian on my fifth birthday.

"Well, you'll have a chance to meet your first real horses this weekend. Max has agreed to take part in a charity polo tournament with my team." In Nick's place, since we haven't yet found a permanent replacement with a similar handicap.

The waiter returns with our wine. He pours a little of the chilled Chablis into my wine glass. I breathe in the bouquet, swirl the wine in the glass then take a small sip. Crisp, just a little tart, perfect. I nod, and the waiter fills both our glasses. Then he clears away the cutlery we won't need and Khara's shoulders lose a little of their tension. I file that interesting titbit away.

"Have you lived in Las Vegas all your life?"

Khara nods, but doesn't say anything more. This conversation is going nowhere fast. Has she never learned the art of making small talk?

"Tell me about it," I prompt.

"There's nothing to tell."

I'm pretty good at reading people. That's why picking up women has always been so easy for me, and why I'm so good at charming clients. So I know that this woman is being deliberately cagey. Now I'm not just interested; I'm intrigued. What deep, dark secrets is she hiding?

"Okay, then, tell me something about Phoenix that I don't

already know," I say, my tone teasing again, changing the subject to easy common ground.

Instead, she clamps her lips together and shakes her head. My eyes widen. Wow, whatever she has on Westerwald's soon-to-be archduchess, it must be good. I wonder if Max knows ...?

But before I can press her the waiter arrives with our meal. Khara eyes the plates with suspicion. "What is this?"

"Veal Entrecôte, and creamy polenta with truffles and Parmesan."

"And again in English?"

I chuckle, and earn another glare. "I guess you could call it rib-eye steak from a calf, and oatmeal with mushrooms and cheese."

"Then why not just call it that?" She takes a tentative bite of the veal.

"Because it sounds better in French. Everything sounds better in French."

She shrugs. "Just sounds pretentious."

We eat in silence for a few minutes and I can tell she's enjoying the meal, despite her initial misgivings. She digs into her food as if she were starving. All or nothing. Does she do everything with that same single-minded focus? My mind strays as I imagine her in bed. Naked. All or nothing. That wild hair spread out across my pillow, its wildness matched in her eyes.

I grin at the vision. It would certainly be a refreshing change from most of the women I've dated. Though maybe calling them dates is an exaggeration. Let's be honest: I don't date them; I sleep with them. But I'll also be the first to admit that's growing old. I've been looking for a fresh challenge lately, and here she is, sitting right in front of me.

As we eat, Khara props the guidebook in front of her on the table and starts to read, effectively walling me out. This time I manage to keep my mouth closed, but I'll admit that I'm stunned. Batting a maiden over, as we say in cricket, is rare enough for me, but this is a definite first. I cannot think of a single moment in my life where any woman found a book more appealing than my company. Most women I wine and dine even put away their mobile phones in my presence.

Still, her supposed absorption in the book gives me a chance to study her. There's something raw about Khara. It's not so much that she lacks polish, but rather a vitality, an untamed quality simmering beneath the surface. She doesn't have that rigid posture and glossy façade that most women in my circle develop somewhere around their pre-teens, nor does she carefully weigh everything she says and does. She makes me feel a deep, primal urge I've never experienced before. It's that physical kick I get every time I touch her, but there's something more there, something I can't identify.

Despite the fact that she keeps shutting me down – or maybe because of it – I actually want to spend more time with her. I want to understand who or what put that chip on her shoulder about men, about me. I want to get to know her. And that is rare enough to be noteworthy.

When we're done with the main course, I summon the waiter for the bill. This is my grand moment; now I'm sure to get her attention.

I whip out my black credit card.

The waiter's eyes go reassuringly big and round. But Khara doesn't even blink. She casts a glance at the card, then closes the guidebook, tucks it away into her big, faux-leather handbag and says, "So where to next, tour leader?"

I choke on my last mouthful of wine. Doesn't she know the significance of a black card? Or does she simply not care? It's that last thought that hits me like a horse kick, as if everything I've ever known has been turned upside down. I've never met anyone before who doesn't care about the money.

I have to clear my throat before I can speak. "I need to get you to your dress fitting, but we're going to make a stop for dessert along the way."

Chapter 5

Khara

The sun on my face feels completely different to the Nevada sun. Milder, gentler, as if the fluffy white clouds drifting overhead are filtering out the heat on its path down to the ground. I lift my face to the sky, feeling the warm prickle on my closed eyelids and my cheeks. I breathe in deeply and smell food, and humanity, and exhaust fumes, ever-present in any city in the world, I suppose. But above all of these is the delicious scent of the man beside me.

The chemistry between us is impossible to ignore. Trust me, I've tried. All morning and all through lunch I tried to ignore this thrum of awareness I get whenever Adam is near. I tried so hard I now have a headache.

I sigh.

"Is it that good?" Adam asks. His voice is doing that purring thing again, making me shiver. Or maybe that's the ice cream trickling down the cone and melting over my fingers. I stop worshipping the sun and rapidly lick my fingers clean, catching the cold droplets dripping down the sugar cone with my tongue.

Adam makes a small sound, a little like a groan, and I flash him a look that I hope says 'In your dreams'.

"Not bad," I answer. "This could even give Ben & Jerry's a run for their money."

He snorts in amusement, and I smile to myself. This rich, creamy, home-made ice cream is way better even than Ben & Jerry's, and I've been involved in a clandestine love affair with Ben and Jerry since my first high school boyfriend (ironically named Ben) broke my heart. I feel just a little as if I'm being unfaithful to them, but this cappuccino and French vanilla ice cream is seriously the best-tasting thing that has ever passed my lips. I take another lick, and moan with pleasure.

Out of the corner of my eye, I notice Adam not-so-discreetly adjusting his chinos, and suppress another smile. No reason why we can't both feel uncomfortable.

I have to admit, Adam's version of sightseeing isn't too bad. From the Guildhall we walked along the embankment of the Wester River which runs through the city. Glass-walled tourist boats ply the river, loudspeakers blaring, while plainer-looking water buses move in a steady stream in and out from the very modern-looking dock. Then he hailed us a horse-drawn carriage, just like the ones in New York City romcoms, and we rode through the increasingly narrow, cobbled streets to this square in the shadow of the cathedral.

Dotted around the square are the quaint wood-and-canvas stalls of a farmers' market, bustling with shoppers, vendors shouting for attention, kids and dogs, and tourists, who are easy to spot because they look just like the tourists we get in Vegas. We eat our ice creams sitting on the sun-baked edge of the stone fountain in the center of the square and a light breeze drifts cool droplets toward us.

Without a doubt, the home-made ice cream stall is the most popular, even more popular than the craft beer stalls. People are queuing for this ice cream, and I don't blame them. Why isn't this in the guidebook?

"Do you come here often?" I take another long lick from my cone, enjoying the way Adam's eyes dilate at the sight. Geez, but men are predictable, no matter where in the world they are, or how much money they have.

Adam shrugs. "I've visited Westerwald off and on over the years, first because my mother is a patron of the Neustadt Ballet and has family here, and then more frequently after I got to know Rik and Max."

That wasn't what I meant, but it tells me more than I wanted to know. A patron of the ballet? I've never even seen a ballet. It just reaffirms that this man who seems to be trying his utmost to win me over is in a whole other league. Still, I can't quite reconcile the man beside me, licking melting home-made ice cream off his fingers as the breeze ruffles his dark hair, with the one I saw earlier, ordering pretentious foods and waving around his fancy credit card and generally acting like a dick. The man I met in Vegas, the one I saw last night, didn't look like the kind of man who'd want to get his no-doubt-designer pants dirty sitting on the edge of a public fountain, as relaxed here among us mere mortals as he looked in the palace library.

Not that Adam could ever be mistaken for a 'mere mortal'. He could be in a room full of the world's most beautiful people and he'd still stand out. Not because of his looks or his fancy button-down shirt that looks like something out of the pages of *GQ*, but because of the way he carries himself, as if he's saying 'I am Someone. Look at me.'

When my cone is done, I trail my fingers in the cool water of the fountain.

"You look more relaxed," Adam observes, flashing me a decidedly wolfish grin. "Have you realized I don't bite?"

I eye him coolly. "You give yourself way too much credit. My being relaxed has nothing to do with you, and everything to do with the place."

He looks at me as if he doesn't understand. I blow out a breath. "These are my kind of people. I belong here, not in a palace." I wave toward the vendors and shoppers.

He looks genuinely confused. "You are who you are, whether you're in a palace or the town square."

Of course he'd think that, safe in his bubble of white male privilege. And being more privileged than most, he'd no doubt feel that same confidence wherever he goes, whether it's a palace, a farmer's market, or a high-priced Vegas casino.

"But in the palace there are all sorts of rules and etiquette you need to know to fit in."

It's more than just knowing how to use a napkin or a fork. In less than a day I've realized it's how I dress, how I walk, even how I talk to servants, that marks me as different. The housemaid was very put out that I made my own bed this morning. How was I supposed to know that would cause offense?

Adam wipes his hands clean in the water. "Etiquette is easy enough to learn."

"I must have missed that day at finishing school." I don't even try to keep the snark out of my tone.

"That's not a bad idea ..."

Since I don't remember having any idea, I stare at him.

"Lessons," he says. "If it worries you, you could have etiquette lessons."

Are there really people who teach this stuff? I shake my head. "Thanks, but no thanks. I can't afford lessons. I'm unemployed as of two days ago, so I need to save my money for more important things, like transport and the gas bill and food." And I'm not going to be here in Westerwald long enough to make that expense worthwhile. Back in Vegas, I'll still have to make my own bed, and I'll only ever use one knife and fork.

Adam holds up a hand to stop me. "This right here is lesson number one – you need to stop doing that."

"Stop doing what?"

"It is considered very poor taste to talk about money. We don't ask about thread counts, or talk about how much things cost, tell anyone we're unemployed, and we certainly don't tell anyone how much we need money."

"But I do need it."

"Lesson number two: don't give away any information that can be used against you."

He rises, offering me a hand to help me up. I'm tempted to ignore it, but that would be rude, wouldn't it? So I place my hand in his and for a moment I struggle to breathe, that sensation of his warm skin against mine flooding my senses. Who would have thought something as simple as a touch could make me feel as if every nerve ending just received a shock? It's as if I can see my life flashing before my eyes, but, instead of my life, I'm seeing flashes of what it might be like to be up close and personal – and naked – with this man.

He pulls me to my feet, but still doesn't let go of my hand and I'm too dazed to pull away.

So much for trying to resist this very inconvenient attraction.

"It's just norepinephrine," I mutter, and Adam gives me an odd look.

It's just hormones. It's not real. It wouldn't last beyond ten minutes after he's gotten what he wanted from you. Hopefully, if I tell myself that often enough, my brain will finally take over and I'll stop feeling so feverish I want to strip off all my clothes. And his.

I pull my hand out of his and fuss with putting the guidebook back in my purse to avoid eye contact.

Adam leads me on a winding route along narrow streets made of uneven cobbles. Thank heavens I don't wear heels. The buildings on either side of us are just as narrow, all identical and rigidly formal-looking, no more than two or three stories high, with red, beaver-tail roof tiles (according to the guidebook). If the other pedestrians weren't dressed in twenty-first century clothing I'd swear I'd stepped into a Jane Austen movie.

Then we round a corner into a wider, tree-lined boulevard, with plush store windows on their ground floors, and every one is a designer brand name. Prada. Chanel. Bulgari. Armani.

I'm so busy gaping at the window displays that I nearly bump into Adam when he stops walking. And there it is, the bridal boutique, only it's not just any bridal boutique. The storefront has one of the most luxurious displays I've ever seen, ball gowns and cocktail dresses and fancy jewelry accessories that I suspect aren't made of paste. The next story up contains the bridal dress display, and these are seriously the most jaw-droppingly elegant dresses I've ever seen, with trains and everything. Rebekah might be right; I don't think these dresses are made for brides who are six months pregnant and headed for the local registry office.

As if sensing my hesitation, Adam nudges me in the back, forcing me to step through the double doors which are being held open by a liveried doorman. Inside, the store is cool and quiet. An attendant steps forward to greet us, but when she takes in my blue-dipped hair, and worn jeans and sneakers, she starts to back off. For a second I wonder if I've stepped out of Jane Austen and into *Pretty Woman*.

"Ms Thomas is here for her appointment with Anton," Adam commands in the same voice he used with the footman. It's a voice that sounds bored, and just a little dismissive. It's the voice I remember from that long ago night in Vegas.

For a moment I envy his self-assurance, the way the attendant blushes and says "Yes, sir," and almost falls over herself in her eagerness to be of service. But I've also been on the receiving end of that tone often enough for my hackles to rise.

The attendant leads us up a sweeping staircase to a private lounge area. Phoenix is already there. "Did you have fun?" she asks, eyes twinkling as she looks between me and Adam.

"It was ... interesting," I answer. "I've seen architecture and art today that I never dreamed I'd see for real. This city is beautiful!"

"See – didn't I tell you this trip would be educational?" She turns to Adam, that sparkle in her eyes looking decidedly mischievous. "And did *you* get an education today?"

"More than I bargained for." He looks around the brightly

lit lounge. The sofas are ivory-colored, as are the walls and even the modern chandelier overhead. The only color in the room is its inhabitants. "I thought bridal fittings were supposed to be accompanied by Champagne?" He sounds hopeful.

He clearly doesn't know Phoenix very well. She has a hard head for alcohol, and could drink most men under the table back when she and I worked together (probably the result of growing up on the road with her hard rocker father) but the one drink she won't touch is Champagne. Says it makes her do crazy things – like marry a man she just met in Vegas. Not that I think that was in any way crazy. Just look at the man she married. Is marrying.

Max isn't a great catch because he's an archduke, because he's rich, or even because he's good-looking. He's a great catch because he's a good man. Not the kind of man who would shirk his responsibilities. When he and Phoenix met, he was working as a winemaker in California. A solid, honest job working with his hands. Then, when circumstances forced him to drop the career he loved, he did the right thing and stepped up to lead Westerwald. That's the kind of man I want for myself one day. Not Prince Charming, just a good, reliable man who can be counted on not to shirk his responsibilities.

"No Champagne," Phoenix confirms. "Besides, we still have the dinner party this evening, so no alcohol allowed until official duties are over."

Adam pulls a face. "If there's no Champagne, I'm going to leave you lovely ladies to your dresses. If I remember correctly, there's a rather nice little bar not far from here that starts happy hour early."

I roll my eyes, but Phoenix laughs. "You didn't read the schedule Max gave you, did you? You're on the guest list for the dinner party, so we'll expect you in the Yellow Drawing Room at six-thirty." She waves an admonishing finger at him. "And don't be late. You always either arrive late at our parties, or leave early."

He grins, his gaze flicking to me. "There just always seems to be some woman at your parties who wants to get me alone."

I can't help it; I snort. Does he seriously think that makes him seem attractive, or that I'd want to be yet another notch on a bedpost that clearly has so many notches it's in danger of collapsing the entire bed? What self-respecting woman would think that was a good deal? So I simply give him the same icy glare I give patrons who get handsy. The same look I gave that cousin of his.

Adam looks away, and it's my turn to grin. Score one for me.

When he takes his leave, sweeping Phoenix's cheek with another kiss, I move away so he doesn't even think about coming close and trying the same with me. His eyes glint, as if relishing the challenge, but he doesn't make a move to touch me. I blow out a breath as he disappears back down the stairs, then I turn to Phoenix. "I'm sorry I was late."

She waves her hand dismissively. "You're not late. I came early so Anton and I could have a catch-up and a gossip."

She pats the couch beside her and I take a seat, grateful to have a moment alone with her. "I've been wanting to ask ..." I gnaw on my lower lip. "What is a royal bridesmaid supposed to do? Aren't I supposed to organize you a bridal shower, or something? The only other time I was a bridesmaid, all I had to do was persuade the bride to borrow one of my dresses rather than get married in jeans."

She laughs. "This time I have more than enough dresses, and having you here is the only bridal shower I need. Claus and the protocol secretary are handling everything else."

"What's a protocol secretary?" I ask, diverted.

"Don't ask!"

"I *am* asking."

"He's the person who tells us where everyone needs to be seated, what order they need to arrive in, how we should greet them ... that sort of thing."

"Sheesh! I am so glad I'm not the one marrying a prince! If I ever get married, I want a quickie Vegas wedding, just like you had the last time."

She sighs dreamily. "Yeah, that was magical. But my point is, aside from Rebekah and Anton, I don't have many friends here. Everyone else I know either works for us or they're important Westerwald families, not the sort of people I want to share a spa day with, or sit up all night eating chocolate with when I get cold feet."

I laugh. "Sorry to tell you this, but it's way too late for you to get cold feet now!"

"That didn't stop me after I married Max the last time."

Our hushed laughter is interrupted by the arrival of Anton Martens himself, followed by a team of seamstresses and assistants. Even I have heard of Anton, fashion icon and one of Westerwald's most famous exports. Phoenix introduces us, and for the first time I really feel as if I'm being presented to royalty.

"Pleased to meet you," Anton says, but he isn't looking at

me. He's looking at my chest, and I'm about to give him that same icy look that quelled Adam when he says, "US size six?"

I nod.

For someone who owns a label that headlines at all the major fashion weeks, Anton is remarkably down-to-earth. While we wait for the assistants to fetch the clothing rail, he chats to us about his favorite binge TV show, the 'greasy spoon' he and his partner Lee like to go to for traditional English breakfasts, and the time he got lost in Paris and nearly missed his own show. When he fits me for my bridesmaid dress, he gets down on his hands and knees to pin the hem himself.

Even unfinished, this dress is the most stunning piece of clothing I've ever worn. The design is deceptively simple – a fitted bodice with a high halter neck and a full skirt that falls in soft folds all the way to my ankles. The only decoration is a high satin waistband the same color as the dress. It's the royal-blue fabric that makes this dress so special – I've never felt anything this soft before.

"Crêpe de Chine," Anton says, lovingly brushing his hand over my hip. "It matches perfectly with your hair and eyes."

"Don't worry about the hair," I say quickly. "It'll wash out before the wedding. And of course I'll be wearing it up."

"Why?" both he and Phoenix ask in unison.

Do I really need to spell it out? Clearly I do. "Because you can't have a bridesmaid with blue hair at a royal wedding." Or frizz. I Googled royal weddings the day Phoenix called and asked me to be her bridesmaid, and everyone in the bridal parties looks sleek and groomed. If I had the soft, bouncy curls of a L'Oréal commercial I might get away with it, but my curls lean more toward wild corkscrew than artful curl. My hair has more kinks than *Fifty Shades*.

"Nonsense," Phoenix says. "This is my wedding and I want it to be uniquely me, and that includes having a bridesmaid who is uniquely you. And I like your hair as it is."

I love her for that, but I shake my head. I don't want to be different. I don't want to stand out. Back home, I see so many people with bright-colored hair that I blend right in, but this entire day I haven't seen one other person with colored hair.

Anton grins. "Did you know that this particular shade of blue is Westerwald blue? Everyone will assume your hair is a patriotic statement."

I bite my lip and turn to the tall gilt-framed mirror. The color is a really good match, and both the dress and the hair bring out the dark blue in my eyes.

Phoenix moves to stand behind me, and I look at our reflections. "A crown of white flowers in your hair and a white bouquet, and you're done."

"I still need shoes," I point out, lifting the hem of the dress to reveal my worn but super-comfortable Keds.

Anton laughs. "Cinderella does indeed need a pair of slippers for the ball." He claps his hands and the assistants jump into action, bringing out an endless parade of shoes. I eye them in dismay. "They all have heels!" I don't even know how to walk in heels. When you're on your feet eight hours every day, trust me, a comfortable pair of flats is worth every cent.

"I'll give you a pair to practice in," Anton offers.

There are other dresses for me to fit, an A-line, knee-length cocktail dress with a deep V-neck in the same shade of blue for the wedding reception ("better for dancing," Phoenix explains), a dusky pink babydoll swing dress patterned with grey roses for the registry office wedding, and a nineteen-fifties vintage-style dress of forest-green crêpe for the banquet.

"You'll need to wear your hair up with this one," Anton says, "to avoid the colors clashing." He twists my wild frizz up into an Audrey Hepburn style, and I hardly recognize myself in the mirror.

"Do I get a fascinator to go with it?" I ask. I always wanted one of those. Something with peacock feathers to match my hair.

Anton shakes his head. "Hats and fascinators are for daytime outdoor events only. Tiaras are for evening wear."

No way am I ever wearing a tiara. I am so not a Disney princess.

"So what do you think of Adam?" Phoenix asks when I'm standing like one of those human statues on a little podium. Anton is back on his knees, pins in his mouth as he nips and tucks at the stiff green crêpe.

"I don't think of him at all," I lie.

She arches an eyebrow at me. I know her well enough to know she won't give up until she has a proper answer.

"He's cute," I say. "But he's a douche."

Somewhere around my knees, Anton chuckles.

"You've barely met him," Phoenix protests.

Then why is she asking what I think of him? For at least the third time today I wonder if she's trying to set me up with Adam, though for the life of me I can't imagine why.

I shrug. "I've met his type before. He's the kind of man

who thinks that just because he has money, he's exempted from behaving like a decent human being."

"You're being hard on him because he's rich."

I remember the way he slid his room key card to me a year ago, assuming I'd go with him just because he had money. And not even bothering to ask my name. The anger I felt then floods through me, fresh as if it happened today. Or maybe it did happen today. The only reason he volunteered to take me sightseeing was so he could get into my pants. "I'm being hard on him because he measures his worth by how much money he has, and how many women he can score with. He's the type who uses and discards women as if they're nothing more than objects for his personal gratification. He thinks money can buy him anything and anyone he wants. It can't."

"You should give him a chance. Get to know him and you'll see that, deep down, he's a nice guy."

I turn to eye her, and she grins cheekily. "It's not as if I'm suggesting you marry him."

As if.

"So what are you suggesting?"

"That you should relax and have a little fun. That's what vacations are for. And you *need* to relax. You're so tightly wound. When did you last do something just for fun?"

I shrug, and Anton scowls at me. "Stand still!" he orders.

"I have fun!" I protest. Admittedly, I haven't dated for a while, not since Raúl and I broke up, but ... Actually, there is no 'but'. I can't even remember the last time I did anything except work or study.

But if I wanted to blow off steam with a man, it certainly

wouldn't be Adam. What I feel around him is definitely not *relaxed*.

When the shoe parade starts again, I hold up both my hands. "Enough! I can't take any more." I look at Phoenix. "Isn't it your turn?"

Back in my comfortable jeans and Keds, I relax on the couch while Phoenix models her wedding gown for me.

It's the kind of dress that little girls dream of, made of thick ivory silk crêpe covered in a gauzy layer of soft silk tulle. The bodice is embroidered with an intricate pattern of roses and decorated with freshwater pearls.

Anton proudly holds out the veil for me to inspect. "It's hand-made Belgian lace."

I gently finger the veil. "Is that a dragon embroidered on it?"

He nods. "The dragon and rose emblem of Westerwald."

I remember the signet ring Max used in place of a wedding ring the first time they married – a blue stone carved like a dragon's head and surrounded by a pattern of silver roses. I had no idea at the time what that ring signified. Did Phoenix?

"What are you wearing for your civil wedding?" I ask.

"Did you pack the dress I asked you to bring?"

I nod, and she grins. "*That*'s the one I want to wear when we marry."

It's the same dress I loaned her for her first wedding to Max, in that Vegas chapel more than a year ago. More Marilyn Monroe than Anton Martens, but if anyone can make it look classy it'll be Phoenix.

Next she models the dress that Anton is still working on,

an ice-blue, lace-and-chiffon outfit that looks like something a nineteen-twenties flapper would have worn.

"My going-away dress," she explains, doing a twirl.

I frown. "Where are you going away to?"

"That's the dress the bride wears to leave the wedding reception, ostensibly to go away on honeymoon, though we won't be taking time off for a honeymoon until Christmas."

My mind is reeling, especially when I consider the cost of all of this. When I met Phoenix she was just as broke as I am. "Who's paying for all of this?" I ask, waving my hand at the rail where all our other dresses are hanging.

Anton makes a choking noise, reminding me I'm not supposed to talk about money, but Phoenix just smiles. "Max's family."

Wow, just wow. I got my first job so I could buy a prom dress, because my own mother refused to pay for it. Admittedly, she was between jobs at the time, as she was all too often throughout my childhood. She was always leaving jobs because she thought she could do better somewhere else. Her attitude toward men wasn't much better. She left all the good ones, and had her heart broken by the ones she left them for, the ones who promised her the world then left her high and dry.

That, more than anything, is why I know what damage a man like Adam Hatton can do. Because I've watched my mother chase that brass ring enough to know what happens when you let a man like Adam into your life. Men like that are after only one thing, and the moment they've had it they're gone.

So if Phoenix plans to set up the best man with her bridesmaid, then she can think again.

Chapter 6

Khara

I have never seen so many beautiful people all in one place. They're all so slim! Sure, there are a few men carrying a little extra weight over the belt, and some of the women could be called curvy rather than thin, but with one look I can tell this isn't a crowd that lives on fast food or instant microwave meals. Even the wait staff are gorgeous.

The guests have a buffed and polished look to them, and there's so much bling it's blinding. I've never felt plain before, but tonight I do. Though I spent more than an hour taming my wayward hair with a hair-straightener and half a can of hairspray, and I'm wearing a dress supplied by Phoenix's stylist, a conservative high-necked dress with a frilled skirt that goes to mid-calf, everyone looks at me as if they can sense that beneath the dress my underwear is from Walmart. It's there in the way the women's gazes slide over me, darting away as quickly as possible, as if they want to pretend I'm invisible. And it's there in the way the men's gazes linger too long, their hungry speculation. I know those looks. It's the way Adam's cousin looked at me. As if I'm an object.

It's like being back in high school all over again.

I wish Phoenix were here with me so I'd have someone to talk to, instead of feeling so spare. Even better, I wish I could slide behind the bar, where I belong. At least then I'd have something to do with my hands.

But Phoenix and Max are playing host and hostess, greeting the never-ending stream of people arriving, filling the Yellow Drawing Room with the buzz of conversation. This massive room, named for its yellow silk wallpaper and gold-leaf decoration, is getting warmer as more and more people fill the space. The jet lag is clearly still affecting me because the room has a surreal, spaced-out feel to it.

I hover near the tall sash windows, pretending to be absorbed in the view out over the gardens. Though it's nearing seven o'clock in the evening, mellow sunshine washes the garden and illuminates the room. I would much rather be down there, breathing in the scents of rose and lavender, than in here with all these beautiful strangers.

The guests gather in little groups of three or four, everyone sipping from crystal glasses of Champagne. They all seem to know each other, but I don't know a soul. Not even Claus and Rebekah are here; they returned to their home in Waldburg this afternoon. Hovering alone on the sidelines is only infinitesimally less awkward than joining one of those groups. Could I escape back to my room without Phoenix noticing?

"You look like you could use a drink." Adam materializes at my side, holding two full Champagne flutes. He offers me one. Damn, the man looks fine in a tux. But he still hasn't shaved. Three-day-old scruff suits him even better than two-day-old scruff.

"No, thanks." I turn away, looking desperately across the room to where Max and Phoenix are in deep conversation with the latest arrivals.

"It's just a drink."

"I don't drink."

"Don't you work in a bar?"

With a sigh, I face him. "Precisely. Can you imagine how good I'd be at serving drinks if I was stumbling around drunk myself?"

"You're not working now."

"When you're surrounded by alcohol eight hours a day, it loses its appeal." Or, more accurately, having to deal with drunk people eight hours a day kills the appeal.

He grins. "Then more for me." He drains one of the Champagne flutes, then the other, and I watch, intrigued despite myself, as he tilts his head back and swallows. Never in my life have I thought that the mere act of swallowing could look sexy. I hurriedly look back out the window, hoping I'm not blushing again.

"What are you wearing?" Adam takes a step back to take in my dress, as if he's only just noticed it. "Should we have a moment's silence for my grandmother's curtains?"

The fabric is rather hideous, dark and patterned with small blue flowers. Even though he's just said exactly what I was thinking, I bristle. "It's from a top British designer. She's very popular with celebrities." Not to mention that I peeked at the price tag before the stylist cut it off. This dress cost more than I earn in six months. I restrain myself from mentioning the price.

"Celebrities aren't exactly known for having the best taste," Adam mutters, shaking his head.

Quite a few not-so-surreptitious glances are coming our way now, especially from the women in the room. Since there's an element of hunger and envy in those looks, rather than just condescension, I assume it's Adam they're looking at, but oddly not all the looks are friendly. Adam doesn't seem to notice. Either that, or he doesn't care. He summons a passing waiter and snags two more glasses of Champagne.

"How much have you already had to drink?" I ask him suspiciously.

"Not nearly enough to cope with all these bores." He hands me one of the glasses, and this time I take it without objecting. I figure it's a public service.

"Nobody's forcing you to be here. You could just leave."

"I wish. But then there'd be an odd number, and Phoenix wouldn't be happy if I upset her table."

I have no idea what he's talking about but ... "If you can't leave, then I guess I can't either." I sigh.

"We could leave together. That way there'll still be even numbers at the table."

For half a second I'm tempted, but then I think of his boast about always leaving palace parties with some woman, and I clamp down on the little ray of hope that I can get out of this torture. I will not be one of those easy women who fall at his feet. I have my pride.

"What's the occasion for this party anyway?" he asks, looking around.

"It's a thank you for the benefactors of the new pediatric wing at the Neustadt hospital."

He wrinkles his nose. "So, in other words, an excuse for Europe's rich and titled to get dressed up and mingle."

"The information was on your schedule," I point out primly.

"I'm not very good with schedules. I don't like to be told what to do or when to do it."

Typical! To stop myself from saying something I'm sure to regret later, I take a tentative sip of the Champagne. The taste tickles my tongue, the bubbles exploding in my mouth, more sour than the Champagne we drank the night Max and Phoenix got hitched in Vegas. The flavor improves as I take a second sip, and then another.

"My two favorite people at this party!" Phoenix appears beside us, looking effortlessly elegant in a figure-hugging lavender-colored sheath dress. With my curves, if I wore a dress like that I'd look like a ten-dollar hooker, but she looks like the princess she now is. Max is half a step behind her, his hand resting at the base of her spine. *Be still my beating heart*. Between Max and Adam, both looking better than James Bond and with the sexy accents to match, it's not just jet lag making me feel as if I've stepped into an alternate universe.

"You must be drunk," I joke back. "It's only me and Adam."

She loops her arm through mine. "Exactly. I can count on Adam to be amusing, and I can count on you to be honest."

"Amusing?" I squint at Adam as if trying to see it, and both she and Max laugh.

It's hard to make conversation as we are interrupted again

and again by people wanting to talk with Max and Phoenix. Adam also seems to know most of the guests, and the conversations flow around me like swift-moving water around a dull, unmoving rock. Phoenix has always had the magical gift of getting people to open up to her and like her, but I'm in awe. I wouldn't have a clue what to say to all these strangers, but she seems to know exactly the right things to say.

After yet another interruption, she lays a hand on my arm. "We'll catch up tomorrow, I promise." Then she and Max head off to circulate among the guests, leaving me alone with Adam once again. I sip from my still-full Champagne glass.

"You know, you really don't need to stay here and make nice with the bridesmaid," I say. "Consider yourself free of that best man obligation. Go mingle with the beautiful people."

"Oh, it's not an obligation, and I'm already mingling with the most beautiful woman at the party."

I roll my eyes. "Bullshit. Everyone else here looks like a movie star. All glossy and shiny and—"

"Fake?" He laughs, and the sound has an unexpectedly bitter quality to it. "It's not hard to look good if you have money. Most of these women spent the entire day at a beauty spa primping for this party. I can guarantee that not one of them went looking at eighteenth century frescoes."

Is a day in a spa seriously all it takes to look like one of them? I eye two women gliding across the room, tall and slender as supermodels, hair and make-up impeccably perfect, graceful even though they're wearing four-inch heels.

"Phoenix did suggest a spa day," I say speculatively. "Maybe I should take her up on it."

He shrugs. "You're better off spending your days looking at frescoes."

What the …? Did he just insinuate I'm so hopeless even an entire day in a beauty salon can't help me? I round on him, indignation firing my blood, but Adam just laughs. "That's why I'm here talking to you instead of working the room: it's refreshing to meet a woman who *hasn't* spent the entire day preening in front of a mirror."

I narrow my eyes at him, not buying this back-handed compliment, and wondering if I should point out that neither Phoenix nor any of the palace staff spent the day preening.

Adam grins. "No, you're right, I'm just being *nice*. You looked lonely and I felt sorry for you. Is that more believable?"

"I'm not lonely," I protest.

"Liar. But don't worry – as soon as they find out you're the soon-to-be archduchess' BFF you'll have more 'friends' than you know what to do with." He leans closer, his voice dropping to a whisper. "But the truth is, I'm talking to you because all the other women at this party know me."

That sounds like the first honest thing he's said all day – and it explains the unfriendly looks. "Do you mean that they already know you're a douche, but since I'm new here you think I might not? Or do you mean they know you in the biblical sense?"

His grin turns to a smirk. "Yup."

Just how many women at this party might he know in the 'biblical' sense?

"Sorry, but you're too late. I already know you're a douche." My smile is so sweet it could cause cavities. It's the smile I use when I feel like stabbing a difficult customer with a fork.

He lays his hand over his heart, looking pained. "I'm starting to get the feeling you don't like me."

I pretend a shocked expression. "Whatever gave you that idea?"

He laughs, throwing his head back, and a couple of heads turn our way. I have to admit that Adam has a really nice laugh, warm and intimate, as if he's letting me in on a secret. It is quite possibly the sexiest sound I've ever heard, even sexier than his purr.

"Adam, dah-ling!" At the interruption, Adam's amused, slightly bored mask slips back into place.

It's the two supermodel types I spotted earlier. Up close, they're not as tall as I thought. I can tell that the brunette has had work done; her features are a little too symmetrical, her lips a fraction too big. Her friend, a classic blond with wide blue eyes, smiles at me in a vague way, but I'm unable to smile back. She reminds me too much of the cheerleader who tormented me all through high school.

Adam leans in to kiss the brunette's cheek. "It's been a while, Elena."

She turns narrow, assessing dark eyes on me. "And who is your little friend?"

Since I'm her height without the advantage of heels, the 'little' is clearly there to put me in my place. Adam hardly seems to move but suddenly he's right there next to me, closing the gap between us, sliding his arm around my waist and pulling me in against his side. When I try to squirm away, he holds me tighter.

"This is Khara. Khara, may I present my cousin Elena, Baroness Cassel."

My tongue feels like it's glued to the top of my mouth. Am I supposed to curtsy or call her 'Your Highness'? Where is Phoenix's protocol secretary when I need him? But Elena isn't even looking at me. Her gaze is laser-focused on Adam, and the desire in her eyes is plain to see.

I hope I don't look at him like that, because it's enough to make me nauseous.

"Very, very distant cousins," she corrects. "And you didn't seem to mind the connection when we were together." Her emphasis on the last word makes my skin crawl. Then her coy smile turns sympathetic, so quickly that I wonder if either emotion is real. "I am so sorry about your cousin Nick. You must all be so devastated."

I glance up at Adam. His easygoing smile doesn't waver, but there's a betraying tightness to his jaw. What happened to his cousin? I remember fair hair and soft hands, but beyond that I can't even picture the man who tried to grope me. Adam left a far more lasting impression.

"There's a rumor that you might inherit in his place ..." Elena leans in, sliding her hand up his arm, as if claiming him.

"You should know better than to trust rumors, Elena." There's a bite to his voice. His other hand slides down from my waist to rest on my butt in an unmistakably intimate gesture. I'm tempted to slap his hand away, but the tension in him stops me. This isn't a man trying to get lucky.

"We should get together again sometime," Elena continues,

not put off in the slightest by the fact that he's groping me right in front of her. "For old times' sake."

"As you can see, I'm here with a date."

Elena's laugh is low and seductive. "That didn't stop us before."

"You know I never come back for seconds." His voice is still so smooth, so polite and full of charm, that it takes both Elena and me a moment to register the hit. Her eyes narrow. I'm pretty sure mine have too. Her friend seems oblivious to Adam's snub.

Elena removes her hand from his arm. "You're right. The rumors can't possibly be true if you're choosing a cold-blood over a thoroughbred. Perhaps Mátyás will be more open to a woman with class and breeding."

I have no idea what she's talking about, but the glance she sends me is enough to know it was a dig at me. I certainly don't feel cold-blooded with the surge of fury rushing through me. I suck in a breath to retort, but Adam squeezes my hip in warning, as if to say 'Don't descend to her level', so I bite my lip.

"I am sure you and Mátyás will be perfectly suited to one another," he says, still smiling. "Now, if you don't mind, Khara and I were in the middle of something."

Elena glares at him, but her parting shot is aimed at me. "Enjoy him while you can, honey, because he won't stick around until morning."

When she and her friend are out of earshot I look up at Adam. "Ew! You dated your cousin?"

"I certainly wouldn't call it dating, and we're only distant cousins. Fourth or fifth, I think. Half the guests here tonight are related in some way, and the other half want to be. European aristocracy is a hotbed of in-breeding."

Our bodies are still pressed together and even though he's wearing a jacket I'm suddenly aware of just how solid and broad his chest is. His hand still rests intimately on my butt, holding me against him. "You can remove your hand now," I say pointedly.

"What if I don't want to?"

"Then I'll make you." I smile sweetly up at him, but my voice is a good imitation of *The Godfather*, and he quickly removes his hand.

I shift away, hoping it's not obvious that I need to place distance between us to get my breath back and my raging pulse under control. Damn hormones! "I'm sorry about your cousin. Were you close?"

He cocks his head, as if he has to think about it. "I was closer to him than almost anyone, but Nick was ... challenging."

I think of that long-ago night in Vegas, of Adam keeping the conversation flowing, smoothing over the difficulties, diverting his cousin away from me. Well, since I've now diverted Elena away from him, we're fair and square.

"And what was that about me being cold-blooded?"

He clears his throat, looking sheepish. "In horse-breeding, thoroughbreds are known as hot-bloods because of their more highly strung temperaments. Cold-bloods are hardier, calmer horses which are bred for work."

I arch an eyebrow. "And that was supposed to be an insult?

I take it as a compliment. I'd rather be a reliable work horse than a high-strung thoroughbred any day."

He laughs. "I think I might agree with you." For the first time since Elena's interruption, the amusement in his eyes looks genuine. "Thank you for playing along. What Elena wants, Elena usually gets, and she would have been a lot more difficult to get rid of if you hadn't been here."

"I can't imagine why she wants you," I tease. "You're not that much of a catch."

Okay, I'm not teasing, I'm flirting. What can I say? After years of harmless flirting to earn bigger tips, it's become a habit. It has nothing at all to do with the way my pulse is still going pitter-pat and my body wants to plaster itself back against him. *Liar*, a little voice in my head whispers.

Adam laughs again, but that bitter edge is back. "It's not me she wants. My cousin died recently in a car accident, leaving ... an inheritance. That's what Elena's after. And she's not the only one. Since the day Nick died, I've been swatting them off like flies."

"Oh, it must be so hard to be you," I mock. But now I understand why he's hanging out here with me rather than working the party like everyone else. It's not because he finds me particularly interesting, or because he feels sorry for me. It's because I'm the only person at this party who doesn't want something from him.

I'm still puzzling out what kind of inheritance would make an already wealthy man seem even more attractive to a baroness when a man more smartly dressed than all the guests, in a black coat, gray waistcoat and long black tie, appears in the doorway. "Dinner is served," he announces in a voice that carries through the room.

Immediately the guests start to move out of the wide double doors at the far end of the drawing room.

"Ladies first," Adam says, gesturing for me to lead the way. I drift after the crowd, nervously expelling my breath.

"You'll be fine," he says in a low voice. "Just remember to work from the outside in."

Chapter 7

Khara

The state dining room is separated from the Yellow Drawing Room by the high-ceilinged vestibule at the head of the grand staircase. The room looks even more impressive than it did when Phoenix gave me the palace tour yesterday. The walls are covered in burgundy silk and hung with paintings of Venice, and the room is lit by three massive, sparkly chandeliers. The table is big enough to seat at least fifty people, and if I thought there was a lot of cutlery and glassware at the breakfast table, that was nothing compared to this table. I gulp, swallowing down panic.

Is it too late to run, to get rid of this butt-ugly dress and escape the palace? *Get a grip, girl. You can do this.*

There are place cards at each setting, with the guests' names written in a curly gold font. Adam helps me find my place, between two complete strangers, then he circles the table to find his own. For a crazy moment I want to call him back, ask if he'll swap places with the man next to me, who looks as if he just swallowed a sour lemon.

I notice that all the way up and down the table, men and

women are seated alternately. Man, woman, man, woman. Now I get what Adam meant about even numbers.

Max is at the head of the table, all the way across the room. Phoenix is closer, but there are still at least four people between us. If I want to talk to her, I'd have to shout. Adam's seat is across from me, a couple places down. Who would have thought I'd actually be sad to be separated from him?

As Adam reaches his place across the table, smiling at the stern-faced, gray-haired woman beside him, an officious-looking young man hurries up to him – the palace's protocol secretary. "I am so sorry, sir. I don't know what happened! You should be seated higher up the table."

Adam glances up the table, toward Max's end. Elena and her friend are both seated in that direction. "Nope, no mistake."

"But sir! You're—"

"Unless you want one of the guests throwing wine in my face, I think I'm better off where I am."

I roll my eyes.

Dinner is about a million times more excruciating than breakfast, and I seem to do everything wrong. When I sit, the stern woman next to Adam glares at me. I hurriedly stand again. We all remain standing as Max makes a short speech, thanking everyone for being here, and for their generous contributions, before he sits. Only then does everyone else sit.

It's almost a shame to destroy the cloth napkin sculpture on my plate. The napkin is stiff with starch, and folded in the shape of a swan. But I copy everyone else, pulling the swan apart to spread the napkin across my lap. In fact, I'm almost scared to touch *anything* on the table. Every item is lined up and perfectly symmetrical.

The first course is a thin, watery soup. Consommé, it says on the gold-lettered menu. I select a knife to cut and butter a bread roll to mop up the soup, earning another glare from the woman next to Adam. What the hell is wrong with her? Did I use the wrong knife or something?

Since Sour Lemon Man is seated on my right, I turn to the man on my left to make conversation, as he looks younger and friendlier, but when I try to introduce myself he turns his back to talk to the woman on his left. How rude!

So I ignore them both and sip on the Champagne one of the liveried waiters fills my glass with. I'm starting to rather enjoy the taste of this Champagne.

When the soup is done, I'm still hungry. The waiters clear away the plates and Champagne glasses and move around the table filling the next in the line of glasses in front of each place setting, this time with white wine. There's another speech, from the tall, thin and exceptionally elegant woman seated on Max's right. Her speech is definitely not short, and my stomach rumbles audibly while she drones on. When she's done at last, the next course is served. Salad.

Lunch seems so long ago. A maid brought a tray of food to my room when I was getting ready, which I thought very odd since I'd had a big lunch and was coming out to a dinner, but I think now I understand why. She knew how meager tonight's food was going to be.

When my stomach grumbles again, I earn even more frosty stares from the guests around me. On the plus side, I finally figure out what Adam meant about working from the outside in. He was talking about the cutlery. We start with the outermost knife and fork, working inwards with each course.

According to the menu, the next course is fish or beef. I expect the waiters to come around and take our orders, like they did on the plane, but we don't seem to get a choice; everyone gets the same small piece of fish, artistically decorated with asparagus. I've never eaten asparagus before, and it's so drenched in creamy butter I'm still not entirely sure what it tastes like. When the young man on my left finally deigns to make conversation with me, I reply with short answers. After all, there's only so much I can say about the weather.

When I hand my empty plate to the server at the end of the course, I earn yet more surprised glances from the people around me. Clearly, I've done something wrong again, but there seem to be a lot of rules I just don't know. It's like I'm playing baseball and everyone else on the field is playing soccer.

Dessert is a watery lemon sorbet and I'm wondering what the chances are Neustadt has a late night McDonalds so I can fill my still-empty stomach, when, after another round of speeches, the next glasses in line are filled with red wine. Turns out that wasn't dessert, and the main course wasn't an either/or, as the servers bring out another course, tiny beef medallions floating in a red wine sauce, surrounded by a perfect circle of strange fluffy green mousse that I only identify as spinach thanks to the menu.

The food finally stops my stomach from making any further

noises, but the room has started to swell around me in a hypnotic rhythm. I have to prop my elbow on the table and my chin in my hands as I will myself to stay awake through yet another speech.

The real dessert is tasty, an airy chocolate soufflé dusted with an icing sugar image of the Westerwald dragon. Gorgeous, but the portions are so stingy that I finish mine in a few mouthfuls. The coffee's really good too, rich and dark, real bean coffee, but I am now so exhausted I don't think even caffeine is going to keep me awake much longer.

At long last this interminable meal is over, and everyone rises to move back to the drawing room for after-dinner drinks and more conversation. As I stand, I wobble on my feet, even though I haven't yet risked wearing any of the heels Anton gave me. The room is definitely swirling now.

I feel a hand on my arm and look up to see Adam. His expression is amused. "I thought you said you don't drink?"

"I don't. I'm just jetlagged."

He smiles. "Sure, if you say so. How about we get you upstairs to bed?"

"If by 'we' you mean 'me', I think that's a great idea." My lips feel numb, and the words sound slurry. Maybe I did have a teensy bit too much of the wine. And the Champagne.

"I'm walking you to your room." His voice is firm, discouraging opposition, but I argue anyway.

"If this is how you seduce women into leaving parties with you, you really need to up your game."

He laughs. "Most of my reputation is well-deserved, but I have never taken advantage of a woman who is ... jetlagged."

I don't want to accept his help but, since the room is swirling even more vigorously, I decide to give in. By the time we reach the door to my room I'm even grateful he walked me all the way here. I would certainly have gotten lost on my own.

He opens the door, waits for me to enter, then says, "Goodnight, sweetheart."

Before I can object to being called 'sweetheart', he has already closed the door on me. I stumble across the darkened room, lit only by a single lamp on the nightstand, and collapse on top of the covers, too tired to even kick off my shoes.

I feel as if I've run a marathon, sat an exam and done a job interview all at the same time. And as if I failed all three.

Chapter 8

Adam

"What the hell are you doing in Westerwald?" my sister Jemima asks when I'm stupid enough (or make that hung-over enough) not to check my caller ID before answering my mobile.

"You're turning into Dad," I moan, ignoring her question. London is a whole hour behind Westerwald, and the caller ID shows she's already at her desk at the office. "You need to get a life."

"I'm at the office," she says crisply, "because it's better than being at home. Unlike you, I can't leave town to avoid the parents."

I cradle my aching head in my hands. "I'm sorry, Jemmy." I really am. Our parents rarely disagree on anything, but since Nick's death my mother has been adamant that I accept her brother's offer, and my father is equally determined that I should stay in the family business. He has this antiquated notion that he's going to pass the business down to me, even though it's obvious to everyone that Jemima is far better management material. For the first time in my memory, they're barely talking to each other.

But my parents are only one reason I'm in Westerwald. Another is that every woman I've ever slept with in Great Britain suddenly wants to reconnect in the hope that I'll make her into a princess. How clueless do they have to be not to realise that if I wasn't interested enough to stick around before, I won't be getting down on one knee now?

It's clearly a major flaw in my personality, this lack of interest in settling down with just one woman. It's not that I don't like women. I adore them. But there isn't a single one I'm not closely related to who doesn't bore me to tears after a few weeks. Well, apart from Phoenix, but I refuse to think of her as a woman because Max would have my balls for breakfast, served up with toast and marmalade, if I so much as looked at his bride-to-be.

And perhaps apart from one mermaid-haired bridesmaid I haven't been able to stop thinking about all night. Though, considering my track record, there's a very large chance that as soon as I sleep with her – which I have every intention of doing before this wedding is over – I'll lose interest in her too.

"You're needed here, so get your arse back on a plane and come home," Jemmy demands impatiently.

"You're not the boss of me," I retort automatically, as I did a million times when we were growing up.

"Until you start behaving like a mature and responsible adult, I *am* the boss of you." Jemima is three years younger than me but has always acted like she's the older sibling. "Do you have any idea what day it is?"

I force a flippant tone. "Wednesday? Thursday?" But I know exactly what day it is.

She sighs. "What is so important that you're going to miss the dedication of Charlie's memorial?"

"Haven't you heard – I'm the best man at the wedding of the decade."

"Max hardly needs you to hold his hand."

"Nope, but the bridesmaid does."

I can actually hear Jemmy's eye-roll down the phone. "You're going to miss the dedication for a shag?"

I'm not going to miss the dedication for a shag, though that would be a nice bonus. I'm going to miss the dedication because I don't want to have to look Charlie's mother in the eye. I don't want to be reminded that I wasn't there when my best friend needed me – that maybe he'd be alive today if I hadn't been so self-absorbed that I didn't realise what was going on with him. Just like with Nick.

I cross my fingers. "It's not like that – I'm helping her. She's American, and completely out of her depth here with all the palace etiquette." At least that isn't a lie.

"And it can't wait until tomorrow? Charlie was your closest friend."

"Charlie's dead. He's not going to care if I'm there or not."

Jemmy blows out a long breath. "Fine. I'll make your excuses. Have you at least decided what answer you're giving Uncle Lajos? If you plan to say yes, I need to replace you at the office."

It shouldn't come as any surprise that I'm that easily replaceable, since I've hardly made myself indispensable, but the truth still stings. "There's no decision to make. You, of all people, know I can't be depended on. You can't seriously think I could be responsible for an entire country."

She's silent for a long moment, as if trying to find the right words. "Yes or no, it makes no difference to me. But, either way, you need to stop blaming yourself for other people's choices. Charlie and Nick were not your responsibility. They were both grown men who made their own decisions."

I shake my head, even though she can't see. Jemmy's one of only a handful of people whose opinions I respect, but on this we'll have to agree to disagree.

"Have you considered that if I accept Uncle Lajos' offer—" I can't yet bring myself to say 'if I become crown prince' because it sounds so fantastical "—then Dad will be more likely to accept you as his heir?"

"Of course I've thought of it. But you can't make this choice for me. You have to make it for yourself. Because, whatever you choose, you need to commit to it. You're either in or you're out. No more of this half life you're living."

"Yes, ma'am," I say meekly. "Oh, and Jemmy – if you need a place to stay to get away from the parentals, you have the spare key for my flat."

She laughs softly. "Thanks, but I'm not a coward like you. I can handle them."

Ouch. I know she didn't mean it to hurt, but it does. I *am* a coward, and I'm not proud of that.

For a long time after she hangs up I sit staring at the phone. Even if it is cowardly, I'm not ready to go back to England, and I am most certainly not ready to face either my family or Charlie's. I need to clear my head, and I can't do it back in England. If I could, I'd have done it already.

The thirty hours I've spent here in Westerwald are the freest I've felt in years. Maybe that's because here I'm free of responsibility – or maybe it's because my thoughts have been distracted by a certain Vegas waitress.

Khara ... *Bloody hell.* Since I wouldn't put it past my sister to check up on me, I'm actually going to have to teach Khara etiquette. But first I'm going to have to get her to agree, even though she's made it crystal-clear she wants nothing to do with me.

When I arrive at breakfast, Max and his personal assistant Jens are the only ones there.

"I didn't see you leave the party last night." Max grins as I settle at the table with a cup of hot, black coffee. "You leave with anyone I know?"

Well, at least he didn't see me leave with Khara. I don't think she'd appreciate that news spreading around the palace. So I simply lift a shoulder. "No offence, but your party was dull so I went out to a club."

'Lost myself in a club' would be more accurate. Loud, pulsing noise in a place where nobody knew who I was, and where there was plenty of alcohol. I left the club alone, though.

"I'd like to take up your offer of a place to stay until after the wedding," I say.

"Sure. As I said the other day, you're welcome to stay as long as you need." Max leans his elbows on the table, steepling his fingers. "But I'm going to ask for something in return."

I nod for him to continue. Everything has its price.

"I need your expertise on a financial matter."

Free financial advice in return for a place to stay seems like a pretty good deal, so I nod again. "Just not today. I have something else I need to do."

Once Max and Jens leave, I ask the maid on duty to prepare a breakfast tray. She glances at the remains of my unfinished cheese and herb omelette, then heads off to arrange it without another word.

Fifteen minutes later, I'm at Khara's door. Balancing the tray in the crook of my arm, I knock.

When she finally opens the door, she looks as if she's just woken. Her wild hair sticks out at all angles, her make-up is smudged and there's a pillow crease in her cheek. She's also cradling her head in a way I know all too well. She groans. "Oh no, not you again. What are you doing here?"

"You missed breakfast, and I thought you might want to eat before your photoshoot. Especially since I imagine you're nursing a massive hangover this morning."

She eyes the tray I hold out to her, torn between temptation and nauseous revulsion. Another feeling I know only too well.

"Thank you," she says, begrudgingly taking the tray.

"Might I suggest you change before you go downstairs? You might not want everyone wondering why you're still in last night's clothes."

She glares at me and when she moves to shut the door in my face I block it with my foot. "I also have a proposition for you."

"Give it a rest. It's too early in the morning for this. I. Am. Not. Interested."

I don't budge. "Actually, it's nearly ten, and you haven't even heard what I have to say."

She squeaks. "Nearly ten already? It's going to take me at least half an hour just to straighten my hair!"

"You don't need to straighten your hair, and this is more important." Since she's no longer actively trying to shut the door on me, I slip into the room. Aside from the wallpaper, it's a mirror of my own.

"You have two minutes." She heads for the sofa, perching on the edge of the seat and balancing the tray on her knees. I follow, closing the door behind me, and take the armchair across from her. She digs into the poached eggs, ham and orange juice. Good, plain, restorative hangover food.

I grin. "I'm going to go out on a limb and suggest that last night's dinner was a tad ... daunting for you."

She nods, attention still focused on the tray.

"There are still a whole lot of formal events planned in the run-up to the wedding, and even more rules and protocols you've not yet been introduced to."

"If you're trying to make me feel even worse, you're succeeding," she says through a mouthful of egg. "And your two minutes are nearly up."

"I want to offer to tutor you."

Her gaze snaps up to mine. "Tutor me in what?"

"Etiquette. How to walk and talk and dress so you can fit in better."

"I know how to walk," she retorts, but the light in her eyes shows she's intrigued. Looks like it's my lucky day.

"But do you know how to walk like a princess?"

"I don't need to be a princess; I'm only here for a few weeks. All I need is to make it through the wedding without embarrassing myself – or Phoenix." She narrows her eyes at me. "Why would you do this for me?"

I concentrate on straightening out a crease in my neatly pressed trouser leg. "I'm bored, and this could be amusing."

When she doesn't answer, I glance up to find her scrutinising me. "Don't you have a job?"

"I do. But right now I'm on an extended leave of absence while I figure out what to do with my life."

"Isn't that nice? That's a luxury no one in my world can afford."

I would laugh at her snarky attitude, except I know she's speaking the truth. It's no different from Jemmy calling me a coward. They're both right, of course, but for some reason I want Khara to think better of me. Which is a scary thought I quickly suppress.

"Do you always say everything you think?" I keep my voice light and amused.

Her eyes hold a glimmer of mischief. "No. In fact, I think I've been very good at *not* saying what I'm thinking."

I lean forward, intrigued. "What are you thinking?"

She leans forward too, to whisper. "I think that you're wasting your time. I'm not going to sleep with you out of gratitude for your help."

Well, there goes that idea. I shrug. "Would you believe me if I told you I wasn't making this offer to get you into bed?"

"Only if you tell me the *real* reason you're here, kicking your heels in Westerwald."

I say nothing for a long moment as she nibbles on a slice of toast. I'm tempted to give her a glib answer, the same glib answer I'd give to the Elenas of the world, but as Khara eyes me expectantly, not letting me off the hook, I experience an urge to do something completely alien, something I almost never do: I want to be honest.

Well, at least partially honest.

"I have to make a decision," I admit at last. "It should be a very easy decision, but everyone is pressuring me to do what I don't want to do ... what I *can't* do. They all expect me to be someone I'm not." I blow out a long breath. "They think I'm a better person than I am. And so I'm hiding here, hoping they'll come to their senses while I'm away."

In her expressive eyes I can see her imagination shift into overdrive. She's probably thinking I was asked to donate a kidney to save the life of a loved one, and I'm too selfish to do it. Which isn't that far from the truth.

But I've already been more honest than I'm comfortable with, so I change the subject. "If you don't get moving, you're going to be very late for your photoshoot."

With a guilty start, she sets the tray on the coffee table, grabs clothes out of the wardrobe and heads for the bathroom. I pace to the windows and pull open the curtains, letting in the bright morning sunshine, and sit on the wide window seat. The sound of the shower starts and, just like that, I imagine Khara standing beneath the spray, naked, eyes closed and face turned up to the water, the gentle curves and dips of her body, her smooth skin ... What can I say? We men may not be the most imaginative creatures, but there are certain things we can imagine very well.

Fortunately, she takes her time before she comes out of the bathroom, enough time for me to exercise the willpower needed to suppress my arousal. Her hair is still wild, her face is completely bare of make-up, and she's dressed in ripped jeans that mould to her curves, beige pumps, and a dusky pink sweater with a deep V-neck that gives just enough hint of cleavage for my body to instantly tighten with desire again.

"That's a vast improvement over that hideous dress you had on," I say. "Let's go."

"But I haven't even done my make-up or hair yet," she protests.

"You don't need to. I arranged a stylist, since I don't trust Phoenix's stylist not to dress you like a sister wife." I hold the door open for her. She opens her mouth, then closes it again, lost for words, and I smile. Making Khara speechless could be my new favourite hobby.

Chapter 9

Khara

"I haven't agreed to anything yet!" I protest when Adam pitches his idea to Phoenix.

I give him the side-eye while a make-up artist paints my lips. I'm seated in a chair in the center of Phoenix and Max's spacious living room, which might look like a regular living room except for the ancient tapestry hanging on one wall and the blue and gold rug on the floor. Aubusson, Phoenix called the rug the first time I admired it. I had to Google what that meant. Turns out they're made in this little village in France – by *hand*.

"It's a great idea," Phoenix says. Then she glances at me, noting my clenched jaw and narrowed eyes. "I'm not suggesting you're not good enough as you are, but when I first came to live here in the palace I was clueless about so many things and embarrassed myself on more than one occasion."

I can't imagine Phoenix ever being embarrassed. She's always so poised and confident.

She shakes her head. "But I had Max to help me, and the palace protocol secretary."

The make-up artist stands back to admire her handiwork.

"Great, then the protocol secretary can give me lessons." I'd rather spend my time with him than with Adam.

Phoenix pulls a rueful face. "Unfortunately, he's all tied up with wedding stuff."

"I could just hide out here in the palace and keep out of sight," I say hopefully. After all, there's that lovely big library I could lose myself in. The only Disney princess I ever wanted to be was Belle, and the Beast's library was the reason why.

"Nonsense!" Phoenix laughs. "Just think how useful your new social skills will be when you graduate and start going for job interviews."

Ugh. Of course, she's right. I'm a realist; I know how competitive the job market is, and if I don't want to be a waitress forever I need every advantage I can get. I throw up my hands in surrender. "Fine, I'll do it." I pin Adam with an icy stare. "But I'm agreeing to lessons only. You keep your hands to yourself."

The make-up artist makes a spluttering noise. I can't work out if she's laughing or in shock.

"Yes, ma'am." Adam keeps a straight face, but amusement lights up his eyes.

Next it's the turn of the stylist. She's a local woman, with a Germanic accent that I'm learning is the local Westerwald accent. The puppy dog look in her eyes every time she looks at Adam leaves no doubt how well he knows her. I'm going with 'in the biblical sense'. I feel sorry for her when I remember Adam's disdain as he told Elena he never comes back for seconds.

She wheels in a rail of clothes, and Adam flicks through

the hangers while Phoenix and I look on, bemused. Neither of us has ever been big into fashion. Since there's nothing on that rail resembling my usual uniform of jeans or hot pants, I feel lost just looking at it.

"No, no, no." Adam discards one outfit after another, then he takes one hanger off the rail and holds it up. It's a baby-blue suit with a knee-length skirt and looks very chic. I can imagine myself wearing it to a job interview. If I were interviewing for a job as a school principal.

I glance at Phoenix and she stifles a chuckle.

For a laugh, I try the outfit on. It makes me look like a politician's wife. "I'd rather be photographed in my pyjamas," I tell Adam. Fortunately, he realizes I'm serious.

By the time I try on the fourth outfit, I remember why I hate clothes shopping. The gray jersey dress makes my figure look stunning, but "too funereal" Adam says. The pretty dusky-pink, feminine floral dress is discarded too.

"But I like that one!" I object.

"We'll save it for Saturday's polo match," he says. "That's going to be your first public outing when everyone knows who you are."

I try to ignore the sudden anxious flutter in my stomach.

He and the stylist finally settle on a plum-colored pencil dress with a wide collar. I scrutinize the stranger's reflection in the portable mirror. I don't feel like myself at all, but I suppose that's the point. The make-up is so subtle it's barely there, my hair has been tamed and pulled back into a neat French twist and the dress makes me look taller, more sophisticated.

"There," Adam says, giving me a critical head-to-toe evaluation. "Now you're ready."

The photographer is waiting for us in the Yellow Drawing Room, which has been cleared of all evidence that it hosted a party last night. I walk there in bare feet, dangling the high-heeled, strappy sandals the stylist gave me from my fingers.

For half an hour the photographer makes me pose in at least a dozen different positions, while her assistant runs around tweaking the lights. I'm exhausted by the end of it, even though I've done nothing but sit and smile or stand and smile. All this for just one photo?

When I see the pictures, though, I agree the fuss was worth it. The woman on the laptop screen looks like a supermodel. My own mother wouldn't recognize me. "Can I get one of these to send home?" I ask.

"You have someone special back home you want to send it to?" the photographer asks with a knowing wink.

Is it my imagination, or does Adam tense, like a dog sniffing the air?

"My brother Calvin. He'll get such a hoot out of this."

Adam relaxes, and I know it's not my imagination. I'm flattered at his interest in me. Then I remember the way the stylist looked at him and it's as good as any cold shower.

When we're finally done I sag back on the antique sofa. "I could murder a coffee." I'd also love to get back into my jeans and pumps. Just standing in these heels has killed my calves.

Phoenix looks apologetic. "I have to meet with the press secretary to go through the press releases for tomorrow, but

I'll see you later. We'll have a nice quiet dinner *en famille* in our apartment, so I'll see you then."

She leaves, followed closely by the photographer and her assistant, and Adam uses the internal house phone to order us tea and coffee. Then he moves to sit in the armchair across from me. "What are you studying?" he asks, casually crossing an ankle over his knee.

"Accountancy and finance."

His eyebrow rises. "An unusual choice for someone with a passion for history."

"There's not a lot you can do with a degree in history."

"How close to graduating are you?"

"One more semester."

"Your brother – is he older or younger?"

"Older."

"Any other siblings?"

"No." Where is this game of twenty questions going?

"The weather has been warm and clear this week."

And what is it with this obsession everyone in Europe has with the weather? I'm saved from having to respond by the arrival of a maid with a tray filled with cups and saucers, two teapots, milk and sugar, all in the same dainty floral-patterned porcelain. She sets the tray on the coffee table between us.

I lean forward. "Thank you, but I asked for coffee."

Adam uncrosses his long legs. "The coffee pot is the taller, thinner one. Tea is the shorter, rounder pot."

Yet another thing I'm clueless about. The maid sends me a sympathetic look, then leaves, and I hide my embarrassment by shifting forward to pour. "Tea or coffee?"

"I'll have tea."

I pour tea into one of the dainty cups and pass it to him, before pouring my own coffee. "So when do we start my first lesson?"

"Twenty minutes ago."

"But all we've done is chat."

"Exactly. Your first lesson is how to make small talk. Conversation is like a game of tennis. I lob a ball at you, and I expect you to pass it back. When I ask if you have a brother, I'm not just looking for an answer, I'm giving you an opening to ask me back. Each question is an invitation. Try to avoid dead-end answers. Expand your answers, or ask a question in return."

"How is talking about the weather supposed to start a conversation?"

"It's an icebreaker, a neutral topic, something that affects everyone. So your response could have been, 'Yes, it has been lovely weather for sightseeing.' That gives the person you're talking to the opportunity to respond with, 'Oh, are you new to Westerwald? What sights have you seen? What did you think of the cathedral?' And that opens another whole avenue of conversation." He sets his teacup down. "Let's start again. Pretend I'm the complete stranger sitting next to you at dinner. So you have a brother – is he older or younger?"

I try to imagine Adam as the rather dull young man at dinner who only wanted to talk about the weather. I can't. "He's a few years older. Do you have any siblings?"

"One younger sister, but she acts like she's the older one. What does your brother do?"

"He's a lawyer." I say it with pride. Calvin was the first person in our family to go to college, let alone graduate.

"My little sister's a lawyer too. She heads up the legal affairs and HR departments in our family firm."

I imagine his sister's job is a whole lot more glamorous than Calvin's. He works for a small non-profit that mostly handles divorces and maintenance battles for women who can't afford legal help. He's overworked and underpaid. I'm going to guess those are both completely foreign concepts in the Hatton family.

Adam grins. "See, that's not so difficult, is it?"

Actually, it is. Making small talk requires a great deal of concentration, as I try to think of ways to keep the conversation flowing without digressing into the forbidden topics of politics and religion (and money), all the while trying hard not to divulge more about myself than I need to. I'm not ashamed of where I grew up or my family but, remembering Adam's Lesson Number Two, I don't want to give him any information that can be used against me. And it turns out direct questions along the lines of "What do you do?" are also considered gauche and American – who knew? There are more things we *can't* talk about than we can.

An hour later, I've not only learned how to make bland conversation with strangers, how to listen and make eye contact, how to sit right (without crossing my legs, keeping my back rigid as a plank), but also the correct way to pour tea if I'm the hostess (milk first, then tea). And I learn that here cookies are called biscuits.

"What's so funny?" Adam asks when I laugh.

"I'm imagining myself serving tea and biscuits back home. We don't get a lot of guests." We don't even own teacups.

"We?" he asks.

"I still live with my mother." His eyebrows lift in surprise, sparking my defences. "Rent is expensive. I could either go to college or I could get my own apartment, but not both."

Trust me, if I wasn't so determined to graduate and make a better life for myself, I would have moved out long ago, but I didn't have the benefit of a football scholarship the way Calvin did. It's not that I don't love my mother, but we're such different people it's hard to believe we're related. She's a hopeless romantic, always believing that the next job is going to be The One, that the next man she dates is going to be her knight in shining armor. By now you'd think she'd realize there's no such thing. You want a job to be The One, you have to stick with it. If you find a good man, you don't let him go, hoping something better will come along. Instead of being satisfied with the good things she had, she's still chasing dreams, and she's still alone.

"Where's your father?" Adam asks, as if sensing the direction of my thoughts.

I shrug nonchalantly. "I have no idea. He took off before I was born."

He bolted the moment my mother told him she was pregnant. I'm not hurt that he abandoned us. Many men leave when the going gets tough, and that's just the way life is. What hurts is the mean voices of the playground bullies telling me I'm not worth sticking around for. I'm a grown-up, I know that's not really true, but sometimes I still hear those voices.

Adam looks at me thoughtfully, and I feel stripped bare again. "You know, with a little less Goth Girl eye make-up and a little more polish, it won't be hard for you to find yourself some rich man so you never have to work another day in your life."

My anger is swift and blinding. *Pretend he's just another drunk gambler who needs to be humored or handled.* It doesn't work. "Are you suggesting I sell myself for money?" My voice is deadly calm. Anyone who knows me would start running at that tone.

"It's not as if I'm suggesting prostitution. People marry for money all the time."

What is this – the eighteenth century?

With shaking hands, I set down my half empty coffee cup and rise. "I am no gold-digger, and not in a million years will I rely on anyone to support me." I turn and, with as much dignity as I can muster in these heels, stride from the room. As soon as I'm out of Adam's sight I pause to strip off the offending shoes and hurry down the main staircase to the front door. I hand them to the footman on duty, ignoring his bewildered expression, and head out into the gardens.

Chapter 10

Khara

Adam was right about one thing: it is a lovely day. Though the temperature is cooler than I'm used to, the sunshine is warm on my face and I breathe in the rich scents of wet soil and flowers. The palace gardens are beautiful – all manicured lawns and fountains, an oasis in the heart of the city. Even though it's late summer, the flowerbeds are full of color, as if it's still spring.

With the exception of the royal family's private garden, the grounds are open to the public, so there are people everywhere. Gardeners, people in suits who seem to be hurrying either toward the palace or away from it, city workers on their lunch breaks, mothers pushing prams on the paths between the fragrant flowerbeds, and the ubiquitous tourists. No one pays me the slightest notice, though one of the gardeners does pause to stare at my bare feet as I dash past. I find a quiet bench under a massive oak tree and gulp down deep breaths.

How can Adam not realize how insulting his suggestion is? I am so sick of rich men assuming that just because I work a service job that means I'll be willing to sell myself. I'm proud of what I've achieved, even though it might not look like much to this man with a black credit card, fancy shoes and an air of entitlement.

I can pay. I still remember every word of that conversation a year ago as if it was yesterday. My hands bunch into fists. I want nothing more than to behave like a stereotypical trailer park tart and wipe that smirk off his face.

Then I hear my stepdad's calm voice in my head. *Violence is only a temporary solution; the evil it does is permanent.* Just thinking of Isaiah soothes the edges of my temper.

Not that he's actually my stepfather. Isaiah's just the man who knocked up my mother the first time round; he's Calvin's father. Unlike my own father, Isaiah has always stuck around. He's the closest thing I had to a dad, and he's also the most decent, hard-working, honorable man I ever met. I have no clue why my mother never married him. She says it's because they didn't have any chemistry, but she had a shit ton of chemistry with my biological father, and look where that got her: a single mom working for minimum wage, growing old alone. If a man like Isaiah asked me to marry him, I'd say "I do" quicker even than Max and Phoenix said the words.

I really hoped Raúl would be the one. I was so sure he was going to propose. Instead, he broke up with me because he said we had no 'spark'. Who wants sparks? Sparks start fires.

I've just calmed to the point where I no longer want to smack Adam, when I see him. I stay where I am, my feet curled up under me on the bench. He approaches like a bomb disposal expert approaching a bomb and comes to a stop just outside my reach. He's carrying the shoes I left with the footman.

"I'm sorry I offended you." He looks genuinely contrite. "So you're not interested in a rich husband. Good to know."

"Do you really think that's all a woman like me is good for?" I bite out.

"No, of course not! I guess I'm just so used to women weighing every man they meet by what he can give her that I assume every woman is like that."

I arch an eyebrow at him. "You know the wrong kind of women, then."

A glimmer of a smile crosses his face. "Clearly." He moves to sit next to me on the bench, still cautiously keeping distance between us. "Well, at least we have one thing in common."

"What's that?"

"You have a chip on your shoulder about men with money, and I have a chip on my shoulder about women who want money."

I can't help myself. I laugh.

He settles back, looking relieved. "You're practical about your studies and your career, so don't you agree that marriage should be practical too? Aren't all good marriages convenient in some way?"

This time my laugh is more like a snort. "You think Phoenix and Max's marriage is convenient? Trust me, she's not marrying him so she can be a princess and live here." I wave my hand at the palace, which is more of a gilded prison than a home, and I think of her schedule and all the duties she now has, how she traded her privacy and freedom to be with Max, when all she ever wanted was a life of travel and adventure. "For Phoenix, this marriage is extremely inconvenient. But it's going to be the best damn marriage ever, because they love each other."

He still looks skeptical. "Please tell me you don't believe in all that soppy hearts and flowers stuff?"

"No, I'm not talking about fairy tales. And it's most certainly not lust or chemistry either. Love is mutual respect, shared interests, a similar sense of humor. Marriage should be a partnership, not a financial arrangement."

I smile as I think back to that morning when Max and Phoenix met. Lust? Sure. But that wasn't what made them walk down the aisle together less than twenty-four hours after meeting. "Within an hour of them laying eyes on each other, I knew they belonged together because they had all those other things in spades."

Adam sits straighter. "You were there when they met? But I thought you'd never been to Europe before?"

Oops. "I haven't." And I'm not saying another word.

"I know how to keep a secret," he wheedles.

"Do you have any other lessons planned for me? Because I'm done with talking for the day."

He frowns, unimpressed by my change of subject. "No more talking today. Next, we're going for a walk before lunch. Have you seen the famous water gardens?" He holds out the shoes to me.

"You are not going to make me walk in those!" I can't hide my horror.

His laugh is pure evil. "Yes, I am."

He gets down on his knees in front of me to strap them on, then helps me to my feet. His touch sends that same breathless shiver through me, but I'm better prepared for it now.

Then he offers me his arm in that way I've learned is an invitation for me to hook my arm through his, and we start off along one of the paths. I have to take small steps to prevent myself tottering, and I'm grateful for the support of his arm. Until he lets me go, that is. Even though the paths are made of densely packed gravel, my heels keep sinking into the ground.

"Is there a purpose to this, or are you punishing me for losing my temper?"

"If you can walk in those shoes here, you can walk anywhere. There are ten steps up from the street to the cathedral doors and, once you're inside, the nave is about two hundred feet long. You're going to be walking that with Phoenix on the big day, with a whole lot of cameras watching your every move."

I huff out a breath. I guess walking through the palace gardens in stilettos is a small price to pay so I don't fall flat on my face on live television.

The water gardens are almost as big as the one at the casino where I work. Long, narrow channels of still water reflect the flowers and the sky, forming neat patterns that eventually merge together into one big pond where an enormous sculpture of a dragon stands, framed by splashing mermaids. From the fountain, the water flows down a stepped terrace into a larger fish pond. There's also a long walkway lined with hundreds of smaller fountains, "modeled on the Avenue of a Thousand Fountains at Tivoli in Italy," Adam says.

At the end of the walkway, the path opens up into a unexpected surprise, a circular garden hidden from view by a wall of cypress trees, and currently deserted. The most breathtaking feature of this secluded garden is the sheer wall of water that falls from a high aqueduct into a wide, shallow pond. The water casts a fine mist up into the air.

"There's a secret grotto hidden behind the waterfall," Adam says. "Want to explore?"

There's a glint in his eyes, as if he's daring me. I glance at the high wrought iron railings that surround the pond, clearly marked with large 'Keep Out' signs in four different languages.

"Sure." I strip off the shoes, because I absolutely do not plan to climb over any railings on the wedding day. "Lead the way."

I glance around, but we're still alone. We clamber over, Adam first, then me, trying very hard not to let the skirt of this fancy dress ride too high.

"Will you please stop objectifying me?" I grumble as I swing myself over.

"Huh?" He sounds distracted.

I enunciate clearly so he can't miss it this time. "You were checking out my ass!"

He smirks. "Of course I was. And not for the first time, I might add. You have a particularly fine arse."

I glower, and he laughs. "I'm a man. It's what we do."

"That is the most entitled thing I have heard you say yet."

He catches me as I jump down on the other side, holding me against him for an earth-shifting moment.

The spray from the wall of water rains down on us, plastering his shirt to his torso and soaking through my dress. I shiver, but not from the chill of the water. I don't think I've appreciated just how fine Adam's torso is until now. My skin feels as if it's burning up. I'm surprised there isn't steam rising off us.

I realize my hand is splayed out on his chest, and it doesn't seem to want to move. Yeah, I'm very aware that right now I'm not only objectifying him too, I'm also enjoying a bit of a grope. That's only fair play, though, right?

He steps away, grabs my hand and pulls me after him. We splash through the pond, ducking under the plunging waterfall into a dimly lit grotto. The walls are made of rough stone, surprisingly dry considering the deluge we passed through to get here.

My hair has started to escape from its fancy French twist and plasters against my face. I wipe it away. "How do you know about this place?"

"Max and I used to sneak down here to drink during his parents' parties."

"What about his brother Rik?" I sit on the rough stone ledge that circles the cave like a bench to place some distance between me and Adam so I can get my breath back.

He pulls a face. "Rik was always the well behaved one. As crown prince, he had to be the responsible son, so he could never sneak off."

It seems a cruel twist of fate that Rik, the dutiful heir apparent, was disinherited, and Max, who was happier making wine at his grandfather's vineyard in California, had to drop everything to take over as archduke. All because of a blood test. Rik was kicked out when it was discovered that he wasn't in fact the previous archduke's son but his mother's bastard from a liaison before she met the archduke.

Adam circles the grotto, running his hand along the face of the rock. As he draws nearer, my pulse picks up in this damned inconvenient dance it does whenever he's close. Why couldn't I have felt this stomach-fluttering attraction to Raúl, who was kind and sweet and steady? Why do my traitorous hormones have to go into over-drive for a man who won't even stick around until morning, as Elena pointed out?

As Adam moves closer, I jump to my feet. Though my intention was to place distance between us, I misjudge and the movement brings us chest to chest. My body stills, like prey awaiting the predator's pounce. The moment hangs suspended between us, then he slowly reaches up and pulls my hair loose, sending at least a half dozen bobby pins clattering to the floor. His hand stays in my hair a heartbeat longer than necessary.

I fully expect him to pull a typical entitled jerk move, like trying to grab me or kiss me, but he doesn't. He seems almost as breathless as I am, and his eyes are wild and dark. Does he feel the same desperate need arcing through him? I hate myself for this feeling. Not just for wanting him, but for wanting him so much I'm even contemplating kissing him.

I have to clear my throat to speak. "You said something about lunch?"

He nods, stepping back, and my breath rushes out. He kneels to gather the bobby pins from the floor, then I follow him back out through the curtain of water into the pond. When we climb back over the railings my hem snags on one of the posts, ripping and creating a long slit up my thigh. I'm horrified, wondering if the stylist will kill me for ruining the dress, but cost is clearly the last thing on Adam's mind. His gaze is on my bare thigh, and his expression is like that of a stoner eyeing a bucket of KFC. I should be insulted by that look, but instead I wonder if fried chicken wings also feel a desire to be eaten when looked at like that.

In silence, we make our way back to the palace. With my body wound so tight, I don't think I could make conversation now even if I wanted to. *It's just chemistry. It's nothing. It's less than nothing.*

By the time we reach the side entrance to the palace, the one that leads to the private apartments and the guest wing, we're still both sopping wet. The footman at the door, the same one who was on duty earlier, does his best not to gape as we step inside.

I'm barefoot, not having bothered to put the strappy sandals back on, and the designer dress seems to have shrunk a size or two on me. "I need a hot shower," I say, shaking droplets from my hair.

Adam's gaze scorches as it roams from the fabric clinging to my breasts down to my bare legs. He grins. "Good idea, but I think mine's going to need to be a cold one."

I race up the stairs, Adam half a step behind me. On the landing at the top of the stairs, we part ways. "See you in the dining room in half an hour," he says.

Chapter 11

Adam

I stand beneath the spray of the shower until the water turns to ice, but it doesn't help. God knows what happened in that moment in the grotto, but it's as if my body has been set alight and the fire can't be quenched. Trust me, I've tried to quench it.

The water drums on my shoulders as I rest my forehead on the cool tiles. I've lusted after enough women to know what desire feels like, and this isn't it. Because in that moment my need wasn't just physical. It was primal. I wanted to possess her, to mark her as mine. And I have never felt that way about any woman before.

Could this uncontrolled hunger inside me be nothing more than the thrill of the chase? It's been so long since I had to do much chasing, I've forgotten what it feels like.

With another woman, I'd assume this was all a game, a tease to make me want her more. But with Khara I know this isn't a game. In the grotto, when I was a hair's breadth away from leaning forward and kissing her, she looked me in the eye, looked deep inside me, as if she saw the real me. And she didn't like what she saw.

My head throbs with a dull ache. No matter what Max thinks, I do have a type, and that type isn't 'easy'. She's shallow. The type of women I usually sleep with don't look at me the way Khara does. They don't care who I am inside; all they care about is the lifestyle, the status, the proximity to a title. They're women who won't tempt me to stick around. Women who won't make me care.

So why don't I just walk away from Khara? I could drop this charade of tutoring her, go out to a bar or a nightclub and find myself someone willing, someone who won't expect anything more of me than a good time and expensive baubles.

I could, but I won't.

And there it is, a prickling at the edges of my awareness, a deep, dark fear I refuse to acknowledge. A fear I felt on that drunken night in Vegas, a fear I've been chasing away ever since. I switch off the taps, wrap myself in a towel and step out of the shower. I know from experience that if I keep moving this fear I don't want to name will go away.

I dress carefully, as if I were going to lunch with my mother, in khaki chinos, a button-down Oxford shirt and a navy pullover. Maybe if I look respectable on the outside, I'll feel less uncivilised on the inside.

When I step into the state dining room, Khara is already there, haloed in the pool of sunlight falling through the tall windows. The long table has been set with just two places and the butler hovers nearby. He nods at my approach, confirming everything has been arranged as I requested. I take the seat opposite Khara and she sets aside the book she was reading, a dog-eared Faye Kellerman mystery. She has changed back into her jeans and sweater, and somehow looks younger and more fragile in her casual clothes with her damp hair loose.

Lunch is not so much a meal as a lesson. I hadn't realised just how many 'don'ts' I'm hemmed in by until I start to teach them to her. There's all the usual stuff: take small bites, don't talk with your mouth full, don't lean your elbows on the table, don't cut bread rolls but rather break them with your fingers, don't hold your knife like a pen. And then there's a whole bunch of other unspoken rules that are completely outdated but woe betide anyone who ignores them, like following the host's pace to eat, never handling the plates or serving dishes, standing every time the hostess or guest of honour stands, making conversation with the person seated to my right during the first course, then alternating with the person on my left for the next course, and so on. I'm only just beginning to understand how excruciating last night's dinner must have felt for Khara.

"What was with the tiny portions they served?" she asks. "And I used to think our hotel restaurant served small portions!"

"Formal dinners are more about the social interaction than about eating," I explain. "Since eating and drinking get in the way of making conversation, the courses are more an excuse for people to be there than for sustenance. That's why you should never come hungry to a banquet or dinner party."

It's clear she's trying very hard not to roll her eyes, and I completely agree. Though for me it's not the food that's in short supply. There's never enough alcohol served at these shindigs for my tastes. When you spend over an hour making polite conversation with a dowager whose sole preoccupation is her latest charity fundraiser to benefit people she's most likely never come within spitting distance of, a half glass of wine per course just doesn't cut it. You don't want to know some of the conversations I've endured in the interest of being polite and engaging.

That night, over a quiet dinner with Max and Phoenix in their apartment, we teach Khara how to shake hands and how to curtsey, the correct way to air kiss (but never hug – that's too informal), and how to address titled guests. As we're served coffee and a cheese platter, Max explains the complicated seating arrangements and order of precedence at formal dinners.

Khara turns a thoughtful frown on me. "So when the protocol secretary wanted to seat you closer to Max's end of the table, it must mean you're pretty important?"

Both Max and Phoenix stay quiet, watching us. I avoid their gazes. "I'm not really important, but my mother is," I hedge.

Max's eyebrow arches and I can practically hear his speculation. He's wondering why I'm not being more forthcoming. But I learned enough about Khara today to know that while she somehow doesn't hold Max's title and wealth against him, in me she sees those same qualities as a major personality defect. Heaven only knows what I did to deserve that prejudice. And, far from impressing her, as it would other women, the revelation that my mother's a princess is more likely to send Khara running than impress her.

And I don't want her to run. Not yet. Despite the way she makes me feel hot and desperate and uncivilised, despite the fact that whatever is stirring between us is far more complicated than I'm prepared for, I don't want this to end.

She's not shallow, she's not easy, but I want her more than I've wanted anything in a very long time.

And it feels so good to want something again.

So I behave like the perfect gentleman all through dinner, treating Khara the same way I treat my sister, the same way I treat Phoenix. Max's sidelong glances, as if he's waiting for me to step out of line, are insulting. He should know me better. I may be a cad, but I'm also my mother's son. I know how to behave in any social situation, I know how to do what is expected of me. And I know how to seduce a woman, even if I haven't had to do it in a while.

When we finally rise from the table and I offer to walk Khara back to her room, Max sends me one of his sidelong glances. "There's the move I was waiting for," he mutters smugly.

I don't deign to give him an answer.

Like the gentleman my mother raised, I say a polite goodnight to her at her bedroom door, careful to keep a safe distance between us, to avoid all temptation. But by the time I reach my own room at the far end of the corridor I could really use a drink, something much stronger than the dry, fruity local wine Max served during dinner.

It's only when I'm sipping on a Scotch, looking out at the

city lights, that I realise with a jolt that I haven't thought of Charlie or the memorial dedication all day. I raise my glass in a silent toast.

I'm woken by a sharp rap on the door. *Coffee.*

But it's not a palace servant with my coffee. When I open the door, dressed only in my boxer shorts, it's Max.

"Good morning!" He sounds way too chipper for this hour of the day.

"Don't you have better things to do than provide wake-up calls for your guests?" I ask grumpily, roughing up my hair in an attempt to get the blood flowing to my sleep-deprived brain.

"I didn't want you to miss our meeting."

"What meeting?" I shut the door and trail behind him to the sitting area of the room. God, I could kill for caffeine.

"You promised me financial advice in return for bed and board, remember? This morning we're meeting with the finance steering committee to discuss how to improve public sector efficiency."

"Sounds thrilling." I move to the table in the corner of the room, where there's a kettle and mugs. It's only instant coffee, but it will have to do. When the kettle boils, I make two cups and carry them across to the sitting area, where I hand one to Max. He looks insultingly wide awake and put together. If I were to accept Uncle Lajos' offer, would I also have to get up early and look as if I've just stepped out of a Brooks Brothers catalogue? Because I can't do it.

I flop down on the sofa and drink the coffee as quickly as

I can without scalding my tongue. "Though it breaks my heart to turn down such a tempting invitation, I have better things to do today."

"If those 'better things' include Khara's etiquette lessons, you're off the hook. The ladies have their spa day today, remember?"

Damn. Now I have no other ready excuse to get out of what is likely to be a very dull meeting. A suspicion forms in my mind. "Did my sister put you up to this?"

Because it would be just like Jemmy to recruit Max to both keep an eye on me and speed up my decision. Not that I've given Erdély or my uncle much thought since I met Khara. I suppress a twinge of guilt.

"No, *you* did. You said your decision was easy because you don't want to think about anyone but yourself. I figured you needed to see the flip side of that: the difference you can make in other people's lives."

I don't bother to respond. He's wasting his time. I'm not going to swap one deadly dull job, which at least offers me the perk of skiving off whenever I can, for another deadly dull job. Even if it's the noble thing to do.

Max empties his coffee mug and stretches as he rises from the armchair. "Get dressed. You'll give my Minister of Finance a heart attack if you show up in boxers. I'll be waiting downstairs for you in my office. You remember where that is?"

I nod.

Twenty minutes later, showered, shaved and dressed, I walk into Max's office. It's a spacious high-ceilinged room with tall sash windows that overlook the woodland area of the gardens.

Aside from the view outside the window, it looks a lot like my corner office in London. His assistant brings us pastries and proper bean coffee, and I sip gratefully as I read the report Max gives me, on the increasing gap in fiscal sustainability, with population growth and increased welfare spending driving up government debt.

The finance meeting is held in the adjacent cabinet room, and isn't as boring as I thought it would be. The challenges the committee faces aren't that different from those faced by many of our company's clients, but the stakes are so much higher, affecting way more than just shareholder profits. If the government doesn't make its spending more efficient, social services will need to be cut. Real people's lives will be affected.

When we leave the meeting five hours later, with some workable suggestions in place, I have to admit I feel a deeper sense of satisfaction than I've felt in a very long time. Not that I'll admit to it.

"Was that so bad?" Max asks smugly as we grab a quick sandwich in his office.

"You got my expertise for free," I grumble. "Do you really need me to like it too?"

He laughs.

The afternoon is no less intense. We sit through an environmental policy meeting to discuss preventing water pollution through pesticide and fertiliser run-off. There are two clear factions in this meeting, those in favour of stricter environmental controls, and those who want to protect business interests. The meeting gets heated and I admire how

Max soothes, suggests and seduces the opposing factions into hammering out an agreement. Without ever appearing to pick sides, he steers the meeting towards greater environmental protections, which I happen to know is his personal mission.

It's not unlike schmoozing clients and though this topic is widely outside my area of expertise I find myself absorbed. Four hours later, with the beginnings of a new policy in place, Max and I are at last alone. His assistant leaves for the day and Max pulls a bottle of Scotch and two crystal tumblers from his desk. "I think we earned this," he says, pouring generous shots into each glass.

"I didn't realise your job was so hands-on." I take a sip. It's damn fine whisky, but what else would one expect from a man who used to make wine for a living? This new job is so far away from his old life in California, and I wonder if he misses it, if he regrets having taken on this responsibility.

Max shrugs. "I can't enact any changes without parliament counter-signing, but all new policy and legislation has to pass through this office. I do what I can. Since I don't have to follow a party agenda or worry about my political career, I can focus solely on this country's future. That's what makes our system of government work." He leans back in his chair, cradling his glass. "Our constitution is very similar to Erdély's."

I should probably know that. But I've never read Erdély's constitution.

"And you do this every day?" I ask.

"Not every day, thank heavens. I get time off for good

behaviour. Tonight's the bachelor party, and I thought tomorrow we could head to the polo match a day early. Take the ladies on a slow drive into France, and stop in at a few vineyards along the way."

Now that sounds more like my idea of fun. "As long as someone else is doing the driving." I plan to have a massive hangover tomorrow.

Chapter 12

Adam

When we set out on our little road trip I'm nowhere near as hungover as I'd like to be.

Firstly, because Max's bachelor party was so tame we might as well not have bothered (yet more proof, if I needed it, that being royal is deadly dull), but more importantly because I'm sharing the back seat with Khara. And because she's wearing another of those cropped tank tops that flashes tanned skin at me. My fingers itch to reach out and touch, to find out if her skin is as soft as it looks.

So I lounge in the rear of Max's luxury SUV, pretending to sleep behind my sunglasses, but I'm aware of every movement she makes, aware of her subtle perfume, a light rose scent that reminds me of my mother's garden on a summer evening, when the sun pricks out the fragile scents.

Max drives and Phoenix is seated beside him, turned in her seat to chat to her friend. If I didn't know there was a car full of Max's security people trailing behind us, this would almost feel like the road trip across Europe Charlie and I did the summer after we graduated. I try not to remember those times too often, but I allow myself a wry smile at the memory.

Khara flashes me a glance when I smile, as if she's as in tune with my every move as I am with hers.

Once we're clear of the city, the road winds along the Wester River, up into the southern hills of Westerwald, where the slopes are dotted with vines. Khara's excitement as she gapes at the view through the windows is contagious. I give up my pretence of sleep and listen as Max, proud monarch that he is, tells us all about the landmarks and his country's history. Perhaps that's why we became good friends; it's not just a shared love of polo and parties and fine Scotch, but the fact that we were both raised on folk tales and history. And we're both pretty good at hiding that geekiness.

Mid-morning, we stop at our first vineyard. The farmhouse looks like a small chateau, a long low double-storey building with half-timbered architecture and a grey-tiled mansard roof. It's too early in the day for wine, even for me, and it's soon apparent that Max isn't here to sample the produce but to talk shop with the winemaker. While he and Phoenix tour the cellar with the owner, Khara and I wait on the terrace that overlooks the steep-sided river valley and sip on strong German coffee.

"How was your spa day?" I ask in an attempt to make polite, civilised conversation.

"Weird."

Not the answer I expected. I raise an eyebrow.

"You don't really want to know, because any honest answer is probably going to be on the list of forbidden topics."

I grin. "Now I *really* want to know."

She sips her coffee, looking out at the view rather than at

me. "They do this thing called a body exfoliation, where a complete stranger rubs body scrub all over you while you're practically naked. After you shower the scrub off, the same person then rubs lotion all over your body. And I mean *all*."

She's just described every one of my fantasies, except that when I imagined her naked in a shower, I imagined *my* hands all over her.

She catches my eye and sends me a withering look, as if she can read my X-rated thoughts. "Where I come from, they have a word for that – and it comes with a jail sentence if you're caught taking money for it."

I laugh. "You Americans are such prudes about your bodies."

She bristles, indignant. "That's what the beauty therapist said when I didn't want to strip off my bra."

"I would have paid good money to see *that*." My grin may be cheeky, but my voice comes out a little rough. She sends me another look that could cut through steel.

"But wasn't it worth it?"

"I guess. The facial wasn't bad. My skin does feel softer and fresher."

"You sound surprised. Surely you've had facials before?" Even my workaholic sister has a facial every few weeks.

She shrugs. "I had one once when I was in my teens and my mother worked at a beauty shop. She got staff discount, but after she changed jobs it wasn't worth it any more."

The drive from Neustadt to the polo ground in Chantilly is only four hours, but it takes us the better part of the day as we stop in at another half dozen vineyards before we even cross the border from Westerwald into France. I listen in on some of Max's conversations with the winemakers. Mostly, the discussions revolve around marketing Westerwald's wine produce globally, but Max also encourages the winemakers to introduce new grape varietals rather than sticking to the usual Riesling grapes.

I wonder fleetingly if Erdély has any vineyards, and whether Uncle Lajos visits his farmers.

Once we're across the border, we hit the Eastern autoroute and make up time. Max is still driving, but I'm in the shotgun seat now so the ladies can chatter in the back. I mess with Max's GPS, changing the accent of the voice every few miles, but it's just an excuse so I can eavesdrop on the conversation in the back seat. They talk about climate change, legislation affecting women's rights, and the books they've read recently. For a barmaid, Khara is surprisingly well read. Or maybe a lot of barmaids are well read. Truth is, I've never stopped long enough to chat to any; I've always been rather preoccupied with other things. Like getting them into bed. That's an uncomfortable realisation.

I also discover that Khara is very fond of her brother, who she mentions at least three times, and not so fond of her mother who, according to an overexcited text she receives while we're circling around Soissons, has just started a new job as a receptionist in a GP's office. I gather her mother frequently starts new jobs.

The downside of getting to understand her better is that it's hard to think of her as just another woman to shag. This is why I prefer not to talk to women. It's easier to walk away in the morning when you don't know anything about them beyond their bra size. Another uncomfortable thought.

No wonder Khara looks at me like she doesn't much like what she sees. I'm starting to not much like what I see either. And that niggling fear is back.

Less than an hour north of Paris lies the elegant old town of Chantilly. Though it's better known for its horse racing and its imposing, heavily renovated chateau, on a large farm carved out of the ancient royal forest is the polo club. Max and I drop the ladies at the hotel on the edge of town, then drive on to the club to check on our ponies. They're already settled in their stables by the time we get there and I make a fuss of Bonney, feeding her carrots and even sneaking her a sugar lump when the groom's back is turned. We take the ponies out for a quick run and the exhilaration of being back in the saddle, with the wind in my face, wipes away all my disturbing thoughts. It's hard to think too much when Bonney and I are flying.

Max is smiling too when we return to the stables, though for him that's a default expression. I bet he's never had to face the unwelcome realisation that he's a much shittier person than he thought he was.

I only see Khara again that evening at the informal cocktail party in the hotel's main salon.

I'm late to the party, as usual, though not for any of my usual reasons. I actually started reading Erdély's constitution and lost track of the time. And now I know that Erdély does have a handful of vineyards, though they only supply domestically.

Max and Phoenix are already mobbed by arse-kissers and attention-seekers, so I grab a Champagne cocktail from a waiter and go in search of my protégée. I find her when I step through the French doors into the hotel courtyard. It's a warm evening but gooseflesh rises on my arms as I look at her.

She is seated at one of the wrought iron tables dotted around the deserted courtyard. Her hair is tied up, pulled back into a bun so only the barest hint of blue is visible. I miss its wild abandon. Her make-up is still a little more nightclub than cocktail party and she's wearing a plain black dress which hugs her breasts and waist, and black knee-high boots. Not standard cocktail party wear, but she looks more attractive than any other woman at this party. She looks unique. Something tugs in my chest, which is certainly unusual. That tug is usually far lower down in my anatomy.

"Have we tempted you over to the wild side?" I indicate the bright pink, cherry-decorated Cosmopolitan she's holding.

She laughs. "Don't tell anyone, but it's a virgin cocktail."

That's my sister's trick. She can drink all night and still be sober at the end of it.

Khara frowns. "I should be wearing that pink floral dress from the stylist. I stick out in there like a lump of coal in a box of jewels." She nods back towards the salon.

"You look gorgeous," I assure her, and I mean it. "And it's better to save that dress for tomorrow, when there are cameras around."

She stiffens, and I reach out and lay a reassuring hand over hers. "Don't worry – those cameras will be pointed at Phoenix, not at you."

"That only makes me feel marginally better."

I laugh. "Are you ready to go mix and practice your new conversation skills?"

She sucks in a breath and squares her shoulders. "Ready as I'll ever be. Let's do this."

I hold her gaze. "Remember: poise is, more than anything else, a result of self-confidence. All you need is to have faith in yourself. You can do this."

For nearly an hour we circulate the room, and I introduce Khara to some of the other guests. She makes me proud. She stands the way I taught her, looking assured and at ease, and I think I'm the only one who can tell she's faking it. She makes polite small talk, without mentioning money or politics or religion, and listens carefully, her whole attention focused on the person she's talking to. I know she's so focused because she's concentrating hard, but the other guests are flattered by her interest. She's a hit.

"Do you know everyone here?" she asks when we get a moment alone.

"Pretty much. Everyone knows everyone else."

"Geez, it sounds like high school all over again, just on a bigger scale, and impossible to fit in unless you were born into it."

I shrug. "You don't have to be born into this world. Marry a title or earn a fortune, and you're welcomed with open arms. It worked for Phoenix." I smile to show I'm teasing. I don't want her to take offence again.

Khara wrinkles her nose. "Thanks, but I think I'll skip it. It takes money to make money, and I don't happen to know any eligible single guys with titles."

Her tone is sarcastic, so I suppress the laugh that wants to bubble up. If she only knew.

"So who is that?" She nods towards a tall, lean man with salt-and-pepper hair.

"The Count of Amiens. He runs a stud farm that breeds highly sought after polo ponies."

"And her?"

A rather buxom woman in a purple dress that probably cost a fortune but makes her look like a giant aubergine. "Marielle Desmarais. She inherited an international supermarket chain, and her husband is a former professional polo player. He's refereeing tomorrow's tournament."

She points out a few more people, and I tell her who they are. I'm rather enjoying this game. It seems I *do* know everyone in the room.

She indicates a man across the room. "And McSteamy over there?"

Maybe this isn't as much fun as I thought. "My team-mate, Mateo."

"Any chance of an introduction?"

At that moment Mateo looks up and spots us. He excuses himself from the leggy brunette who's trying to wrap herself around him and strides towards us. Mateo is not only tall and fit for his age, but he's got that silver fox thing going for him – and I haven't yet met a woman who can resist his Argentinian accent. It's never bothered me until now.

"You're new," he says to Khara, holding out his hand to her while he gives her a head-to-toe scan, lingering a moment too long on her chest. I flex my fingers to avoid curling them into fists. From his slow, heated smile it seems he likes what he sees. And it's clear the interest is mutual.

"I'm Khara Thomas." Her voice is breathless as she places her hand in his.

Mateo bows over her hand in a way I never could. I'm too English to get it right.

"Mateo Alvear de Villegas. Do you need to be rescued from this English rascal?"

"Only half English," I mutter, but they both ignore me.

Khara smiles up at him. "Thank you, but that won't be necessary."

I blink. Mateo seems unsure whether that was intended as a brush-off or not. But he smiles again, with that smooth Latin charm that's as natural to him as breathing. "Not necessary, maybe, but it would be my pleasure." He's still holding her hand.

"Actually, Khara and I were about to head out to dinner," I say brightly. "So if you'll excuse us?"

"We are?" She looks at me blankly, and I frown meaningfully at her.

"There's still at least two hours of sunlight left. I thought you might want to go out and explore a little of the town before dinner."

"You have not been to Chantilly before?" Mateo asks.

She laughs, extricating her hand from his. "I haven't been *anywhere* before. It was a pleasure meeting you."

I place my hand in the hollow of her back and guide her through the crowd towards the hotel reception, eager to leave the party and the stifling conversations and sideways glances.

"Very few women say no to Mateo." I keep my tone conversational.

Khara darts me an amused glance. "Very few women say no to you too, yet somehow I manage it."

I forbear to point out that I'm the one she's leaving the party with. Nor did she refuse to have dinner with me. "I thought you were attracted to him?" I ignore the swift tug of an emotion I can only imagine is jealousy. It's not something I've ever felt before.

She shrugs. "I was. Until he bowed."

"You don't like men who bow. I'll add that to the list of things you don't like."

"I don't trust smooth-talking men, that's all," she corrects. "I grew up in Vegas, where smooth-talkers are a dime a dozen. They come in all shapes and sizes, from all walks of life, but they all have one thing in common."

"Oh?" The doorman opens the hotel's front door and we step out of the air-conditioned foyer into the warm evening.

"Men like that leave."

Her father took off before she was born, I remember.

A stone's throw from the hotel entrance is the grand stone archway that leads to the famous Chantilly chateau. I guide her in the opposite direction, into the town, and we wander down the main street, taking in the sights. It's a Friday evening and even though it's late summer, and soon the leaves will be turning, the air is balmy and the sky is still blue as the sun dips down towards the horizon. The pubs and restaurants are full, music and laughter spilling out onto the pavement. We explore the town, making easy conversation as we stroll through the lengthening shadows. Away from the room full of strangers in elegant clothes, Khara relaxes, loses the tension from her face and her shoulders, smiles more. She has the prettiest smile, rare enough to be magical when it finally emerges. It makes her eyes sparkle.

"I think I've died and gone to dessert heaven." Khara sighs. "So far I've counted at least two bakeries, a pancake shop, an ice cream shop, and *four* chocolate shops."

When it's nearly dark, we choose a pub-like bistro with an outdoor seating area. The place is packed, but we find a small table for two outside on the pavement. I order – in French – but this time Khara doesn't roll her eyes. Maybe because it sounds less pretentious when you're shouting to be heard over a babble of voices. We order burgers and fries, and the meal is surprisingly good.

The sexual tension still simmers between us, but it no longer burns. Maybe forced proximity is the cure for what I've been feeling. Or maybe it's because this feels like a date, and I know where dates usually end. In bed. Or in the shower. Or up against a wall. And when that happens I'll stop obsessing over her and be able to get my head back on straight. Get back to what I'm supposed to be doing, which is figuring out what I'm going to do with the rest of my life. But thinking of that gives me a headache, so I top up my wine glass.

Despite the noise, we manage to converse, talking about everything and nothing, about movies and books, polo and international politics, swapping stories about our lives. When she tells me she grew up in a trailer park, I'm careful not to let my shock appear on my face. Khara is nothing like the stereotypes I've seen on TV.

The stories she tells, of a tight-knit community, of eccentric neighbours and good friends, changes everything I thought I knew about people who live in trailer parks. Her childhood sounds just as happy as mine was. And her high school years sound every bit as awful.

She cups her chin in her palm. "I was 'lucky enough' to attend a private charter school. It had an excellent academic record, but didn't score high on diversity, and no one wanted to be friends with the charity case from the trailer park."

She doesn't sound bitter when she says it, but I'm starting to see where she got that chip on her shoulder. I can only imagine how lonely she must have felt. But there has to be something more ... Surely she didn't develop such a deep mistrust of people with money just because she felt like an outsider in school?

"But look who I'm talking to!" She laughs. "Your school would probably have been even worse."

I laugh. "Socially, my posh public school might have been more diverse than yours. Since it was a boarding school, we had boys from Africa, China, Russia, the Middle East. And a massive bursary programme to attract the best kids from all walks of life. But it was a very rigid school. Hundreds of years of tradition and discipline." I grin. "Needless to say, I was never very good at doing what other people expected of me."

As we talk, the strange funk I've been in for nearly a year

disappears. I don't usually talk this much with the women I date. Perhaps because most of the women I've dated aren't this interesting. Or this interested.

I'm surprised when I look round and notice that the restaurant has slowly emptied around us. It's later than I realised.

The crowning glory of the meal makes Khara's eyes light up. A verrine with layers of chocolate mousse alternating with the local delicacy, thick, vanilla-flavoured crème Chantilly and topped with fresh strawberries.

"This is the best whipped cream I've ever tasted," she moans. "This definitely doesn't come out of a can."

"This is the *original* whipped cream." I lean across the table to wipe a small dollop from the side of her mouth. Her pupils go large and she holds herself still at my touch, but doesn't shift away. I sense victory as I lick the cream from my fingers.

We walk back to the hotel in the dark, not touching, though our hands occasionally brush as we walk. The streets are quiet, and the temperature has dipped. I give her my jacket to keep warm as we walk. I certainly don't need it, not with the desire heating my blood.

The hotel lobby is empty, the cocktail party long over. I walk her to her room, wishing I had more of that Chantilly cream so I can lick it off her when I get her naked.

She opens the door, but doesn't step inside. Instead, she turns to face me, shrugging out of my jacket and handing it to me. Still lost in that vision of creamy skin, a great deal more of which is now visible, I take the jacket from her.

"Thank you for the lovely dinner." She smiles, that too-sweet smile that sets off warning bells in my head. "But this waitress is still not on the menu."

She steps through the door and, while I'm still trying to puzzle out the smile and the words, I find the door shut in my face.

I stare at the closed door and do a double-take.

Not a victory after all. Instead, her words set off an echo in my head, like a distant memory I can't quite catch hold of. I shake my head to clear the nagging thought.

I could do what I usually do – head to the hotel bar either to see if some other woman is up for a little fun or to drown my sorrows. But I do neither. I head to my own room, to a cold shower and an empty bed, wondering where the hell this date went wrong, and whether I'm losing my touch.

Chapter 13

Khara

Neither Phoenix nor I have the foggiest clue about the rules of polo.

"There are four players in each team, and the match is divided into six sections called chukkas, which are seven and a half minutes each," she explains. "And that's the extent of my knowledge."

The playing field is a vast, manicured lawn which has to be the size of at least eight football pitches. The crowds gathering about the edges are dressed in classy casualwear, not a pair of jeans in sight. The men wear khaki pants and blazers, the women elegant pantsuits or sophisticated sundresses, and everyone wears practical sun hats. My pink floral dress blends in perfectly, and I send up a silent thanks to Adam for insisting I save it for today. Many of the spectators have brought picnic blankets and baskets, but we're in the VIP enclosure, seated on plastic chairs beneath a white awning which flaps in the light breeze. There's a bar, where Champagne is flowing like water. Both Phoenix and I stick to real water.

There are cameras and cell phones everywhere but, since most are pointed at the field, I manage to relax a little.

The first match is a women's event. For such large animals, the horses are astonishingly fast and agile. Players and horses move as one, poetry in motion.

At half time, when the players lead their horses off to be watered and rested, Phoenix grabs my hand and pulls me to my feet. "This is the fun part!"

We join the crowd surging onto the field. Apparently it's a polo tradition for the spectators to spend half-time behaving like excited kindergarteners, running around the field stamping down the clods of earth and grass that the horses' hooves have kicked up. "It's called the divot stamp," Phoenix explains.

Not that she gets much chance to join in the fun. Everyone wants a piece of her, a moment to bask in the attention of the soon-to-be archduchess. There are even a few who ask to have their picture taken with her, and I obligingly act as camerawoman, being careful to frame every picture I take with the half dozen top-of-the-range cell phones so that Phoenix looks good in every one. She told me on the drive here that she never lets anyone take selfies with her, as she can't be sure what awful pictures will end up on the internet. It makes me laugh, the thought of complete strangers lining up for selfies with her, when I remember her carrying trays of beer or washing glasses or wiping up red wine spills. Or the lazy afternoons we spent at the side of the public swimming pool, the visits to the library, the supermarket, the laundromat. She'll probably never go to a library, supermarket or laundromat again in her life. Unless she's there to cut a ribbon to open it.

"How do you cope with all the attention?" I ask when we're safely back in the VIP enclosure.

"It's the price I have to pay if I want to share my life with Max, and since I can't even imagine life without him ..." She shrugs. "We cope because we're in this together. We're stronger because we have each other."

It sounds cheesy, but it isn't. Not if you know them, and I sigh with envy. I so want what they have – a true partnership. Though I think I'd miss being able to go to a real library, or do my own grocery shopping, I wouldn't miss doing laundry.

After the break, the players return to the field with fresh horses, the teams swapping sides. When the ladies' match is finished (and I have no clue which side won) it's Adam and Max's turn. Their match starts when a stunning woman in a figure-hugging sage-green dress throws the ball into play.

Phoenix and I giggle together as we make up our own commentary to go with the action happening on the field. "And then Max takes the quaffle from Adam and runs with it," she says.

"Oh, no! But look – the man on the brown horse has taken it," I continue. The crowd cheers. "Does that mean someone spotted the Snitch?"

The play moves away down the field and I squint into the sun. "He feints, he shoots, he ... no! He *doesn't* score. Looks like he overran the quaffle. I could really use a pair of Omnioculars right now."

Phoenix squeezes my arm. "This is so much fun. I wish you could stay longer. Are you sure you have to go back to Vegas so soon after the wedding?"

The look I give her is the only answer she needs. When the clock strikes midnight, everyone knows what happens to Cinderella's coach and ballgown.

I turn back to the match. The ground shakes as the horses thunder past. I may not know anything about the sport but it's certainly exciting to watch, with the horses covering the massive field almost as fast as ice hockey players. But, unlike hockey players, polo players are dressed in a uniform that displays their assets rather well. There's a lot of eye candy out on that field.

Max. Mateo. The fourth member of their team, who is barely twenty years old but looks like a supermodel. Despite how many other buff men there are to look at, and despite my best efforts not to, my gaze is constantly drawn back to Adam. Their team is dressed in white pants, riding boots, and forest-green polo shirts. The pants are just tight enough to give a good eyeful, especially when Adam stands in the stirrups and swings himself from the back of one horse onto another, a move that has me anxiously holding my breath until he's safely reseated.

The close-fitting shirt perfectly outlines his broad shoulders and tapering torso, showing off those defined pecs I had my hand on in the grotto. The man really is perfection. I sigh. *Yeah, I'd like to do him.*

Phoenix sends me an amused glance, and I blush. "Did I say that out loud?"

"You didn't have to." She laughs. "I've never known you to hold back from having a little fun if you like a guy. So why not let loose and have some harmless holiday fun with Adam?"

Because with him it wouldn't just be harmless fun. When the dice are so heavily loaded in one person's favor, someone always gets hurt. I shrug, keeping my gaze on the field. "Because he's a man whore."

"Less than everyone thinks." She suddenly jumps up, clapping and cheering wildly. I'm also on my feet by the time I spot the Flagger behind the goals raise his flag to indicate a goal. From the celebratory dance Max is doing in his saddle, I assume he scored the goal.

From an inauspicious beginning, their team have now pulled level with their opponents. The last chukka is going to be nail-biting.

The action moves closer to us now, and the thud of horses' hooves, the whack of the bamboo mallets against the ball, and the voices of the players and the crowd all rise together to make my heart hammer with the thrill. I'm just as gripped as the rest of the crowd, gasping, cheering, clapping.

The scores are still neck-and-neck, with only a minute left in the game, when one of the umpires blows his whistle for a foul. Play stops instantly and the crowd grows quiet. Adam takes the penalty shot. The spectators are silent, holding their breaths. He swings his mallet. It thwacks against the ball, which flies through the air. And straight between the goalposts.

The crowd roars, Phoenix and I are both on our feet, cheering ourselves hoarse, and the game is over.

The men trot casually toward us. When they remove their helmets, they look tired but happy. They dismount as they draw near, then lead their horses closer. Phoenix, fearless as always, leans over the white picket fence to pat Max's horse on its forehead, but I hang back. Up close, the horses look even bigger and I'm more than a little daunted, especially when Adam's horse snorts and shakes its head wildly.

"That's my girl," Adam croons, rubbing her forehead affectionately. She nuzzles into his hand and he laughs softly. My heart does a stupid little leap.

Then he catches my gaze, and winks. I blush. I'd like to say it's just the warm day and the sunshine or something, but I won't lie. I'm blushing like a stupid, giddy teenager who has just been noticed for the first time (the only time) by the school jock. *Get a grip, girl.*

"Khara, I'd like you to meet my best girl, Bonney," he says. "Named for William Bonney."

"You named a girl horse after Billy the Kid?"

"In the National Pony Society's Stud Book, she's listed as Wilhelmina, but that's such an old lady name. My sister suggested Billy, but that didn't seem right either for this beautiful girl, so I call her Bonney." He pats the horse's side, looking at her in a way I suspect he has never looked at any human woman.

What is it about men who get mushy over animals, and what they do to feminine hormones? Or maybe it's the shirt plastered to his back with sweat, which shouldn't be sexy but absolutely is. Or the way his dark hair is tousled and all over the place. He must be the only man on the planet who can make helmet hair look sexy.

"Want to give her a sugar lump?" He holds his hand out to me.

Ignoring the flutter that has settled yet again in the region of my stomach, I take the sugar cube he holds out, shivering as my fingers accidentally stroke his palm. I reach toward the horse, which snuffles at my fingers, then daintily picks the sugar cube off my nervously outstretched palm with her lips.

Braver now, I stroke her forehead and she blows softly, as if in pleasure.

"And now you can say you've met your first pony," Adam says softly.

"This is just a pony? She's massive!"

"In polo, our horses are always ponies, whatever their size," Max answers. Then he rubs his hair, which has gone dark with sweat. "I need a shower."

"Need help?" Phoenix asks coyly.

He holds her gaze, his eyes darkening with desire, and I can almost see the sparks between them.

"You read my mind," he says. Then he glances around. The crowd is slowly drifting to the pavilion where the luncheon will be served, but there are still people milling around within earshot. He sighs. "But I'll have to take a rain check."

I glance at Adam and see that for once we're thinking the same thing: what a drag it must be to be royal, and to always be on your best behavior.

While the men head off to shower and change, Phoenix and I make our way to the big glass pavilion where the luncheon is being served. There is a carnival atmosphere away from the field: food stalls, music playing on loudspeakers, bouncy castles and other entertainments for kids.

Inside the pavilion, the air is cool and more subdued. A uniformed waiter shows us to our seats. There are already a few people seated at our table – an older gentleman with kind twinkling eyes, his elegant wife, and the stunning woman in sage-green who opened the men's match. The elderly gentleman, president of the polo club, introduces us. Turns out the woman in green is Amalia Lecroix, one of France's most famous actresses. Yup, not only am I sitting at a table with royalty, but also with a movie star. In seven years working the casino floor and the occasional shift in the restaurant, I haven't seen this many celebrities.

Phoenix engages the elderly gentleman in conversation. I have to admit, I didn't know she spoke French. I watch as the room slowly fills with other guests and recognize some of the people I met at the cocktail party last night. There are smiles and hugs, air kisses and laughter, as the guests drift to their seats. It feels a lot like lunch break in our high school cafeteria, but with one crucial difference: here, some of the people I met last night actually stop to greet me as they pass by. They're not so intimidating when you get to know them.

The tables are already full when Adam, Max and Mateo arrive in the pavilion. Heads turn as they wend their way between the tables. Three gorgeous men, all slickly dressed as if they just stepped out of a Ralph Lauren commercial. Be still, my beating heart.

"Where's your fourth?" Phoenix asks as they reach us.

Max grins. "His girlfriend came with him for the weekend. Last I saw, they were making out in an empty horsebox. I don't think we're going to see them until after lunch."

"He's young. It might not last long." Mateo winks. He offers his hand to me again. "It is a joy to see you again, Khara.

Perhaps after lunch I can tempt you to take a walk in the paddock enclosure with me?"

There's a wicked glint in his eyes, and I wonder if that's supposed to be a euphemism. Then he turns to Amalia, the same suggestive smile in his eyes. "*Enchanté*, *madame*."

She smiles, and flutters her eyelashes.

The club president performs the introductions again. When he introduces Adam to Amalia there's a distinct chill in the air. Phoenix's sharp eyes catch it, Max shakes his head, and Mateo's eyebrows lift.

"You slept with her?" I murmur in an undertone when Adam takes the seat beside me.

"I don't think much sleeping was done," he whispers back with a swift grin. "But my memory is hazy. It was a long time ago."

"She still hasn't forgiven you."

He grins. "She still hasn't got over me."

I roll my eyes.

His arrogance may have been a tad premature. Mateo and Amalia flirt throughout lunch, and she seems very over Adam.

The food is gourmet, which means small portions arranged artistically on the plate. But it tastes good, and I'm even able to enjoy it. I'm getting the hang of all the cutlery, know how to fold the napkin in my lap so it faces the right way and how to hold my hand over the wine glass to say 'No, thank you' when the waiter comes around to offer more, and I don't feel so awkward making conversation. Not that I need to make much effort at conversation. Both Phoenix and Amalia are vivacious, larger-than-life personalities, and with them around

I can fade quietly into the background, which is my preferred place to be.

You'd be excused for thinking I'm an attention-seeker. After all, I have blue-ombred hair and wear hot pants to work. But those are just me being practical. Hot pants and short skirts get me bigger tips, and colored hair ensures the patrons remember who their waitress is because, let's face it, we can all look alike, especially to gamblers, whose focus is on the slot machines rather than on the person handing them a beer.

But I was the girl in the high school cafeteria sitting alone with my nose in a book. I wish I could do that right now, take the paperback out the bag at my feet and disappear into its pages rather than have to pretend I want to be here.

I give in to Phoenix's suggestion and try a Pimms and lemonade, a light and refreshing alcoholic drink, which helps settle my nerves. Adam is right. I can do this. Everyone here is just human, after all, even the actress. Up close, I can see she has lines around her eyes and her skin isn't perfect. We're all perfectly imperfect.

The cheerful, lively atmosphere lasts until dessert, puffy balls of choux pastry filled with that same Chantilly cream we enjoyed last night, though this version has a delicate hazelnut flavor.

"Is it true you are your uncle's heir now that your cousin has died?" the club president's wife asks Adam. The table falls silent. I wonder how much wine the woman had to drink. Doesn't she know it's rude to talk about money in polite company?

"I can't comment," Adam replies quietly, his shoulders

suddenly stiff with tension. "The announcement will only be made after the funeral."

"Oh, of course," the woman says, her tone conciliatory. "Protocols must be followed."

The conversation resumes, but the air is changed and it doesn't take me more than a moment to realize why. Amalia is no longer flirting with Mateo. She is so busy eyeing Adam speculatively that she doesn't even acknowledge when Mateo leans in and whispers in her ear. No one else seems to notice, though. Max and Adam are teasing each other about the size of their horses, and Phoenix has engaged the club president and his wife with a funny story about the first time she attended a polo match. I catch Mateo's eye across the table, and he shrugs ruefully. Then he folds his napkin in neat squares, places it on his side plate to indicate he's leaving, and rises.

"*Pardonnez-moi*," he murmurs to Amalia and she nods and smiles at him, then he is gone, striding away across the room. He's clearly not one to waste time on a lost cause. Silently, I applaud him.

But then I wonder – just how big an inheritance is this that even women who know what a cad Adam is are willing to throw away their pride for a chance at it?

Chapter 14

Adam

Out on the polo field, life is simple. Everything comes down to the ball, the goals and the horse beneath me. There is no time for thought or emotion, just reaction. It's when I get off the field that everything crowds in on me again, the need to be Someone, though I'm not entirely sure who that someone is – the game-playing, the undercurrents.

The walk from the stables into the pavilion is like walking from one world into another. In the stables, my only concern is the wellbeing of my ponies. When I'm surrounded by animals, I don't feel a need to question who I am or whether life has meaning. I just am. Ponies have no artifice, and they don't judge. They accept us completely, as we are.

I look around the pavilion, at the flirting, the posturing, the jockeying for attention or position, and I feel bone-weary. Off the field, I've played these games my whole life and I can't figure out why. Is it because it's expected of me, or because without them I feel insubstantial, as if I'm nothing more than a shadow? Just a trust fund and my family name.

I glance around the table, at the animated conversations, the polite laughter, then my gaze snags on Khara. As usual, she's quieter than everyone else, steadier. She looks up, meets my gaze, and I smile. It's a cliché, I know, but her eyes really are dark pools. I could lose myself in them. It's not the colour, but the honesty in them. Here is the one person I know who doesn't play games. She has that brashness Americans have, but it's more than that; it's a rawness, a sense that what you see is what you get.

I start when I hear my name. I break Khara's hold on me and force a smile as I turn to Amalia. "Sorry, I missed that?"

"I was asking if you remember that party where we met? Whose party was it?" She's twirling her hair and looking at me coyly, and it takes a great deal of effort not to roll my eyes. Not her too? What is it with all these women who want to be princesses? I blame movies and fairy tales for creating unreal expectations.

"I have no idea," I answer curtly.

Amalia giggles. "It was at the yacht club in Antibes, and your cousin wanted to move the party onto a boat, so we picked one and climbed on board. And we found that bottle of Dom in the fridge, and Nick said it was as if it was there waiting for us, but then, just as we opened it, the captain arrived and threw us off."

I glance around the table to see who else might have heard her reminiscence. The only person paying any attention is Khara, who arches an eyebrow at me.

"Not my proudest moment," I murmur so only she can hear. That bottle of Champagne cost fifteen thousand quid, and I had to pay about the same again to persuade the captain not to press charges.

I'm relieved to see that, with the luncheon over, most of the VIP guests are drifting back towards the field for the afternoon match. Max, as the highest titled guest at this event, has been invited to open the mixed men's and women's event by tossing in the opening ball, so he and Phoenix rise to leave too. I still have a full glass of a rather superb Loire Valley Chenin Blanc, and am in no hurry to join them – and I'm rather relieved to have a quiet moment in the emptying pavilion – until Amalia slips into the empty seat to my left.

Khara is rising too, to follow Max and Phoenix. I reach out and grab her arm. "Please don't leave," I mouth at her, nodding as subtly as I can in Amalia's direction. I don't want to be alone with her. I may say – or do – something I later regret.

Khara sighs, but slides back into her seat on my right.

"I have missed you." Amalia lays her hand on my arm in a gesture I've used many times myself. It's the initial contact that says 'Hello, I'm interested'. "We had fun together." Her voice is heavy with suggestion as her elegant manicured hand strokes down my arm in sexual invitation. "And we can have fun again."

She's a good actress, with the awards to prove it, and she's an even better seductress. A few weeks ago I might have gone along with her act without a second thought, but with Khara seated beside me, radiating disapproval, I find it much easier to think with my brain rather than my other head. I shift away so that Amalia's hand falls from my arm. "I thought it was Mateo you wanted to have fun with?"

"Mateo is very charming, but he isn't you."

I open my mouth to respond, but Khara beats me to it.

"You do know Adam never comes back for seconds, don't you?" She sounds cool and amused, and I have to give her credit for that. Most women would have made a line like that sound bitchy.

Amalia turns wide, surprised eyes on Khara, as if only now realising she's there. "Who are you?"

"No one."

That she certainly is not. I wrap my arm around her and pull her closer before I turn back to Amalia with a bright smile. "Haven't you heard? Khara's my girlfriend."

I expect Khara to stiffen and try to pull away, as she did that time I used her as a shield against Elena. But she surprises me. She leans closer and slides her hand possessively along my thigh.

Amalia looks back at me, employing her trademark pout. In the past, it was that pout that did it for me. Now I feel absolutely nothing. Well, not nothing. I'm feeling a hell of a lot, but it's all concentrated in my groin, and on the spot where Khara's hand rests against my thigh.

"I didn't know you were seeing anyone," Amalia says.

"Clearly I am." I trap Khara's hand with my free one, determined to keep it where it is. My trousers already feel tight enough. If she so much as moves an inch, my stirring arousal is not only going to be uncomfortable, it's also going to be obvious.

Amalia's beautiful almond eyes narrow. "Are you sure?" She turns to Khara. "Because with Adam you're only his girlfriend if you last long enough for it to make the papers. If the press don't know about it, you're nothing more than a shag."

My temper is starting to fray at the edges, a rare occurrence. As if sensing my dangerous mood, Khara gives me a sharp pinch between the ribs, out of Amalia's line of sight, but I can't resist one more dig. "You and I both know the papers don't know everything. I'm pretty sure they haven't heard about your rather interesting little fetish."

Amalia pales. With a toss of dark, silky hair, she rises and walks away, back ramrod-straight. Okay, maybe that last comment was uncalled for.

"For a moment there I thought I was protecting you from an obvious gold-digger, but now I'm not so sure who needed protecting. Geez, but you're *mean*." Khara shifts away from me.

I rub my head, still not letting go of her hand which is trapped beneath my other. "I've had about as much as I can take of women kissing up to me because of my family name or my family's fortune."

She rolls her eyes. "Poor little rich boy," she mocks, pulling her hand out of my grip. "If you didn't exploit your name and fortune to get into women's pants in the first place, maybe you'd have better luck."

That's the kind of thing my sister would say.

I blow out a breath. "You are nothing if not honest."

"And you're not."

I arch an eyebrow, waiting for her to explain.

"What is this inheritance that everyone wants to get their hands on?"

I don't want to tell her. Is it because I'm afraid she's going to turn out to be like every other woman and suddenly find me more desirable? Or because she won't?

I blow out a long breath. "The inheritance my cousin left me is the opportunity to replace him as Crown Prince of Erdély."

I search her face for the sudden piquing of interest I've seen in the faces of so many other women, but it doesn't come. Instead, she looks at me steadily, the same way she did when I flashed my credit card, and something pulls tight in my chest. It's that feeling that twisted my gut for the first time in Vegas a year ago: the fear that everything I have, everything I am, means nothing.

"I haven't heard of Erdély," she says, tone thoughtful.

"You, and at least nine-tenths of the planet. It's a tiny micro-state on the border between Austria and Hungary."

"Like Westerwald?"

"Even smaller. It's about a third of the size, and only has a population of about a hundred thousand people."

"What's it like?"

I can rattle off the country's GDP, the key dates in Erdélian history and name every ruler since the sixteen-hundreds (backwards), but that is the one question I can't answer. I shrug. "I don't know. I haven't been there in at least twenty years."

She arches an eyebrow at me. "And that's the big decision you face, the one you're trying to avoid – whether or not to take your cousin's place?"

I nod, and she purses her lips in a way that reminds me of Uncle Lajos. "But you don't want to, because it's too much responsibility and will put a dent in your self-indulgent life-style?"

It's not really a question, more of an answer. How the hell does she know that?

"What's the alternative, if you say no?" she asks.

"I go back to my job schmoozing clients for my father's firm."

"I meant the alternative for Erdély." Jemmy could take lessons from Khara in how to put me in my place.

"Then my cousin Mátyás will inherit when my uncle dies."

She holds me pinned with that steady gaze. "Is this the same Mátyás you said would be a perfect fit for Baroness Elena?"

I nod again.

"And you think the people of Erdély deserve that?" There's a glimmer of humour in her eyes now, as if she's enjoying baiting me, enjoying my discomfort.

"I think Erdély deserves better than me." That feeling is back, making it hard for me to breathe. I stretch and rise. "I'm done with this event. Want to blow this joint?"

"I need to go back out there and pretend to be the perfect bridesmaid."

"You already passed with flying colours. Let's go play tourist some more."

The family name opens a lot of doors. At Chantilly's chateau, it opens very literal doors. The curator falls over herself to give us a private tour, even escorting us through rooms that aren't usually open to the general public. The elegantly furnished state apartments are even more lavish than those in the palace in Neustadt, with walls decorated in ornate gold leaf, and the collection of artworks is second only to the Louvre. As our guide leads us from one gallery to the next, Khara is speechless again. There are masterpieces by Raphael, Poussin, van Dyck and Giotto, an endless list of the masters which means little to me, but clearly means a great deal to her.

"Does your family have a palace like this?" she whispers as we stroll down the Psyche gallery, a long hall displaying the forty-four stained glass windows depicting the life of the goddess Psyche.

I shrug. "There's a recent nineteenth century castle, and an older seventeenth century hunting lodge, but I'm going to guess neither is as elaborate as this one." Nick used to call the castle 'the farm' and did everything in his power to avoid spending time there.

Khara laughs. "I think your idea of 'recent' is a little different to mine."

In the chateau's Reading Room, which is not nearly as impressive (or as comfortable) as the palace library in Neustadt, the curator shows us the collection of ancient illuminated manuscripts. "This belonged to one of your ancestors," she says, donning gloves and opening a glass cabinet to retrieve a Book of Hours, a religious devotional richly decorated with gold leaf.

"Wow," Khara breathes. Then she glances up at me. "I guess that makes your ancestors kind of important?"

I shrug. "I remember one of my ancestors married into the Bourbon-Condé family, though that had to be at least four centuries back."

I study the yellowed pages, the bright ink and burnished gold of the manuscript. I have no idea which of my many, many forebears this belonged to, but I'm struck suddenly by the sense of that life, lived centuries ago, still remembered in the pages of this book, this tangible reminder of a life once lived. What legacy will live on when I'm gone? Will I be like Nick, nothing more than an embarrassing memory best forgotten?

"All the royal families intermarried, so of course you're related to a lot of important European historical figures," the curator says. She probably thinks she's being helpful, but please, please don't let ancient history do what a black card and a title couldn't. Please don't let it turn Khara's head. It's suddenly very important that she sees *me*, not my history.

Khara gazes at me thoughtfully. "Now I know why you are the way you are. From what I recall of European history, most of those old time royals were complete douches. It must be in the genes."

The curator gasps, a horrified look on her face, but I laugh, relieved. "Spoken like a true American," I say, taking her hand. "Shall we go and look at the gardens?"

The chateau is surrounded by a French-style water garden, immense geometric mirrors of water reflecting the sky and formal fountains. Beyond that lies a parkland, and the less formal Anglo-Chinese garden with its dense vegetation and quaint cottages, and the romantic English Garden with its temple of Venus and Island of Love, where an afternoon wedding is in progress. We hover, watching from a distance as the bride and groom exchange vows beneath a bower of roses.

"A dream wedding," I comment.

Khara shakes her head. "Not mine. I want a wedding just like ... like one I attended in Vegas last year. Simple, no fuss, just a handful of close friends sharing a magical moment."

"How can you sigh over art, but not have a romantic bone in your body?"

"It's not romantic to spend your life savings on a dress you're only going to wear once, and on feeding a whole lot of people you're not even that close to. There are much better things to spend money on, like college tuition, or a mortgage on a new home, or the chance to travel like ..."

She bites her lip, and I wonder what else she was going to say.

"What if money wasn't an obstacle? Would you want the big white wedding then?" I press.

She turns on me. "What does it matter? I'm not going to marry someone rich, so there's no point even going there. All I want is someone kind and good and dependable."

"Do the two have to be mutually exclusive?"

"In my experience, they usually are."

I arch an eyebrow at her. "This is more than just feeling left out at school, isn't it? What happened to make you so cynical?"

She narrows her eyes at me, as if I should already know the answer. Then she blows out a breath and shakes her head. "The first time I met a guy like you, I was in high school. You know the type: super rich family, the popular kid in school, good at sports, a little bit dangerous."

She's right. That does sound like me.

"I was so thrilled when he noticed me. Me, the girl that no one ever saw." She blushes and looks away. "I was thrilled right up until he told the entire school he did it as a bet to get into my pants."

Did he win the bet? I'm too afraid of what the answer might be to ask.

"The worst of it was that I really should have known better. I've had a lifetime of watching my mother date men like that. You want to know what I learned from her?"

I shake my head.

"Men like that don't marry women like us. They'll happily screw us, but when they marry they choose women from their own social circle, and they break our hearts."

"Max is marrying Phoenix."

She laughs softly. "Max is different. Besides, Phoenix blends into his world. She knows the right things to say, how to act in social situations. She wasn't always a cocktail waitress, and she doesn't live in a trailer."

I want to deny it, to tell her that the men I know aren't all like that. That *I'm* not like that. But I can't. I've screwed my way through enough waitresses, receptionists, and hotel front desk staff whose names I haven't even bothered to ask, to recognise that I'm one of those men. She has every right to call me a douche.

The vows are done, and the wedding guests stand and clap as the bride and groom walk down the petal-strewn aisle hand in hand.

As the guests move to the reception marquee set up on the

lawn, Khara smiles up at me cheekily. "I told you my deep, dark secret. Now you tell me yours."

"I don't have any secrets," I lie.

"Ha! Tell me why you *really* offered to tutor me."

Ouch. Do I have to? But fair is fair ... "My friend Charlie died a few years ago. His parents donated a new sports centre to our old prep school as a memorial, and this week was the dedication. I wanted an excuse to get out of it."

She eyes me, and it's that moment in the grotto all over again. She wants me, but she doesn't like me. I can imagine what she sees: a self-centred man who'd do anything to avoid taking anything seriously. I can't blame her.

And yet I want to prove her wrong. Madly, desperately, I want more than just to get Khara into my bed. Don't get me wrong; I still want to sleep with her. I want to see her hair spread out across my pillows, and I want to see her eyes go wild and dark, and I want to lick Chantilly cream off her skin.

But there's something else I want even more: I want to prove to her that I'm a better person than she thinks. Better than that jock in high school who humiliated her.

She turns away and starts walking back in the direction of the chateau. I have to hurry to catch her up.

"What do I have to do to convince you that I'm not like every other rich man you've ever met?"

She pauses to look at me. "Care about something or someone other than yourself. Do something real and useful with your life. Something that involves rolling up your sleeves, not the kind of job that involves taking a pay check for doing nothing."

She mistakes my silence for disagreement, sighs and shakes her head. "I thought so. You know, most of the population goes to work every day. It's really not that hard."

It's not holding down a job that's hard.

That old, dark fear raises its ugly head again, and this time I know what it is. It's the fear that if I care about anything or anyone, if I invest too much of myself in anything, then I will be vulnerable again. It is easier to be shallow, to hide behind the external trappings, behind the gloss of my family's wealth and reputation, than to let anyone or anything in. That is why I can't accept Uncle Lajos' offer. Because then I will have to care about an entire nation.

I cared about Charlie. I cared about Nick. I can't, I won't, let myself care about anything that way again.

Chapter 15

Khara

By the time we get back to the hotel, which now seems incredibly modern after seeing the eighteenth century chateau it's modeled on, Phoenix and Max are already in the bar, surrounded by what seems like an impromptu party.

"Where did you two disappear to?" Mateo shouts over the music and voices, drawing the entire room's attention to us. Maybe not the entire room. Their younger teammate is on a sofa in the corner, a blonde in his lap, and they're not paying attention to anyone but each other.

"We went to look at the art at the chateau," I answer.

"Looking at art – is that what you're calling it these days?" Phoenix asks with a sly wink. Max has his arm around her, and they're both smirking. I've never been more convinced that they've deliberately thrown me and Adam together than I am right now, though I can't figure out why. Wasn't Max the one who told Adam I wasn't his type?

Deliberately misunderstanding Phoenix, I launch into a description of everything we saw at the chateau. It's not hard for me to gush, and the way their eyes glaze over gives me immense satisfaction. But I'm also talking too much to cover the fact that Adam has barely said a word since we left the chateau's English garden. He barely looks at me.

"Poor you, mate," Max commiserates with Adam when I pause to draw breath. "After all that art and history, I'm sure you could use a drink."

Adam grins, but it seems forced. "Whatever it is, make it a double."

If anyone thought we left the polo match early to hook up, they sure aren't thinking it any longer. Adam takes the drink he's handed and, without even a glance at me, moves to join Mateo to admire the glass trophy their team won.

Phoenix looks at me enquiringly, and I shrug. I have absolutely no idea what's gotten into him. All I suggested was that he invests himself in something. Was that really so bad, and why did he ask if he didn't want my opinion? It's probably yet another one of those etiquette 'rules' I just don't get.

I look longingly at the woman serving drinks behind the bar, and wish we could trade places. Back there, mixing drinks, serving customers, staying invisible, I know what I'm doing. Out here on this side of the bar, everything is just so complicated.

As soon as I can do so without looking like a party pooper, I slip away to my room. But it's a long, long time before I fall asleep.

Adam doesn't join us for breakfast next morning. The concierge brings up the Sunday morning papers and Phoenix flicks to the society page (I didn't even know that was a thing). There are color pictures from the polo match – Max and Adam on the field, Max and Mateo accepting the trophy, Phoenix and me in the VIP enclosure. I breathe out a sigh of relief. I look just like everyone else at that polo match. Better yet, I look like a royal bridesmaid.

"Of course, there'll be pictures all over the internet as well, mostly fashion sites," Phoenix says, "but I never bother with those."

My heart thuds at the thought of strangers all over the world speculating about my clothes or my hair, and then I laugh. One of my high school tormentors runs a successful fashion blog. It's going to kill her, seeing me in the VIP enclosure at a high society event, all dressed up in designer clothes. That thought just made this entire trip to Europe and losing my job worthwhile.

The return drive to Westerwald later in the day is much quicker than our initial trip. Max claims that the cracking bruise he received on his shin during the polo match has made him an invalid, so he and Phoenix take the back seat and Adam drives. It's immediately obvious that Max and Phoenix only wanted the back seat because they can't keep their hands off each other. I catch Adam's eye and he grins.

He seems determined to keep things light and casual between us. He doesn't refer to his inheritance or his family once, and instead I find myself talking to fill the void. By the time our little cavalcade draws into Neustadt, I've had more practice at making small talk than any one person needs for a lifetime, and I also have a headache from trying to figure out what's going on with him.

When he doesn't join us for dinner, I'm relieved.

No, that's a lie. I'm not relieved. I'm mad.

I've known the man less than a week and in that time he's gotten under my skin in a way no other man has before. He's annoying and arrogant and entitled, and I shouldn't give him a moment's thought, but I can't stop thinking about him. I'm not sure I can keep blaming it on hormones.

For the next few days I hardly see him because Phoenix keeps me busy with royal wedding stuff. This wedding is so much more than dress fittings, floral arrangements and seating plans, as this isn't so much a wedding as a diplomatic event. Phoenix has included elements of all Westerwald's neighboring countries in the ceremony and reception: there are Dutch tulips in the church and in her bouquet, Belgian lace for her veil, a French croquembouche wedding cake, and the party favors for the reception guests are German almond-based marzipan sweets made in the shape of Westerwald's dragon and wrapped in blue and white chiffon bags, the colors of Westerwald's flag.

Phoenix lets me sit in on her meetings with the security heads to plan the final motorcade route, and with the protocol secretary to discuss seating inside the cathedral. She even insists on personally viewing the royal carriage and meeting the horsemen who will accompany the procession. I tag along, but those horses are scary big so I stay well back.

We attend the opening of the palace's merchandise pop-up store, where I hold Phoenix's bag and jacket while she does the official ribbon-cutting and makes a speech (in the local Westerwald dialect, which earns her rapturous applause). There are porcelain plates and mugs, tea towels and oven gloves, branded chocolates, flags, collectors' coins, plush toys, and even baseball caps with Max and Phoenix's faces emblazoned on them. I'm the shop's very first customer. I buy a plate for my mother, a set of mugs for Calvin, and a coffee tin for Isaiah – plus a set of proper porcelain teacups for myself. When I mentally convert the price back to dollars I experience a momentary qualm, but when Phoenix offers to pay I insist on paying for them myself. After all, the proceeds go to Westerwald's biggest children's home.

The store manager looks at me like I've grown another head. I suppose royal bridesmaids aren't supposed to act like common tourists, buying souvenirs to take back home, but that's what I am. And my brother is going to have such a laugh drinking out of a mug with their faces on it, considering less than a year ago Phoenix asked him to help her get a divorce from Max. It's a long story but, needless to say, the divorce never happened and Calvin was very careful to destroy all the evidence.

We spend half a day at a hair salon owned by a friend of Anton's, which closes just for us. Khara insists I touch up my blue ombre, and I'll admit I feel more like myself with the vivid color. Her own blonde highlights look so natural I swear not even an expert will be able to tell they're not.

Another day, Phoenix and I take a break from wedding duties to attend the official launch of a new adventure park just outside the city. There's a treetop obstacle course and a zip line (Westerwald's first) and, after yet another ribbon-cutting and more posing for the cameras, we actually get to do the course. There are still cameras following our every move, but once we're in our harnesses and navigating the suspended bridges and rope swings more than fifty feet above the ground I stop paying them any attention and just have fun with Phoenix, the way we used to in the old days. I wish Adam were here. He'd love this course way more than looking at art.

Even though Max and Phoenix requested that donations be sent to their favorite charities in lieu of wedding gifts, presents have still been steadily pouring into the palace. We spend an entire afternoon sorting through them – what to keep, what to give away to charity or to palace staff, and what to send to the national museum (like the antique black Chantilly lace shawl sent by the pony-breeding Count of Amiens, and a book of hand-written poems from a local primary school). Some of the gifts also have to be returned, obvious promotional items that companies are hoping Max or Phoenix will use in public to market their businesses, like the set of branded golf clubs.

Max is horrified when we tell him over dinner that night. "How can anyone think I play golf?"

The sun sets late here, later than I'm used to. We eat dinner in the private garden as the shadows grow longer, the garden turning softly blue at the edges then fading slowly into darkness, a slow, creeping sunset with none of the dramatic fire of our Nevada sunsets.

When Max leaves us to go back to his desk to catch up on work, it's only just past dark. A servant places citronella-scented lamps on the table and brings us a fresh bottle of the low-alcohol Moscato wine I'm developing a taste for.

"Has Adam gone back to London?" I ask casually.

Phoenix eyes me, but says nothing. The look in her eyes, as if she can see right through me to the desperation underneath, is distinctly uncomfortable.

"It's just that I haven't seen him around these last few days," I add hurriedly. "I was wondering if he plans to give me any more etiquette lessons?"

Because I don't feel anywhere near ready to sit at a formal banquet with hundreds of VIP wedding guests.

Okay, okay, I know I said I don't lie to myself. I'll admit it – this has nothing at all to do with napkins or cutlery. I just want to see him. Heaven only knows why.

"What happened between the two of you?" Phoenix asks at last.

"Nothing. Less than nothing."

"Then why are you avoiding each other?"

"I'm not! *He's* avoiding *me*."

Oops. Too late I realize that was as good as an admission that something *did* happen, though I'm still not entirely sure what it was. She holds my gaze until I relent. "We were watching this wedding in the chateau grounds, then he asked what he had to do to prove he's a decent guy, and I told him he should do something worthwhile with his life."

"Ah."

"What does that 'ah' mean?" She made it sound like a revelation.

"Do you know what Adam has been doing this past week?" she asks at last.

How could I, since I haven't seen him? I shake my head.

"He's been job shadowing Max."

I say nothing, and she raises an eyebrow. "You do know his uncle is the ruling prince of a little country called Erdély, and that Adam is a possible candidate to become his heir?"

"He told me after the polo match."

She leans forward, resting her chin in her cupped palm. "He wasn't even considering saying 'yes' until you told him to do something worthwhile."

He can't possibly be doing this because of something *I* said. Could he?

I watch a moth beat itself against the glass of the lamp. Phoenix is still watching me as if she's waiting for me to say something. Eventually she huffs out a breath. "His room is just down the corridor from yours."

I narrow my eyes at her. "You've been trying to get us together from the moment I landed – why? I mean, I know he's nice to look at ..."

She splutters. "Nice to look at?! He's hotter than a blowtorch – and if you ever tell Max I said that, I'll deny it."

I laugh and shake my head. "But we're completely unsuited to each other. We come from completely different worlds."

"Maybe he's just what you need. And clearly you're exactly what he needs."

Goddess, save me from happily married women who want to see everyone else around them paired up.

We chat a while longer, until the Moscato bottle is empty and the air grows chill and drives us indoors. We part inside, in the grand vestibule with its black-and-white marble floor and sweeping staircase. A sleepy security man is on duty where the footman usually stands during the day.

I give Phoenix a quick hug, then watch as she disappears through the side door that leads to the apartment she and Max have shared for nearly a year, even though they're unmarried as far as the public is concerned. I'm far too wide awake for sleep, but after a quick wave to the security officer I head upstairs to the guest wing.

At the top of the stairs, I pause. My own room lies down the corridor to the right. Instead, I turn left. Phoenix told me Adam's room is at the end of the hall. I hover outside the door, screwing up my courage. Twice, I raise my hand to knock. Twice, I pull it away. I don't want Adam to think this is a booty call.

Third time, I just do it. I wait, wondering if maybe he was already asleep, but then the door opens. My breath catches in my throat.

He's dressed in sweatpants and a tee-shirt, and he's barefoot, the most casual I've ever seen him. His hair is mussed, like he's been running his hands through it, and he sports several days' worth of scruff. But it's the black-rimmed glasses that make my pulse do all sorts of crazy things.

"I didn't know you wear glasses," I blurt out.

He removes them, as if he'd forgotten he was wearing them, and rubs the bridge of his nose. "I usually wear contacts."

The epitome of pure masculine perfection actually has a flaw. Just when I thought he couldn't get any hotter. I shift my weight from foot to foot. "I'm sorry if I'm disturbing you."

"You're not." He steps back, opening the door wider in invitation. "Come on in. I could do with a break."

I step inside and look around. The bed is strewn with papers, and the duvet is crumpled where he was sitting. He shuts the door behind me and I suddenly realize I'm alone with him. In his bedroom. Late at night, when everyone else has gone to bed. I wouldn't blame him for thinking this is a booty call.

"Wine? Coffee?"

"Coffee, please." I don't want to be tempted to do anything more stupid than I'm already doing.

He moves to the tray in the corner.

"Hey – you have a coffee press! That's so unfair! My room only has instant coffee." And an electric kettle, which Phoenix had to teach me how to use.

Adam grins. "I bought my own because I can't stand instant."

While he makes the coffee, filling the room with the delicious, rich scent of Italian roast, I move to the bed, perching on the edge to look at the papers spread out there. It's mostly financial stuff, annual budgets and treasury reports. The numbers are easy enough to read but the words are in a language I don't recognize. Erdélian, I assume.

Adam brings two cups of coffee to the bed and hands me one, then sprawls beside me. I take a sip. Milk, no sugar, just the way I like it.

"I'm sorry I've been neglecting our lessons," he says. "The days have just sort of run away with me."

I wave at the papers. "You've had more important things to think about."

He smiles. Not his usual arrogant grin, but a softer, warmer smile that melts what little is left of my common sense. "Not more important than you."

I have no idea what to say to that. As lines go, that's a pretty good one. And spoken in that intimate, husky rumble, I can see why women fall for him so easily. I'm falling for it too.

"So what have you been up to?" he asks.

I tell him all about the treetop adventure course and the zip line, and he laughs at the golf clubs. "Anyone who knows Max knows he's far too much of an adrenalin-junkie for golf."

"And what have you been busy with?"

Careful not to spill his coffee, Adam rolls onto his stomach. I stretch out beside him and look at the papers he spreads out for me.

"Should you be showing me these? Aren't they top secret, or something?"

He laughs, a warm, low chuckle. "I got these off the internet. My uncle runs a very transparent administration."

In the mellow lamplight, we read through the various reports together, occasionally using Google Translate when he doesn't recognize the Erdélian words. The country has a healthy tourism sector, "Mostly outdoor activities, like skiing, hiking and cycling," he explains, "but the economy is primarily agricultural. There were copper, iron and manganese mines, but they shut down in the twentieth century. The biggest challenge seems to be that much of the existing infrastructure is ageing and needs maintenance, but the country isn't bringing in enough revenue to cover the costs. There's no major deficit, and they'd like to keep it that way, but there's not much room for growth either. The country needs outside investment."

I roll on my side to face him. "And you just happen to be an investment broker."

"It's not that simple." He rubs his head, mussing up his hair even more. I'd love to run *my* fingers through his hair.

"If Erdély were just a client, I'd have no problem saying yes to my uncle's offer. Because if I get bored I can hand off the account to one of my juniors. Clients come and go, projects come and go, but Erdély has just always been there. And it will still be there long after I'm gone. I'm not the right person for that kind of responsibility."

"You told me I should have faith in myself. Perhaps you should take your own advice."

He holds my gaze, and I lose myself in the cool gray-green depths of his eyes. Then slowly he leans forward and presses his lips to mine. I have every opportunity to move away, to stop this from happening, but my limbs are too liquid to move. My eyes flutter closed, all my senses focused on the feel of his lips brushing mine. My heart pounds so hard it deafens me. I open my mouth, inviting him in, but suddenly he's not there any more.

I open my eyes, breathless, dazed, and more than a little mortified. Adam rolls off the bed, collects our empty coffee mugs and carries them across the room to the coffee tray.

"I'm sorry," he says, his back turned to me. "I shouldn't have done that."

I'm not sorry.

He sets the mugs down and turns to look at me. "This is

new for me. I've never been just friends with a woman before, but I like it, and I don't want to mess this up."

He's friend-zoning me? To say that I didn't see that coming is an understatement. What happened to him trying to seduce me? Involuntarily, I touch my fingers to my lips. That kiss was magical, but what if it wasn't good for him? What if he's changed his mind? What if he doesn't feel this same sudden high which is zinging through my veins? Is that why he's been avoiding me all week – to spare my feelings?

Hot humiliation surges up into my cheeks. "It's getting late," I say, pushing off the bed. "And tomorrow's going to be another busy day."

I walk to the door, and Adam follows. He reaches for the doorknob, but doesn't turn it. "Will I see you tomorrow?"

"Of course. Tomorrow night is the ballet fundraiser we're all expected to attend."

"Of course." He still doesn't turn the knob, effectively blocking me in. My heart races again.

"So, we're still friends, then?" he asks.

I force a bright smile. "Yes, we're still friends."

Chapter 16

Khara

What am I supposed to wear to the ballet? I stare at the open closet, at my meager assortment of clothes. The borrowed dresses have all been returned to the stylists, and the closet looks very bare. Aside from the ivory-colored dress I brought for Phoenix, my only other dress is the black skater dress I usually keep for first dates. It's the same dress I wore the first time I ever met Adam, the same dress I wore to the cocktail party the evening before the polo match. I really don't want to wear it again. What are the chances I can wear jeans tonight? I certainly have enough of those. Or I could go out shopping. It would mean dipping into my tuition money, but that's better than asking Phoenix for yet another favor.

There's a knock on the door, so I slam the closet door shut and hurry to open it.

Adam is leaning up against the doorframe, and he's carrying a garment bag. "I have a gift for you." He grins and holds up the bag.

Hoping desperately it's not the school principal's suit, I unzip the bag, gasping as the dress within is revealed.

"I can't accept this!"

"That's a pity, because I'm never going to be able to wear it."

I frown. "You could return it."

He shrugs. "Too much effort. So you might as well take it."

He holds the bag out to me, and I take it, holding it reverently. "Thank you."

"See you later." And he's gone, leaving me holding the most beautiful dress I've ever seen. The taffeta under-dress is plain, with a figure-hugging bodice and full knee-length skirt. But over the top is a gauzy ankle-length layer of pale grey chiffon, embroidered with multi-colored flowers.

A few hours later, I'm finally dressed, with my hair carefully straightened and tied up in an intricate bun courtesy of a YouTube tutorial. I'm adding the finishing touches to my make-up, hoping I've achieved the subtle, barely-there look that Adam's make-up artist gave me, when he's back at the door.

"You look stunning."

Hard as I try, I can't stop the blush that heats my cheeks. He looks pretty darn stunning himself. Last night's scruff has been shaved off and he looks very debonair in black and white evening dress. And he smells even better.

I drag my gaze away and do a little twirl to show off the dress. "Oh, this old thing. I just threw it on. Only took me about five ... hours."

"That sounds like a quote."

"It is. From the funniest romcom ever. Now, can we please get to this fundraiser so we can get it over with?"

"Don't you enjoy the ballet?"

"Ask me again in another couple of hours."

He gives me an amused glance, but wisely holds his tongue. He offers me his arm and we head down the hall to the staircase. "By the way, I love the shoes."

Another blush. I'm wearing the same strappy sandals I wore for our walk in the gardens.

The drive to the theater is nothing like our casual road trip in Max's SUV. There are two black luxury sedans pulled up at the palace entrance, each with a chauffeur and a personal protection officer up front. Adam and I go in the front car, and Max and Phoenix in the other. The security officer holds the door open for me. It's one of those fancy cars where the door opens backwards, which I've only ever seen on TV.

"Looking good tonight, Khara." He flashes me a smile and a wink.

"Thanks, Lukas."

I slide into the long leather bench seat and Adam slides in beside me. "On a first name basis with the bodyguard?" he asks in a low voice.

I flash him an annoyed look. "Don't be such a snob. Lukas has been driving with us all week. Of course I know his name."

"I'm not a snob, and it's not his name that worries me," he mutters.

The look I give him now definitely isn't annoyed; it's amused, and maybe a little hopeful. "You're not jealous, are you? Because *friends* aren't supposed to get jealous."

"I am not jealous!"

Could have fooled me. Against my better judgment, that makes me feel all mushy and aglow on the inside.

There's an entire reception committee waiting in line in the theater's foyer to greet us. I concentrate on doing everything Adam taught me, standing up straight without fidgeting, smiling politely, making small talk, but the butterflies in my stomach are throwing a rave. As soon as we can, Adam and I slip away up the grand staircase to the 'retiring room', a waiting room outside the royal box with white walls decorated with gold-painted plaster moldings and midnight-blue velvet sofas. I collapse down on one of the sofas, relieved to take the pressure off my feet. When I get back to Vegas, I'm never wearing high heels again.

"Take this." Adam pours two glasses of Champagne from the ice bucket set ready for us. "It'll settle your nerves."

I don't expect the alcohol to calm me but surprisingly it does, without dulling my senses. Is that why it's the drink of choice at these fancy events?

"This theater was built in the 1850s," he says, "to replace the original theater, which has now been converted into a restaurant. This was one of the first public buildings in Neustadt to be fitted with electric light."

I hide my smile. I already read all about the building in my guidebook, but it's sweet of him to have made the effort.

When Max and Phoenix finally join us we enjoy a few moments' peace in the privacy of the retiring room while the rest of the audience fills the auditorium. Then the orchestra starts to tune up.

"That's our cue." Max holds out his hand to Phoenix and leads her out into the royal box as the orchestra plays the opening bars of Westerwald's national anthem. I grab us a few bottles of water from the table and follow them out.

The auditorium is breathtaking, all royal blue and gold, and an enormous chandelier hangs overhead from the gilded ceiling. The place is packed, with row upon row of seating both below us and around the walls, and the audience is on its feet, clapping, every head turned in our direction. I suck in a breath. *They're not looking at you*, I remind myself.

Adam and I wait at the back of the box as Max and Phoenix pose at the front, waving to the crowd while camera flashes pop. At last they take their seats, and Adam and I sit in the stiff high-backed chairs just behind them.

The lights dim, the music swells, and the curtain rises. Tonight's performance is *Giselle*, one of the classical ballets. I'm entranced by the costumes and the music and the dancing, so drawn into the story that when the curtain falls I'm in tears at the death of Giselle. I hope I haven't smudged my make-up.

"Is that it?" I ask Adam as we head into the ballroom, where drinks have been laid out for the VIP guests.

He chuckles, helping himself to two glasses of Champagne from a passing waiter. "That was just the first act."

I accept the glass he holds out to me, even though I don't plan to drink it. Better than letting him drink both glasses, the way he did at the palace dinner party. Though I flush when I remember he wasn't the one who got drunk that night.

"How can there be a second act when the title character's dead?"

"She comes back as a spirit to save Duke Albrecht from the vengeful spirits of other betrayed maidens."

"Why would she do that? He's a liar and a cheat. He deserves to be punished. She would have been much better off with the simple gamekeeper."

"But the heart wants what the heart wants," a woman's voice says behind me. I turn to see an older woman in a black and white evening gown, with her fair hair artfully tousled and laughter lines around her eyes. It's the eyes that tell me who she is. They're Adam's eyes.

"Hello, Mum." Adam steps forward to kiss her cheek.

For a moment I'm paralysed, trying to remember how I'm supposed to address a princess. I should have known she'd be here. Didn't Adam tell me his mother was a patron of the ballet? I should've practiced curtseying in these damned heels this afternoon.

"Mum, this is Georgiana's friend, Khara Thomas." It takes me a moment to remember he means Phoenix. Georgiana is her birth name, but she hates it and prefers the nickname her parents gave her, though I don't suppose it's very royal-sounding.

He turns to me. "And this is my mother, Her Royal Highness Princess Krisztyna Eszterháza de Erdély Hatton."

She sends him an arch look that makes me want to laugh. Instead, I curtsey, relieved when I don't fall over and make an idiot of myself.

"Oh, don't bother with all of that." She waves her hand. "Just call me Krisztyna."

I don't think so.

Her direct gaze sweeps over me, but her smile is reassuring. It reaches all the way up to her eyes, making them crinkle, and she doesn't look at me as if she knows my underwear is from Walmart. Those etiquette lessons must have paid off.

"Are you the reason Adam has stayed here in Westerwald so long?" she asks.

I choke. "Hardly. He's been working with Max."

That cool green gaze turns on Adam. I never thought I'd see him squirm, but he does now. "You did make me promise I would give serious consideration to Lajos' offer," he says defensively.

"I did indeed." She turns back to me. "Are you enjoying the performance?"

Though my tongue still feels stiff and my mind is blank, I remember just enough not to give a one-word answer. "I love it! And it's much less stuffy that I thought."

"Oh?" She raises an elegant eyebrow.

"I mean, the audience gets so involved, clapping whenever the dancers do something amazing."

She nods. "Yes, we like to show our appreciation. Are you enjoying your stay in Westerwald?"

I can do this. I'm having a conversation with a real live princess (Max doesn't count as royalty as far as I'm concerned) and I'm not face-planting. "Oh, yes! Europe is just incredible. And Adam has been so helpful, taking me to see museums and art galleries."

She glances at her son. "Has he?" Then she smiles, another warm smile that makes me feel less gauche and awkward. "It has been a pleasure meeting you, Khara. You should get my reprobate son to take you to visit Erdély some time soon too." The arch look she sends him suggests the invitation is aimed more at him than me.

Then she gives him a quick hug, looking for a moment

more like a mother than a princess, and moves off through the crowd, to do whatever it is that princesses do. I let out a long breath.

"That wasn't so scary, was it?" Adam teases.

"It was terrifying."

After the second half of the ballet, I'm still convinced Giselle would have been better off with the gamekeeper who loved her than with the fickle aristocrat who was engaged to another woman.

There's a party in the ballroom after the show, the dancers coming in to mingle with the wealthy guests who've paid a fortune to be here tonight. A bar has been set up at one end of the room, and a small orchestra plays. There are quite a few people I recognize from the dinner party and the polo match, and Adam was right – now that they know my connection to Phoenix, everyone wants to be my friend. It's flattering and tiring in equal measure.

Adam doesn't stay glued to my side, and I suppose that's for the best. I certainly don't want to appear on those society pages for the wrong reasons, but it means I have to fend for myself with the Elenas of the world. And yes, Elena is here, much friendlier tonight than the last time we met.

"Is that dress Valentino or Zuhair Murad?" she gushes, air kissing my cheeks. "It's gorgeous."

"I don't have a clue," I confess.

I'm rescued by Adam's mother, who invites me to meet the ballet dancers. Elena makes a big show of being an old friend of the princess', but there's a look in the older woman's eyes, a stiffness in her shoulders, that makes me think she finds the conversation tedious. It's the same look Adam gets in polite company.

The princess certainly doesn't look bored when she talks to the dancers. She chats animatedly, sweeping me along with her, and it's clear she's passionate about the ballet. I wonder if that's how Adam would look when he's excited, and I realize I've never seen him truly passionate about anything. Nothing ever burns through that slightly amused, slightly bored façade.

With their royal duties done, Max and Phoenix take to the dance floor alongside a few other couples, twirling around in the kind of dance I've only ever seen on *Dancing with the Stars*. Then Adam joins them, dancing with a blonde who looks as groomed and as indistinguishable as that trio he was with in Vegas. But boy, can they move. Where did he learn to dance like that?

He sweeps her around the floor and they look so perfect together I feel almost ill. It's no wonder he thought kissing me last night was a mistake – I can't hope to compete with that.

Politely excusing myself from the dancers and the princess, I head for the bar. Just this once, I could really use a drink.

"A Negroni, please," I say to the bartender. He mixes the Cinzano, vermouth and gin, then adds flamed orange peel. I wrinkle my nose, tempted to show him how to make it properly without the burnt orange overpowering the delicate botanicals, and have to hold myself back. That would definitely make me look like a Giselle in a world of Albrechts.

"You don't like the drink?" Adam appears at my side just as I take my first tentative sips.

I shrug. "The barman was definitely chosen for his looks rather than his cocktail-making abilities."

Then I turn to face him, urgently in need of an answer to something that's been bugging me all evening. "You're not engaged, are you? You don't have a marriage of convenience planned to some titled heiress?" Like Albrecht.

He laughs. "I most certainly do not."

I've barely had two sips of this drink, so I can't blame this sudden tightness in my chest on alcohol. "If you're going to be the *Fürst* of Erdély one day, you'll need to marry and have an heir."

Judging from the look of horror on his face, I'm guessing that thought hadn't yet occurred to him. "Well, I guess I'll just have to make my sister my heir. Sorted."

"Is the idea of settling down with just one woman so repugnant to you?"

"You've met the women I know. Would you want to marry any of them?"

I laugh. "There must be at least one half-decent woman who'll have you."

"Phoenix is already taken, and I'm guessing you'd turn me down."

"Damn right I would."

He removes the glass from my hand, takes a long sip and pulls a face. "You're right. It doesn't taste quite right. Would you like to dance?"

"No, thanks. I can't dance."

"Everyone can dance."

"Sure, bouncing around in a nightclub, but not like that."

I wave at the dance floor, where Max and Phoenix are now partnered with Giselle and Albrecht. "I thought this kind of dancing only existed in movies."

"We'll need to remedy that, since there'll be 'this kind' of dancing at the wedding reception." He holds his hand out to me in invitation and I take a step back, out of his reach.

"No way! I am not going out there and making a fool of myself in public."

"Don't you trust me?"

"Do you even have to ask?"

He looks pained. "Okay, I'll let you off the hook for tonight, but I want you in the palace ballroom at nine o'clock tomorrow morning for your first ballroom dance lesson. And I'm not taking no for an answer."

"Fine." I know I sound like a moody teenager, but dancing might just be even scarier than learning to make small talk. At least conversation doesn't require bodily contact.

Chapter 17

Khara

Life slows down in the palace on weekends. Since this is their last weekend before the arrival of Max's relatives and the madness of the wedding, Phoenix and Max take off for the castle upriver at Waldburg, to visit with Claus and Rebekah, and ride their bikes in the countryside. They deserve time alone after the hectic few weeks they've had, but I wish I was going with them. Anything would be better than dance lessons with a man who should come with a health warning: liable to cause heart flutters and irrational thinking.

Nevertheless, I ask the maid who brings me breakfast to show me to the ballroom, where Adam is ready and waiting. On the plus side, we're left completely alone, so no one is around to witness how often I get breathless when I'm in his arms. Or how often I step on his feet, or move in the wrong direction.

"I clearly don't know what I'm doing," I moan. I must have inherited my dance ability from my father rather than my mother, whose first job in Vegas was as a showgirl, before she fell pregnant with Calvin.

"You need to trust me!" Adam throws up his hands in

exasperation. "Stop trying to plan the steps ahead of time and let me lead."

"Let me dance barefoot, at least," I beg.

He shakes his head. "You can't take off your shoes at every ball you attend."

"It's only one ball. Are you sure I have to do this?"

He pulls a sheet of paper from his pocket and I see it's another of the palace's typed schedules, but this time it's a list of dances. Geez, even the wedding reception is scheduled down to the last minute.

After Phoenix and Max have their first dance, they're supposed to dance with their parents. Since both of Phoenix's parents are dead, she'll dance with his grandfather, and he'll dance with his mother. That's when Adam and I are supposed to join them. Then I'm supposed to dance with Max's grandfather, while Adam partners Max's mother. I scrunch up my nose. We're going to be on that dance floor for at least ten minutes with only two other couples and an audience of over three hundred invited guests. Please remind me why I agreed to be Phoenix's bridesmaid?

Adam holds out his hand to me again, and when I place mine in it he pulls me up against him. He settles one hand on my lower back and holds my other hand.

"Just keep looking at me," he says. "Not at your feet."

He starts up his MP3 player again, and we start to move. I do what he says, keeping my eyes on his, and surprisingly it works. I get so lost in his gaze that I lose the ability to control my feet. His hand is firm on my lower back, guiding me as we sweep around the ballroom. When the song ends, he stops moving. I feel dizzy, and I don't think it's from dancing.

"See," he says triumphantly. "When you stop trying to direct everything and go with the flow, you dance really well."

I'm exhausted by the time we break for lunch. Not that it's much of a break. We eat alone in the breakfast room, with only a maid serving us rather than the terrifying butler, but Adam insists we observe all the correct table manners for a formal dinner. There's so much to remember – the correct distance to sit from the table (two hands' width), the correct place to lay a napkin or a fork to send a message to the servers, the correct way to use cutlery so they don't clink against the plates or cups.

"I can't do this!" I moan, sinking my head down onto the empty placemat after the sorbet course has been removed – which I've now learned is a palate cleanser rather than dessert. "Please let this week be over."

Adam takes pity on me and gives me the afternoon off. I curl up on my bed, determined to finish the Faye Kellerman mystery I'm reading. My eyes grow heavier, until I'm suddenly startled awake by a loud knocking on the door. The room is dark, illuminated only by a shaft of pale blue moonlight. I fumble my way to the door. It's Adam. Of course.

And he's dressed in jeans and a plain black shirt. It's the first time I've seen him in jeans.

I rub my eyes. "Am I late for dinner?"

"Nope. I gave the staff the night off. I'm taking you out on the town tonight."

"Just promise me no bars."

He arches an eyebrow, and I groan. But I give in. I'd rather be in a crowded place, with loud music and lots of other people, than alone in this very big, very empty palace with Adam.

Neustadt is as magical by night as it is by day. There are bars and restaurants everywhere, with lights and music and laughter. The shops stay open late, there are food and craft beer stalls on the street corners and the sidewalk cafés are full. We wander along the river, stopping at a food truck for a dinner of döner kebabs and local *weissbier* which we eat sitting on the stone balustrade of a bridge as the tour boats pass beneath us, lit up with multi-colored lights.

The bar Adam takes me to is the Landmark Café. It looks very different at night, with electric-blue light reflecting off the brushed-steel bar. There's live music, and people are dancing out on the terrace overlooking the river. We find an empty sofa in a corner of the bar, and Adam orders us the Landmark's signature blue cocktail. It's not as sweet as it looks, and I drink it down rather quicker than I should.

By the second drink, I let him cajole me onto the dance floor. The music is fast-paced and loud, making conversation impossible. This is my kind of dancing, gyrating to a beat rather than having to think about where to place my feet. The music is new to me, with German lyrics and a beat made for dancing. It pulses through me, in time with the swirling light. The dance floor is packed and we're pushed close together, our bodies swaying in rhythm, thighs and hips and arms touching until my hormones are drunk on the sensation.

By the third drink, I can't remember why I didn't want to be alone with Adam tonight. In fact, I really, really want to get him alone. Because the things I want him to do to me can't be done in a very public bar.

He calls for a palace car to fetch us home, and I don't argue. I want this. I want him. I really, really want him. Those fancy blue drinks clearly cause amnesia, because I can't remember a single reason why I ever thought being just another notch on Adam Hatton's bedpost was a bad thing.

In the back of the car, with the dark glass separating us from the driver up front, I lay my hand on Adam's thigh. He doesn't push it away. Instead, he lays his hand over mine, trapping my palm against his leg. His long fingers intertwine with mine, and his thumb brushes the back of my hand until my whole body is a molten mess. We sit like that for a long time, as the streets blur past, until the car slides between the massive palace gates and rounds the building towards the private entrance.

He only lets go of my hand when we climb out the car, but when I stumble, my low heel snagging in the loose gravel, he catches me, wrapping a strong arm around my waist, his fingers warm against the bare skin between the top of my jeans and the sparkly sequinned crop tank top I'm wearing. *Yes!* The warmth and strength of his hand against my skin promises pure pleasure.

His hand stays there, all the way past the sleepy security officer who opens the front door to us, all the way up the stairs and to my bedroom door.

But when I open the door and hold it wide in invitation, his hand falls away and he doesn't step across the threshold.

"Do you want to come in?" I ask, draping myself against the door like a provocative silver screen siren.

He clears his throat. "That wouldn't be a good idea. Just friends, remember?"

Friends. *Right*.

"I'll meet you in the ballroom at nine." Then he turns and strides away down the corridor toward his own room. I shut the door and throw my purse at it. Lip gloss, tissues, and my phone rain down as the bag bursts open. I sag to the floor and sink my head into my hands. How is it possible that a man with a reputation like his didn't take advantage when it was offered to him?

If I were thinking at all rationally right now, I'd probably hate myself for wanting him. But my body is wound so tight I don't care. Because that feeling I had when I first laid eyes on him in the library nearly two weeks ago is now ten times stronger than it was back then. *Yeah, I'd like to do him.*

Since we only got back to the palace in the early hours, I've hardly slept by the time I meet Adam in the ballroom. My head hurts, and my muscles ache. I didn't realize ballroom dancing uses so many muscles. Adam has thoughtfully supplied bottles of water which at least relieves my dehydration, even though it does nothing for the pain in my head. The headache has nothing to do with last night's cocktails and everything to do with the fact that I spend the better part of the day in Adam's arms, our bodies constantly touching and swaying together.

By the time Max and Phoenix return from their weekend escape late that afternoon, I've mastered the basics of the waltz, rumba, cha-cha, foxtrot and quickstep. I draw the line at learning to tango. I am never going to need to dance a tango.

With their return, the palace goes from silent as a grave to humming. The next morning there's an official debrief for the bridal party and all the heads of staff in which Claus runs us through every step of the processions, ceremonies and even the speeches. This is suddenly very real. Though I've been working on my speech since I first received Phoenix's call, I pray for a lightning strike or other act of God to get me out of it.

On Tuesday the palace is overrun with staff, preparing for the arrival of the first wedding guests – Max's family.

Phoenix's anxiety feels almost like a living thing, and I share the feeling, though for entirely different reasons. Tonight, we'll be sitting down to dinner with a whole bunch of royalty. This will be my first real test since that disastrous dinner party. But for Phoenix, her anxiety isn't because of the titles or the etiquette, but because they're family. By lunchtime she's a wreck.

"I've met them all before, and they're wonderful people." She folds her napkin over and over. "But it's just so ..."

Overwhelming. I get it. Her mother died when she was young and she was raised by a single father, just like I was raised by a single mother. Neither of us even knew our grandparents. Suddenly finding herself in a large family of in-laws and grandparents and cousins has to be pretty intimidating.

"My mother sent a long text this morning," I say, ready to provide a distraction. "She's dating the GP she's working for."

Phoenix laughs. "Oh, no! That is so not going to end well. And I thought she was really enjoying that job?"

"Me too." I sigh. "Her eyes are always so full of stars, she can't see straight."

Which is exactly how I feel about Adam.

We gather in the private drawing room for pre-dinner drinks. This is a long room with French windows opening straight into the private garden. The walls are painted a soft periwinkle blue, and the ceiling is decorated with plaster molding painted in gold. The scent of roses drifts in through the open doors.

When I enter, running late because it took me an age to straighten and tame my hair, the room is already packed with people. Phoenix comes forward to welcome me, squeezing my hand in mutual support, before she introduces me to everyone.

Max's mother was a supermodel before she married the former archduke. She's still beautiful and effortlessly glamorous, with a tanned glow that suggests her new life in California agrees with her, but there's a sadness in her eyes too. Phoenix once told me Max's parents were desperately in love, and her husband's death really knocked her.

His American grandparents are down-to-earth, and when his grandfather shakes my hand I can feel the roughened work calluses on his palm that remind me he's still a wine farmer.

Then there's Max's older brother Rik, as dark as Max is fair. His hair's a little over-long and tattoos peek out beneath his sleeves, making him look more like a marauding pirate than a dethroned prince. I cannot believe that once upon a time he was the dutiful brother, the one raised to be archduke. Rik's new bride, Kenzie, is a 'commoner' like me and Phoenix, and she makes me feel less like a unicorn in this room of beautiful people. She's petite and fragile-looking, with ginger hair, freckles, and sparkling blue eyes. She's also heavily pregnant.

"Yes, I was an enormous bride." She giggles as she rubs her belly. "I can't wait for the baby to come. The sooner he or she arrives, the sooner we can go home."

"Where's home?"

"We live on an island in the Caribbean called Corona, but we'll be staying with my parents in England until after the birth. Rik thinks I should have my mother close by." She rolls her eyes. "I love my parents dearly, but they also drive me nuts."

Trust me, I get it.

Max's other brother, Christian, is the newcomer in the family, the late archduke's son by the girlfriend he had before he met Max's mother. He's also an A-list movie star, and I've swooned over that face and those hypnotic blue eyes more times than I can count. What red-blooded woman on the planet hasn't?

His wife makes me think of Grace Kelly, with her grace, poise and ice-blonde good looks. They really are an intimidatingly gorgeous couple, but Teresa takes my hand and leads me to a sofa, plying me with good-natured questions about how I'm enjoying my visit in Westerwald.

"I grew up here in Neustadt," she says. "I really miss it,

especially now as the seasons start to change. California's year-round summer is lovely, but I do miss the autumn leaves and winter snow. You really must come back at Christmas time. The markets and the festive lights are magical."

If only. I sigh. "Everything about this place is magical! Even the bars. Adam took me to the Landmark Café, and it's nothing like any bar I've ever been to."

She laughs, glancing toward where her husband and Adam stand in conversation beside the drinks trolley. "I know that bar."

As if sensing her gaze, Christian turns to look at her, and his eyes light up. I don't even bother to hide another sigh. I've never had a man look at me like that.

Dinner is a loud, casual affair, even though it's served in the formal dining room. The conversation flows naturally and I find myself relaxing, not worrying about small talk or if I'm going to embarrass myself. I'm seated close to Max's grandparents, who are exactly the kind of grandparents I used to wish for. I never met any of my father's family, and my mother's parents were extremely conservative and cut her off when she came to Vegas to dance. That's another thing Phoenix and I have in common.

Adam is seated down the far end of the table, with Rik and Kenzie, and though there's a lot of laughter and chatter between us, I notice a reserve between Adam and Kenzie.

"Please, please tell me you didn't sleep with her?" I whisper to Adam as we make our way back to the drawing room after dinner.

"Oh God, no!" He looks genuinely horrified at the thought.

"She used to date my friend Charlie a long time ago, back before she met Rik."

There's a look in his eyes when he mentions his friend, something more than grief, and I wonder if he even knows it's there. He turns away quickly, smiling at the room, but his smile seems forced.

Max's grandparents head off to bed, and his mother soon after, leaving the rest of us to keep the party going. Since the servants have packed up for the night, I station myself at the incredibly well-stocked drinks trolley and do what I do best: mixing and serving drinks until eventually the party breaks up. Max and Phoenix head to their apartment, but the rest of us are all staying in the guest wing so we walk up the stairs together, parting with hugs and warm goodnights.

Chapter 18

Khara

On the morning of the wedding rehearsal Phoenix and I visit the palace vault with Max's mother. Anna, she insists I call her. The head of palace security accompanies us, but Anna unlocks the door with her own key. The heavy door opens slowly and Anna switches on the lights. I gasp.

The windowless room looks like a museum, with low lighting and velvet-lined glass cases around the walls. Each case has its own light, illuminating what seems like hundreds of items of jewelry. I follow them hesitantly into the room, pretty sure I shouldn't even be here.

There are necklaces, bracelets, earrings, and brooches – and more tiaras than a Disney movie. Not the glitzy plastic-looking tiaras you see in bad TV movies either, but really old antique-looking ones.

In a tall case in the center of the room is a gem-encrusted crown. "Max wore that for his coronation," Phoenix tells me.

"That was the day he proposed to you, wasn't it?" Anna asks.

Phoenix flashes me a conspiratorial look. "That was the day Max made his very public proposal, yes."

Way to go, Phoenix. Not quite the truth, but not a lie either.

As we wander from case to case, Archduchess Anna tells us the history of each piece. Some came into the family as parts of dowries, some were gifts from other royal families, and others were wedding gifts from husbands to their brides. There's even a case of Fabergé jewels.

I have a sudden image of Phoenix doing this one day, walking her own daughter or daughter-in-law through the history and significance of each piece.

"This one—" Anna points to an especially elaborate necklace of rubies and diamonds, almost vulgar in its ostentation "—started a war. Archduke Willem had it made for his mistress. Some say it was this necklace that was the last straw. After he presented it to her, the people of Westerwald rose up in support of his queen, who was kept a virtual prisoner while he flaunted his mistress to the world, and there was a very bloody civil war."

"Max told me the story," Phoenix says. "When the war ended, a sorceress cast a spell on the royal family so that every royal marriage from that time forward would be blessed with true love."

She and Anna exchange a satisfied, secretive look that makes me feel even more like I'm eavesdropping on a private conversation.

Anna gives us a lesson in tiaras, and I learn a whole lot of new words I'd never heard before – drops and toppers and festoons, and the difference between bandeaus and wishbones and circlets. There are tiaras that can also be used as necklaces, and others that can be taken apart to form brooches, and one with interchangeable gems to match any outfit. We pore over the cases, and Phoenix finally settles on a simple bandeau tiara, a scrollwork of vine leaves made of silver and diamonds.

"Very apt when you're marrying a winemaker," Anna says. "Now don't wash your hair for at least a day before the wedding, or the tiara will slip around on your head. And make sure your hair is already lacquered before you put it on, or the tiara itself gets sticky. You also need to ensure that your veil isn't attached to the tiara, or the weight of the veil will pull it backwards off your head."

I stifle a giggle, and both women look at me. "So, behind all the glamour that the rest of the world sees, this is what real princesses talk about – practical things like hair-washing and lacquer?"

Anna laughs. "Yes, nothing is ever as glamorous as it seems. Now, what about you?"

"What about me?" I ask, immediately self-conscious. "I'm wearing flowers in my hair. No tiara necessary."

"But you'll need earrings and a necklace," she points out.

I'm so dumbstruck that the other two ladies continue without me. Phoenix describes my bridesmaid dress and they pick out a pair of sapphire chandelier earrings for me to wear, and a delicate emerald necklace for the banquet.

"I can't!" I whisper, but they ignore me.

The head of security takes meticulous notes of which items we'll be wearing with each outfit throughout the festivities. It's his job to ensure the jewels are brought to our rooms in time for each event, and that they're safely locked away again afterwards. I'm still shell-shocked when we finally leave the vault, and Anna hands Phoenix the ancient-looking key. "It's yours now," she says simply.

The cathedral is closed to the general public until after the wedding, but the place is a hive of activity. TV people swarm all over, laying cables and rigging cameras and microphones. Church staff polish the candle sconces, and specialist window cleaners are up on scaffolding cleaning the stained glass windows. Security officers guard all the entrances, searching everyone who enters and exits.

Phoenix and I walk the long length of the uneven, flag-stoned nave, both wearing the same shoes we'll wear for the wedding in a couple of days. Up front, Max and Adam wait for us. Max smiles at his bride as if no one else in the world exists, but it's Adam I'm watching. A small smile curves his mouth as his gaze meets mine, and he no longer seems to have that bored air he usually wears.

The archbishop runs us through the ceremony, and when it's all over we return to the palace for afternoon tea.

"Where's Adam?" I ask, when I notice he hasn't joined us in the drawing room.

"His uncle and aunt have arrived for the wedding. They're staying at one of the hotels in town, and Adam has gone to see them," Rik answers.

An anxious knot tightens in my stomach. Has he made a decision yet whether to accept his uncle's offer? Could he be announcing his decision right now? Though I have no right to feel this way, I'm hurt he hasn't told me any of this. *Just friends, remember?* Yet somehow I thought we'd become very good friends. The kind of friends who tell each other things.

He doesn't join us for dinner either. Since tomorrow is the civil wedding, everyone heads to bed early. I'm just stepping out of the shower, ready to get into my pyjamas, when there's a knock on the door.

"I have the chocolates ready, but you better not have cold feet," I say as I swing open the door. But it isn't Phoenix, come for a late night chocolate-binge. It's Adam, dressed in a navy three-piece suit and looking breathtakingly debonair.

"I'm not sure why I'd be getting cold feet, but I won't say no to chocolate."

"I was expecting someone else," I stammer.

One dark eyebrow arches. "You were expecting someone else in your room at this hour, dressed like that?"

He waves a hand at the towel, which is the only thing covering my assets.

"Phoenix, but that doesn't matter. Please get inside before anyone sees you here."

He grins and steps into the room. I quickly shut the door, but now I realize I'm practically naked and standing less than a few feet away from Adam. He seems to be thinking the same thing. His eyes kindle.

So maybe he is still interested?

My heart hammers loud enough inside my chest I'm sure it's audible.

"Give me a moment." I rush to collect my pyjamas, and dash into the bathroom to change. Plain grey sweatpants and a thin camisole top. Why didn't I think to grab something sexier?

My hair is still steamed-up from the shower and untameable. Since I can't hide in here all night while I straighten it, I'll simply have to leave it as it is. I brush my teeth, add a dash of lip gloss, and return to the main room.

Adam is seated on the sofa, flicking through the new novel I picked up in the library earlier, this time an Alisha Rai romance with a semi-naked man on the cover. I would blush, but Anna recommended the book and if it's good enough for an archduchess I'm not going to be embarrassed to admit I'm enjoying it. Adam sets the book down when I draw close, and his eyes darken. God, I wish he didn't want to be just friends.

What are the chances that 'friends with benefits' could be an option?

"I had dinner with my uncle this evening," he says, patting the sofa beside him. I fetch the box of chocolates I had ready in case Phoenix showed up, before I sit on the sofa, carefully keeping distance between us.

"How did it go?"

"He suggested I visit Erdély before making a decision."

I nod. "That's sensible."

"So I'm going to leave the day after the wedding to spend a few days there."

My heart catches in my throat. The day after the wedding. That's two days away. Just three more sleeps before he leaves and I most likely never see him again. I don't trust myself to speak, so I nod again.

Since I now need chocolate a great deal more than Phoenix will, I rip away the packaging and open the box, offering Adam one before I blindly help myself.

The bittersweet taste of dark chocolate and strawberry liqueur hits my tongue. After the wedding, I have just one more week here in Westerwald before I'm due to fly back to Nevada. Phoenix and Max planned to take me to the castle in Waldburg which I've heard so much about. I was looking forward to seeing it but, without Adam there, it suddenly feels very unappealing. I can't even imagine being here in Westerwald without Adam down the corridor, or holding my hand (metaphorically) through every event.

"Another?" I ask, offering up the chocolate box.

He takes one. I take two; hazelnut praline and something darker-flavoured, coffee perhaps. I couldn't be bothered to read the box.

He holds my gaze until my breath squeezes tight in my chest. I memorize every line of his face, the slight crinkles that are developing at the corners of his eyes, the tiny gray flecks at his temples, the five o'clock shadow on his strong chin. His lips, full and tempting.

He leans forward, twining his fingers into my hair. "I like your hair like this, free and unconstrained."

I wrinkle my nose. "It's a pain in the ass."

He grins. "Just like you then."

I can handle the flippant, easy banter. But his fingers are still in my hair. He tucks the strands back behind my ears, his fingers brushing my cheek, and my eyes drift closed. This, I *can't* handle. Why did he have to touch me?

Because now my body is coursing with the electricity of his touch. I know chemistry can't be trusted, but it's impossible to ignore. I want him even more now than I did that first night in the library, before I knew who he was. I want him more than when I was drunk on cocktails.

And he's leaving in two days.

"I should leave you to sleep." His voice is a low hum, and I open my eyes. "I just wanted to tell you that I'll be leaving soon."

He rises from the sofa and heads to the door, leaving me still seated, clutching the box of chocolates.

"Sweet dreams," he says from the door. Then he lets himself out.

I switch out all the lights and climb into the enormous bed. Alone, still clutching the chocolates. All I can hear is Elena's voice: '*... he won't stick around until morning*'. I can't even get him to stick around for the night.

Chapter 19
Adam

"This tie feels like a bloody noose." Max runs his fingers inside his collar, as if to loosen the tie.

"Feeling nervous?"

"No, I just hate wearing ties."

He is nervous, though. "Trust me, she won't back out now," I reassure him. Our conversation is hushed as the wood-panelled city hall chamber is rapidly filling with guests. Since this is only the civil wedding, there's no music, no pageantry, no bouquets or fancy floral arrangements, and no important dignitaries, just family. Admittedly, on Max's side that family includes two heads of state and a good many titles. I'm probably one of the lowest ranking people in the room.

Max fidgets with his collar again. "That's not what I'm worried about. I'm trapping her in this life. It's not the one I originally promised her."

What the hell does that mean? I thought he met her in Waldburg when she was backpacking around Europe. He was already archduke by then, so what other life could he have offered her?

But Khara told me she was there when they met, so that must have been in ...

I don't have time to follow that line of thought through to its conclusion, as the guests are rising and everyone turns to face the door, where the bride has just appeared. Phoenix is wearing a sleeveless, cream-coloured dress that looks more Marilyn Monroe than the dress of an archduchess, but she's easily one of the most beautiful brides I've ever seen. Probably because of the radiant glow on her face. Max finally stops fidgeting, mesmerised as his bride walks towards him. I glance at him and he has honest-to-God tears in his eyes as he looks at her. My gaze slides past Phoenix, and my own chest squeezes tight.

I'd say that Khara cleans up well, except that she has always looked beautiful. That first morning we met in the breakfast room, when she was dressed in ripped jeans and with her hair loose, she was just as striking as she is now.

But something has changed. Maybe it's because I know her better now. God, I wish I didn't. It would be so much easier to take her to bed if I didn't know her. If I didn't know that sleeping with her and walking away was only going to prove to her what dicks men like me are.

Just two more nights. I need to get through just two more nights without giving in to temptation. How hard can that be?

Her hair is pulled back in a sophisticated French twist, and her dress is pink with grey flowers, soft and floaty, the skirt ending just above the knee. My gaze trails down her bare legs then slowly moves back up to her face as she sits in the chair beside me. She's glaring at me.

I'm relieved to see that flash of fire in her eyes. For a moment I wondered if this stylish, self-possessed woman was the same outspoken, wild waitress I've been fantasising about every night.

"Focus!" she mouths, and with a rueful grin I turn my attention to the Mayor of Neustadt, who is already greeting the assembled guests.

Max and Phoenix are seated at the table before the Mayor. The ceremony is simple: bride and groom affirm under oath who they are and that neither is married to anyone else. They exchange vows and rings, Max moving her engagement ring from her left hand to her right in the Germanic custom, and Phoenix sliding onto his right hand a simple engraved titanium band. Then it's time to sign the register. Max and Phoenix sign first, then the Mayor and her deputy, and finally Khara and me as witnesses. When Khara bends over the documents to sign, she glances up at the bridal pair with a cheeky grin and Max winks at her, as if they share a secret.

The guests precede us out of the chamber, to wait below the city hall steps. Further back, there's a security cordon beyond which a horde of photographers and flag-waving well-wishers have gathered. As we reach the main entrance and the noise of the crowd hits us, Khara flinches. I take her hand and give it a reassuring squeeze.

As we step out into the sunlight I reluctantly let go. We take our places on either side of the entrance, and then Max and Phoenix step through. In a break from tradition, the guests throw handfuls of eco-friendly bird seed instead of confetti, the cameras flash, the cheers rise to fever-pitch and the bridal couple smile and wave. Then there's the anticipated kiss for the cameras, which is pretty tame by Max and Phoenix's usual standards.

When they're done, Max and Phoenix move towards the crowd to meet their fans but, before they do, Max catches Khara's hand and pulls her close. "Thanks for the dress," he says, so low I'm only just able to catch the words. I raise an eyebrow in enquiry, but Khara merely shakes her head and smiles.

The cars are already waiting to take us back to the palace, a vintage Rolls-Royce Phantom for the bride and groom, prosaic minibuses for the rest of us. I find myself squashed into the back seat of a bus with Khara on one side and a British duke on the other. Up front, Teresa is sitting in Christian's lap to make space for other passengers.

"Our lives are not always as glamorous as they seem," I whisper to Khara and she chuckles, though she tries hard not to.

The drive is far too short for my liking. I rather enjoy having Khara's thigh and arm pressed up against mine. I itch to do something about it, the way I would have done a few short weeks ago, but I behave, even though it causes me actual physical pain.

We pose for the official photographer on the grand staircase of the palace, first the bridal party, then the family, then all forty plus invited guests. When we're done I look around for Khara, but she has disappeared. I frown.

I know we're not joined at the hip or anything, but she usually wouldn't leave without at least acknowledging me.

After the photographs, we make our way onto the terrace for drinks. Late afternoon sunlight angles down across the flower beds, and the scent of lavender and roses perfumes the air. The guests mill around the garden, sipping Champagne and being beautiful.

I catch a glimpse of Khara across the garden, talking to Teresa and Christian, and start to make my way towards them, but I'm waylaid by Rik. "Not planning to leave the party early again?" he teases. "Or are you still scouting for a likely candidate to leave with?"

"Neither. Haven't you heard? I'm a reformed man these days." I look again for Khara, but she seems to have moved away.

He looks at me askance. "Is that code for 'I've already slept with every available woman at this party', or does it mean you're seriously considering your uncle's offer?"

"I know for a fact I *haven't* slept with every available woman at this party, and yes, I'm considering it."

Rik grins. "Good for you. You'll make a much better ruler than Mátyás and, for that matter, a much better ruler than Nick." He frowns. "Am I allowed to say that about the dead?"

I shrug. "Why not? Far worse has been said about him. I gather his death is something of a relief in Erdély. His gambling habit was becoming very hard to keep under wraps. Do you know he was barred from two Vegas casinos last year? And in one of the seedier dives in the city he started a bar brawl. It wasn't pretty."

"And I'll bet you were there to bail him out." Rik's expression is serious now. "You've always been a really good friend."

Not always.

"Where's your wife?" I ask, which isn't really a change of subject.

"Upstairs, having a nap before dinner. I offered to stay with her, but she says I'm a distraction." Rik chuckles. He's hardly the same man I remember from our uni days. He used to take himself so seriously, but these days he's more likely to be the one joining me in the grotto to drink illicitly.

And thinking of the grotto ... I turn to search the garden again. Since there's no sign of a pink dress with grey flowers, I give up looking. "Let's get a drink and get this party started."

From the terrace, we move inside to the Yellow Drawing Room for yet more drinks. It's still light outside and all the tall sash windows are open, which is a relief as the room is getting very crowded and stuffy. More guests have arrived, mostly palace staff and representatives from some of the charities the royal family supports, who've been invited to join the evening banquet.

Phoenix and Max are at the entrance to the drawing room, greeting the new arrivals. I grab two bottles of water from the temporary bar set up at one end of the room and head over to them.

"You're a lifesaver," Phoenix says, popping open the bottle I hand to her.

"Have you seen Khara this evening?" I try to sound casual, but the look she gives me suggests I've failed miserably.

"Last time I saw her, Teresa was introducing her to some people."

That's *my* job. Though, admittedly, Teresa is probably related to even more people in this room than I am.

I only see Khara again when we meet outside the state dining room to take our places for dinner. She has changed into a more formal evening outfit of forest green, in a classic style that accentuates her curves, making her look like a glamorous fifties movie star.

"You look beautiful."

She smiles, but her focus is somewhere over my shoulder. A sense of unease grips my stomach. She's avoiding me, won't even look me in the eye as I offer her my arm to lead her into the dining room.

The tables have been set up in a horseshoe shape to accommodate all one hundred dinner guests. The staff have worked for two days to lay the tables and get this room ready, and the amount of silverware and crystal is dazzling.

Once all the other guests are at their places, the six of us who will be seated at the head table make our grand entrance. Following the past years' scandals in the royal family, Max decided to avoid controversy and seated his family elsewhere. There are also no politicians or religious leaders at the high table. Max is turning out to be a master of diplomacy.

He and Phoenix lead the way to polite applause, then the Mayor and her partner, with Khara and I bringing up the rear. The only hint that the confidence she exudes is only skin-deep is the way she grips my arm.

"You're avoiding me," I say in a low voice as we progress down the long room, smiling at everyone. "Was it something I said?"

"Nope."

"Something I did?"

She smiles as if she hasn't heard me.

"Is it because I'm leaving?"

Her jaw tightens. Bingo.

"You're the one who told me I should do something constructive with my life. Why are you upset now that I'm doing something about it?"

"I'm not upset about it." But she says it through gritted teeth.

We reach the high table and I escort her to her seat. I really want to carry on this discussion, and get to the bottom of why she's mad at me – because, whatever she says, she is clearly mad at me – but my seat is at the far end of the high table and if I don't take my place we'll hold up the entire dinner.

Once I reach my chair, Max indicates for us all to sit. He remains standing to welcome the guests to dinner. Thankfully, it's a short speech, then the first course is served.

Khara glances at the array of cutlery and wine glasses (seven at each table setting) and briefly meets my gaze.

"You can do this," I mouth.

And she does. Despite the fact that we are on full view to the entire room, she keeps her poise, looking every bit as relaxed and at home as Phoenix. My heart swells with pride. This Vegas waitress is most definitely not a coward.

Throughout dinner, Khara and the Mayor keep up a lively conversation, though I can't hear a word from where I'm seated. I wish I were with them. Instead, through the first five courses, I'm grilled by the Mayor's partner, who turns out to be a political analyst who knows more about the current situation in Erdély than I do. When she hears I plan to visit, she's vocal in her support of the idea. "The country doesn't want to lose its independence, nor do they want to be ruled from afar by someone who doesn't give a damn about them. Your uncle managed to win them over, but they won't accept any less from his successor. They'll choose union with Hungary rather than a bad ruler. You'll need to commit to this."

I don't tell her that I've never committed to anything in my life. Or that I can barely commit to keeping my hands off a beautiful woman for more than a couple of days.

When the liveried footmen clear away the plates from the main course and all the Champagne glasses are filled, ready for the toasts, Max rises, striking a crystal glass for attention as if this were any ordinary wedding.

Then he nods to Khara and she moves to the microphone at the lectern. My hands clench anxiously for her beneath the table.

"This should be the Father of the Bride speech but, as most of you know, Georgiana's parents are no longer with us." Her American accent seems more pronounced coming through the speakers. Aside from the little wobble in her voice as she starts to talk, I can hardly tell she's nervous. "I am honoured to be here today in the place of her family, but I'm also terrified, so I'm going to keep this short." The guests laugh, and Khara turns to look at Max and Phoenix. "I don't know what your father would say to you right now, but a good friend once told me, just as she was about to walk down the aisle to marry the love of her life, that she knew he was the one because being with him felt like coming home. I hope for the two of you that you will always be 'home' for each other, that you will continue to grow stronger because you are together." She turns back to the audience and raises her glass. "I invite you all to join me in a toast to those who can't be with us here today."

Phoenix wipes away a tear. From where I'm sitting, I can see Max take her hand beneath the table. The guests raise their glasses, murmuring in response, and I get to my feet. As Khara passes me to go back to her seat, I give her arm a quick squeeze. Then it's my turn to stand at the lectern and look out at the audience. I pick out a few familiar faces from the crowd.

I glance down at the speech on my phone. "I'm sure it won't surprise most of you to know that I wasn't Max's first choice for best man. But, since everyone else was already taken, I got lucky." There are a few nervous titters from the audience. "It was an incredible privilege for me to stand beside Max today. He's truly one of the nicest people I know. We met when Rik and I were at Oxford together. Back then, Max was just my friend's annoying kid brother we let hang around with us because we needed a fourth member on our polo team." I pause, screwing up my face as if thinking. "Actually, not much has changed." The titters are more genuine now. "Because Max was so easygoing and fun to have around, he kind of grew on me, and I'm very proud now to count him as a friend. But, no matter how nice he is, Max was always going to need a very special woman at his side, someone who shares his spirit of adventure, someone who puts up with his appalling taste in friends—" more laughter "—and someone who can support him in his role as archduke. I think Max really lucked out when he met Georgiana. Because no one could be more perfect for him than she is." I lay down my phone and turn to the happy couple. "Together, you are a formidable team, and Westerwald is very lucky to have you." Then, turning back to the guests, I raise my Champagne flute. "I ask you all to raise your glasses to the Archduke and Archduchess of Westerwald."

There's a scraping of chairs, a loud chorus of 'Hear, hear' and 'Cheers' in a number of different languages and, from Rik and Christian's end of the table, the sound of drumming on the tables and one loud whoop.

Once the toast is done, I move back to my seat and Max takes the microphone. He has to wait a few moments for everyone to take their seats and grow quiet again.

"My wife and I—" he glances at Phoenix, his eyes crinkling "—are saving our speeches for tomorrow night's reception, so I'll keep this quick. The jobs we do can be lonely. It is so important that we have friends we trust and can rely on, and we have been blessed with some very good friends." With a sweep of his arm, he takes in his family, and Claus and Rebekah. "Tonight I'd like to thank both Adam and Khara for taking time out of their busy lives to be here for us these last few weeks."

Phoenix rises and moves to stand beside him, and Max gestures for me and Khara to join them. From under the lectern, Phoenix takes two navy blue jewellery presentation boxes, one long and thin like a necklace case, the other square like a ring box. She hands the square one to me and the long thin one to Khara, giving us each a hug as she does so. We take our seats and the noise levels in the hall rise as normal conversation resumes.

I wait until the footmen start to serve dessert and coffee before I open my gift from Max and Phoenix. Inside the box, nestled against a bed of blue velvet, are a pair of gold cufflinks. I lift one out of the box; it's in the shape of the royal crest of Erdély. I raise an eyebrow at Max, but he just grins.

"No pressure, mate, but I hope you accept your uncle's offer. You'll make a good ruler some day."

No pressure? Right.

I glance down the table to where Khara is opening her gift. She pulls out not a piece of jewellery but a folded sheet of paper. She unfolds it and her mouth drops open. There are tears in her eyes when she looks at Phoenix, then at Max. "You shouldn't have." Her voice sounds choked.

Phoenix lays a hand over hers. "It's traditional for the bride and groom to give the bridesmaid a gift. Or would you really have preferred jewellery?"

Khara wipes her eyes. "Are you kidding? Where would I wear fancy jewels? This is perfect. Thank you."

She gives Phoenix a quick hug, then, with an emotional sniff, she's on her feet and heading for the door. I'm tempted to go after her but, with so many people watching us, I don't think she'd appreciate me drawing attention to her departure.

After dinner, many of the guests leave. Though we have to be up early again tomorrow to do this all over again, this time for the general public, there's still a bar open in the Yellow Drawing Room. Max and Phoenix are surrounded by his family, but there's no sign of Khara. I need to know she's okay.

I'm chatting to the British duke, another polo-playing buddy, when I see a flash of green out of the corner of my eye. Khara, heading out onto one of the small verandas that have been opened up to let in fresh air.

The duke turns to follow my gaze, just in time to see Mateo follow her out.

"Too late, mate," the duke says. "Looks like Mateo beat you to it."

Over my dead body.

I cross the room, ignoring anyone who attempts to snag my attention as I pass. The closer I get, the more my blood pressure rises. I push aside the heavy velvet curtain and step out onto the veranda. Mateo is leaning over her, boxing Khara up against the wall. Blood thunders in my ears. Why doesn't she push him away, or give him that icy glare to make him back off? He's a gentleman. If she says no, he'll walk away.

Which means she hasn't said no.

Neither of them notice my approach.

"You have beautiful eyes," Mateo says as I draw close enough to hear.

Really? That's the best line he could come up with?

Khara laughs, a soft, sexy chuckle. She doesn't look as if she's been crying. She looks ... playful. "Are you flirting with me?"

"Only if you want me to." He leans in even closer.

"Get your hands off her," I growl.

He straightens, looking surprised.

My fists clench. "Leave the lady alone."

The lady in question places her hands on her hips. "Butt out, Adam. This has nothing to do with you."

"Hell it doesn't."

She turns to Mateo. "Would you be so kind as to fetch me a glass of Champagne?"

He looks uncertainly between us, then with a nod he heads back into the drawing room. Khara rounds on me, that familiar icy glare in place. Now why couldn't she look at *him* like that? "What's got into you?"

"I'm your friend. I'm looking out for you."

She arches a skeptical brow.

"He's a player."

"You are such a hypocrite." She leans towards me, her voice low and dangerous. "You can't have it both ways. Either we're *just friends*, and I'm free to flirt – or have sex – with any man I want. Or we're not."

I wish she hadn't said that, because the images in my head are not pretty. "You are *not* having sex with him."

"Oh, really?" She draws in a shaky breath. "I can do whatever – or whoever – I want. Isn't that how you live your life – come and go as you please, without a thought for anyone but yourself?"

This isn't about Mateo any more, is it?

When I don't answer, she smiles. That smile may look sweet, but there's steel in it. "It's your choice, Adam. Are we just friends, or aren't we?"

I really don't want to have to choose. I want to be the better man, but if that means letting Mateo sweep her off her feet

… A dark, possessive hunger grips hold of me. I'm close enough to feel her breath. Close enough that all I have to do is lean in and kiss her.

But I don't. I step back. The pregnant silence hangs between us, the voices in the room beyond muted behind the curtains.

She shakes her head. "I thought so. There's nothing in your life that you care about enough to step up for, is there?"

Before I can stop her, she pushes through the curtain into the drawing room, leaving me alone with my fists still clenched and my mind a roiling mass of regret and frustration.

Chapter 20

Khara

The second time my neighbor Carly married, she had the big white wedding. Of course, her idea of 'big' and Phoenix's are a little different, but in many respects their weddings are just the same. We all piled into Carly's parents' trailer to get ready for the wedding – her sister and cousins, her bridesmaids, me, her mom, my mom. The noise was something else, and you can't imagine the clutter. Make-up and shoes and dresses everywhere. There wasn't an inch of space to spare.

Space is the one thing this palace has plenty of. The suite we're in is at least four times the size of that entire trailer, but it's just as cluttered with shoes and make-up and dresses. Almost all the women in Phoenix's new family are here – Anna, Kenzie, Teresa. Rebekah's here too, and she and Kenzie are deep in conversation about birthing plans and midwives. There are also four hair and make-up stylists in the room, one of whom appears to be an old friend of Teresa's. Apparently they worked together on the same film set where Teresa and Christian met.

While a hair stylist works on my hair, carefully pinning in

place the crown of real white tuberoses and dainty baby's breath, I sit quietly, listening to the noisy conversations going on around me.

I should be happier. After all, my tuition fees are paid up. That was very generous of Max and Phoenix, but they're right – that means more to me than any piece of bling. I feel as if a massive weight has lifted off my shoulders. When I get home I can find a part-time job to support myself until I graduate, something that doesn't involve eight hours on my feet with the sound of slot machines dinging in my ears all day. No more sloppy drunks putting their hands on my ass.

I should be happier, but I'm not. Maybe if I'd gotten lucky last night I'd be smiling today, but you didn't really think I'd let Mateo do anything more than boost my dented ego, did you?

"You're very quiet today." Phoenix slides into the armchair in front of me.

"I'm quiet every day."

"Nope. This is different."

I am not about to admit that Adam Hatton has me tied in knots. That every time I close my eyes I picture him standing in my bedroom doorway, dressed in a suit and looking delicious enough to eat. Right before he told me he was leaving. Is it entirely stupid of me that I'd started to think there might be something more than chemistry between us? Well, he made it perfectly clear last night that there isn't.

But this is her wedding day and I refuse to let my issues with that selfish jerk spoil her day. So I manage a smile. "I'm about to walk down the aisle with live television cameras following my every move and commentators discussing my hair, my dress, and my background. Aren't you the least bit nervous?"

"No, I'm not. Can I tell you a secret?" She leans forward, dropping her voice to a stage whisper. "We're already married. Today is just for show." She laughs, throwing back her head. "Do you have any idea how good it is to be able to say that?"

I laugh with her. It must have been hell keeping their marriage secret for an entire year. It was hard enough for me and I wasn't here, living this lie every single day. But now she can say it out loud: she's Max's wife. Archduchess Georgiana of Westerwald.

"You're done." The hair stylist pats me on the shoulder.

I grin and hold out my hand to Phoenix. "You ready to go walk down the aisle again?"

She looks at the slip she's wearing and grimaces. "First, I'm going to need a crowbar to get me into that wedding gown. Whose bright idea was it to have a seven course banquet the night before I have to wear that thing?"

"You'll have to go back at least a hundred years to find someone to blame for that tradition," her mother-in-law Anna says from the adjacent chair.

Fortunately, it doesn't require a crowbar to get Phoenix into her dress, just Anton Martens with a needle and thread. He's not in the least fazed by half a dozen women in their underwear, trying to squeeze into layers of tulle and silk and lace. I wonder if the backstage area at Fashion Week is anywhere near as chaotic as this.

When the bulk of the wedding party finally head downstairs, Max's assistant Jens is at the door with a clipboard and a countdown timer, marshalling everyone into cars. Max's mother, Anna, travels in the first car with her parents, Max's Californian grandparents. Then Fredrik, Christian and their wives leave in the next vehicle.

"Shouldn't we go round to the cathedral's back entrance in an unmarked car?" Fredrik asks, eyeing the luxury sedan parked ready to take them.

"Nope." Jens is all efficiency. "Max's orders. You're part of this procession whether you like it or not."

"Well, at least it's not an open carriage, so I can't get pelted with rotten tomatoes."

"No one is going to pelt you with rotten tomatoes," Teresa says. "Just because you were disinherited doesn't mean the public don't still love you. They watched you grow up, after all. You're still their prince, even if you're not their archduke."

Next there are the page boys and flower girls, three of each, under the supervision of Rebekah and their mothers, all of whom Teresa introduced me to at the party last night. One duchess and two countesses, all on Max's side of the family. The boys are in royal blue uniforms that match my own dress, the girls in white dresses with blue satin sashes, and hooped tulle overlays filled with blue petals. Their crowns match mine. The attention to detail at this wedding is astonishing.

When they're all gone, piled into yet another luxury car, the vestibule echoes with the sudden silence.

Jens turns to me. "You can tell Phoenix that her car will be at the door in two minutes and thirty seconds."

"Don't we need to wait for Max and Adam to leave first?

You know, so the groom doesn't see the bride on the wedding day and all that." Though they did have breakfast together in their apartment this morning, before all this commotion started.

Jens doesn't look up from his clipboard. "They'll be leaving from the garage in one minute and fifteen seconds, so no need to worry."

Which means I won't get a chance to speak to Adam before the ceremony. Not that I have any clue what I'm going to say. I keep veering between 'I'm sorry I was a bitch last night' and 'You're such a douche.' Maybe both. Either one is better than 'I don't want you to go.'

I head up the stairs and knock on the door to call Phoenix and Anton down. When the door opens, I grin. Phoenix really is the most beautiful princess I've ever seen. Okay, so my experience of princesses is a little limited, but she certainly looks regal. She has her hair done up in soft curls, with a few bouncy strands loose around her face and the tiara firmly in place.

"Your carriage awaits, Cinderella."

The Rolls-Royce Phantom is waiting at the front door when we get downstairs. I take a peek inside and breathe in the scent of luxury.

It takes Anton, Jens and I to get Phoenix into the back of the car without crushing her dress, though I admit I'm not much help. The royal blue bridesmaid dress is such a snug fit that if I even breathe too hard I'm going to pop a seam.

Anton arranges Phoenix's veil and then we're off, waving to the crowds who've gathered to line the route. For a weekday in such a small country, there are a *lot* of people who've come out to watch. There are blue and white flags everywhere, and quite a few Stars and Stripes too.

The crowds roar as we pass, and then the car sweeps into the main avenue that leads to the cathedral and there are uniformed soldiers lining the street in a guard of honor.

"There are only eight hundred soldiers in the entire Westerwald army," Phoenix tells me. "Every one of them must be here."

It's so surreal, I can't even be nervous. After all, this has got to be just a dream. If anyone pinches me, I'm going to wake up back in my bedroom in that trailer park in North Vegas.

The car pulls up in front of the cathedral and a military officer steps forward to open the door for us. Anton hands us our bouquets, a small bunch of white roses for me and, for Phoenix, a simple arrangement of blue tulips mixed with myrtle for good luck. He climbs out and turns to offer me his hand to help me out, then together we help Phoenix step out, straightening her skirts and her train.

Cameras flash and the crowd screams, but Phoenix looks as calm and confident as if she were out for a stroll in the palace garden. Her serenity calms me too.

"Okay, let's do this thing," she says, looking up at the cathedral doors.

Ten steps up from the street to the doors, Adam said. I count them, and he's right. We make it up all ten without tripping on our heels or our hems. Phoenix pauses in the doorway to wave to the cameras, then we step inside. It takes a moment for our eyes to adjust from the bright sunlight to the darkness inside. We're in the ante-chamber, the flower girls and page boys are all lined up and the organ is playing.

"This is where I leave you," Anton says, air kissing Phoenix's cheek through her veil. "I'll be in the cheering section." He slides into the back of the church, moments before the music changes and the children start their procession two-by-two down the aisle.

In the vestibule, it's just me and the bride and a half dozen ushers who are probably protection officers in disguise. Though there are six hundred guests waiting inside that nave for us, Phoenix isn't in any hurry.

"When my dad was in chemo, he used to tell me how much he wished he could walk me down the aisle. Not to give me away but just to share the moment with me. He'd say, 'Princess, you make sure the man waiting for you down the other end of that aisle is worthy of you.' He'd have liked Max."

I squeeze her hand. "Your father's right here with us."

This being Phoenix's wedding, I didn't expect the traditional Mendelssohn wedding march, but now I realize that it's not the church organ playing. It's a cello, and I laugh as I recognize the song. It's Bruno Mars' *Marry You*, the same song that played when she walked down the aisle to Max in that little chapel in Vegas a year ago.

I'm sure I'm not supposed to be laughing as I make my way down the long nave, but I can't help it. The uneven floor is patterned with the rainbow light falling through the stained glass windows, but I'm no longer afraid of tripping over my own feet. Instead, I hear the lyrics in my head as I bounce to the jaunty tune.

When I near the front of the church, I see that Max is laughing too. He's dressed in uniform, like Prince Charming in *Cinderella*. Our eyes meet and we share a smile, then his gaze moves past me and the expression on his face is the one every woman wants to see on her husband's face when he looks at her.

Yeah, her dad would like Max.

I finally let myself look at the best man. He's dressed in a morning suit, pinstripe pants, black cutaway jacket, blue-gray waistcoat and a silver-gray ascot tie. He's all cleaned up for the day too, clean-shaven, his thick dark hair groomed back and catching a stray ray of light from one of the high windows. I've never believed a man in a formal suit could look so sexy, but he does.

His gaze meets mine and holds me captive. His eyes look very green today. Maybe it's a trick of the light falling through the stained glass. I move to stand to the left of the altar, take Phoenix's bouquet when she hands it to me so that Max can lift her veil, then I move to sit in the pew on the left. Since Phoenix has no family, her stalls are filled with important dignitaries, but I barely register who they are. I sit when required to sit, stand when everyone else does, but the ceremony is a blur.

I should be paying attention, making note of every detail, but I figure I'll have to watch the replay on YouTube sometime, because it all feels like a dream. One of those enchanting, golden dreams you never want to wake from. I'm hyper-aware of Adam in the stalls across from me, aware of every move he makes, of his gaze, which keeps coming back to mine. It's like there's an invisible magnet pulling us toward one another. Every nerve ending in my body hums with the awareness.

How can he not feel it too? How can he believe we can simply be friends? This hasn't been simple from the very beginning, from the first time I laid eyes on him in that private dining room in the hotel in Vegas. I've discovered that chemistry, while it may be unreliable, and a very, very bad basis for a relationship, cannot be denied.

One more sleep.

I don't need a relationship with this man. But what I do need is to give in to this dark throb of desire between us. I need it so much that I don't care if I'll be just another notch on his bedpost. He won't be just another notch on mine.

One more sleep.

I don't care that he's leaving tomorrow. Okay, that's a lie. I care, but it's not something I can change. He was always going to leave, because that's what men do.

Adam was never going to stick around until morning anyway.

But that doesn't mean we can't have tonight. And if he isn't going to take what he wants, I'm not going to let that stop me. I am not going to leave Westerwald with any regrets.

The cathedral reverberates with sound as the Archbishop declares Max and Phoenix man and wife. Though the service was conducted in the local dialect, even I understand that much. The noise of the cheering crowd outside the cathedral is so loud we can hear it in here, over the applause of the assembled guests.

Max and Phoenix kiss, a far less demure kiss than they

shared on the city hall steps yesterday, then hand-in-hand they face the cathedral nave. I move to Phoenix, buss her radiant cheek with a congratulatory kiss and pass her the bouquet, then take my place behind her.

Adam holds out his arm to me and I loop mine through his, enjoying the rush of heat between us. He looks down at me, his bright gaze searching, as if he can sense my decision, the change in me.

I don't walk down that aisle; I float.

The smiling faces on either side of us merge into one long shifting pattern of color. Then we're in the ante-chamber, and the ushers rush to open the heavy bronze doors which are green with age. Max and Phoenix step out into the sunlight, Cinderella on the arm of Prince Charming, and the crowd outside goes wild.

Adam and I hang back, allowing the crowds and the photographers to have their moment. Max kisses Phoenix, sweeping her into a graceful choreographed backbend. She's laughing when they break their kiss.

The soldiers lining the stairs raise their bayonets, or whatever they are, and suddenly there's a bang, and gold glitter rains down over the royal couple. Phoenix does a double-take, the crowd explodes, but Max is laughing. I can't help it. I start giggling too.

This wasn't on the official schedule, but it's the perfect touch. Glitter guns, just like we had in that Vegas chapel, except then it was Calvin and me firing glitter all over the newlyweds.

Phoenix shoves Max with her shoulder and she's laughing

too, and I can't imagine what photographs are going to make the front pages of tomorrow's newspapers, with the bride and groom both in stitches. The flower girls and page boys flock around to see what the excitement is all about, while the ushers try ineffectively to marshal them back into line.

I struggle to get my giggles back under control, and Adam looks at me, bewildered.

"Inside joke," I say as we step out the doors and follow the bridal couple down the stairs.

Max leads his bride down to the waiting carriage, the same open landau he and Adam arrived in. They drive off, waving to the crowds, and the Rolls-Royce Phantom pulls up in its place.

Adam holds my hand as we walk down the stairs to where an officer is holding the car door open for us. He doesn't let go as he did yesterday when we emerged from the city hall. He doesn't let go until we're seated and the door is closed, and I pull my hand out of his so I can strip off my heels.

"Ah, that's better!" I stretch my cramped toes, and Adam smiles. My insides turn to jello.

We wave to the crowds as the car slowly makes its way down the long avenue of flag-waving spectators, and no one outside the car would know that inside our fingers are again entwined.

Surely any moment now I'll wake up.

Chapter 21

Adam

Khara no longer seems to be mad at me. I have no idea what changed, but the temptation she offers is irresistible. I'm like a runaway train, storming down the tracks, knowing that the light up ahead isn't the end of the tunnel but an imminent train wreck. I don't think I can stop it. I don't want to stop it.

But I can't manage to get a moment alone with her either.

The bridal party, including Max's brothers and their wives, his grandparents and a whole bunch of extended family, gather on the balcony outside the Yellow Drawing Room, the same balcony where Khara and I had our fight last night. Our first fight and we haven't even had sex together – yet. That's something of a novelty for me.

While we wave to the crowds that have gathered in the palace forecourt, I have to be on my best behaviour. I can't touch her, can't even hold her hand, though the temptation to put my hands all over her is overwhelming. Especially when I catch a glimpse of the trainers peeking out beneath the hem of her bridesmaid dress. Who'd have thought a pair of ordinary trainers could get my heart thumping like a jackhammer?

The balcony appearance seems to go on forever, though in truth it's probably not much more than twenty minutes. All this posing and pageantry is new to me. Erdély's way more relaxed. In all my years as the grandson of the *Fürst*, or hanging out with Nick, I've never once witnessed this kind of rabid attention. Admittedly, maybe that's because I haven't been there since I was a kid. Will I be greeted there with flag-waving fans, with angry protestors or with indifference? I'll find out tomorrow.

After the balcony appearance, we gather in the private drawing room for the official photographs, with the same photographer who took Khara's portrait pictures. There are hair and make-up artists on hand to ensure we look our best for the pictures. The attention to detail is mind-blowing; Claus deserves a knighthood for putting this wedding together.

Then, just when I think I can get a moment alone with Khara, she's whisked off on bridesmaid duties, she and Phoenix disappearing up to the private apartments to change outfits.

The pre-reception drinks for today's event are on the Orangery Terrace. The Orangery is a long conservatory at the rear of the palace which opens onto the formal garden. With its skylights and wall of French windows, the room is flooded with late afternoon sunlight. I stride between the round tables, set ready for the informal dinner that will take place before the ball, and head to the terrace where Champagne is being served.

Years of training kick in. Armed with a glass of Champagne, I circulate among the three hundred plus guests who've been invited to the reception, greeting old school friends, polo friends, diplomats, business moguls, celebrities, aristocrats and royals. And yes, I know and have met almost all of them at similar events over the years. I smile as I think of the game Khara and I played in Chantilly, when she tested my knowledge of the guests. Given the chance to attend a few more of these functions, she'd probably get to know most of them too.

Most of my extended family are here, even Mátyás, though I go out of my way to avoid him. I don't think that's cowardly; it's strategic. It's while I'm avoiding him that I bump into Jemmy.

"Hey, bro!" She greets me with a hug and a kiss. "I hear you've been keeping busy?"

"Am I the only one in this family who doesn't have access to some top secret intelligence network?"

She laughs, linking her arm through mine. "Mum told me you've been working with Max. Does that mean you're seriously considering becoming crown prince?"

"I promised her I'd consider it. I'm travelling to Erdély tomorrow to check the place out."

"How does the bridesmaid feel about that?"

I stop walking to look at her. "Did Mum tell you that too?"

Jemmy grins. "Nope, the morning papers did."

"*What?*"

"This morning's cover photo in the local papers was of Max and Phoenix on the steps of the city hall. And there, in the background, probably only recognisable to those of us who know you, you and the bridesmaid are holding hands."

"Her name is Khara."

She looks at me strangely. "You usually don't bother with their names. It's their bra size that interests you."

I drop her arm and glare at her. "I am not that shallow."

She arches an eyebrow.

"Okay, I *was* that shallow. But I'm trying to be a better person." Or at least I was until Khara looked at me in the cathedral today as if I was the last drink of water on a hot day in the desert.

"If she's Phoenix's friend, I'm going to assume she's not your usual type. Just be careful with her, okay?"

"She's not a gold-digger."

"I didn't mean you should be careful about her hurting you. I meant you should be careful *you* don't hurt *her*. Have you considered what it will do to your friendship with Max and Phoenix if you break her heart?"

Nope. I rub my head. Doing the right thing stinks.

But I'm not sure I can walk away from Khara now. I've waited more than two weeks to see that invitation in her eyes, and now that it's there I'm probably going to prove her right, that I am just as big a douche as she always thought me.

Jemmy shakes her head as if she can read my mind. "I'm not saying you can't have something with her, just that maybe you need to rethink your usual MO of being a bastard afterwards."

"It's not like I try to be a bastard."

She grins. "So it just comes naturally to you? Your problem is that when you see something you want, you go after it like a heat-seeking missile. But once you've got it, you lose interest. Clients, cars, women. Just once, why don't you try seeing something through? At the very least, please promise me you'll be careful with this one?"

"What is it with everyone in this family wanting me to make promises?"

Jemmy doesn't back down. She holds my gaze, and I'm the one to look away first. "Fine. I promise I'll try not to be a bastard." I'm just not sure how. I haven't had much practice at it. "But don't get your hopes up. This isn't going anywhere. I'm leaving tomorrow. And in less than a week she flies back to the States."

"For someone as bright as you are, you can be really dumb sometimes. There's always another option."

I narrow my eyes at her. "You know, you and she have a lot in common. You both give me a hard time."

She laughs and links her arm through mine again. "I can't wait to meet her."

The dinner seating plan is a work of genius. There is no head table at this dinner, and seating at the round tables has been determined not by rank but with an eye to everyone's enjoyment. I'm seated at a table with a Middle Eastern sheikh I was at school with and his Oxford-educated wife, the head of the European winegrowers association, and one of Max's cousins and her German prince husband, both of whom work in mountain rescue. Ours is a lively table, and the only thing missing is a certain mermaid-haired waitress. Want to guess where she's seated? Next to my sister.

They don't seem to stop talking. I would give anything to overhear that conversation. Or at least to be able to moderate it. Who knows what nonsense my sister is filling Khara's head with?

Khara has changed out of the body-hugging ankle-length bridesmaid dress, into a shorter, flirtier cocktail dress in the same shade of royal blue, the same colour as her hair and her eyes. She no longer wears the crown of flowers and tendrils of hair have started to escape her fancy updo. My gaze keeps drifting back to her, no matter how hard I try, as if she exerts a gravitational pull on me.

The dinner itself is a modest four courses: soup, starter, main and dessert, and the portions are far more generous than most official banquets. My constant glances reassure me that Khara looks poised and at ease. She's fitting in beautifully. Better than that, she looks like she's having a good time.

My chest tightens, and it takes me a moment to identify the baffling feeling. It's pride. And possessiveness.

Neither are emotions I've felt towards any woman before.

What makes her so different from other women? On the surface, she's no different from a million other women, apart perhaps from her aversion to men with money. Am I only drawn to her because she's the one in a million who hasn't fallen at my feet?

Then Sayid says my name, drawing my attention back to my own table.

Once the last of the plates have been cleared away, it's time for the speeches. The newly elected Prime Minister makes a surprisingly heartfelt tribute for a politician – and a mercifully short one. Then it's Phoenix's turn. God, this woman is amazing; if she had a clone, I'd marry her. Her entire speech is in the local Westerwald dialect, and the translation is shown in three languages up on the two large screens.

"The day I met Max, I knew he was someone special. I knew he was someone I wanted to spend the rest of my life with. What I didn't know was that marrying him was going to take me on the biggest adventure of my life. Never in my wildest dreams could I have imagined that this was what our future would hold." She sweeps her arm to take in the room filled with beautiful, glittering people, royalty, celebrities, diplomats and senior government officials from across Europe. "But even if I were to wake up tomorrow and discover that all of this was just a dream, Max is still the man I'd choose to marry." She turns to her new husband and blows him a kiss. "I love you more every day, Max."

When Max stands to talk, he has to clear his throat to speak. "If I look overcome with emotion, it's because I am. I am a very happy man today, and I have to thank my wife for that." He looks out into the distance, as if making eye contact would be more than he can handle in this moment. "Years ago, my father told me something I've never forgotten. He said that I'd know when I meet the right person for me because it would be the person I love in the same way I want to be loved. The day I met Phoenix I knew she was my person, because I wanted her to be loved and happy more than I wanted to be loved or happy."

There's hardly a dry eye in the room when he's finished, though luckily they're mostly tears of laughter.

Unlike the British weddings I'm used to, the cake isn't cut

before we dance. That ritual only happens at midnight so, when his speech is done, Max invites us to move to the ballroom. My pulse kicks up a notch as the guests move across the domed vestibule to the ballroom. Tonight, this room looks nothing like the empty, cavernous space where I taught Khara to dance. The room glitters with the light of a thousand tiny fairy lights and the heavy scent of flowers fills the air. I move through the crowd, just like that heat-seeking missile my sister called me.

Khara and Jemmy still have their heads bent together.

"Don't believe anything she tells you," I say as I come up behind them.

Khara blushes, but Jemmy just grins.

"Ready for our moment of glory?" I ask Khara.

"No. But maybe I'll get lucky and twist my ankle or something on the way to the dance floor, and be spared the humiliation."

"You'll be great. After all, I taught you."

Jemmy rolls her eyes. "You're both doomed then."

"Ha ha." I turn to Khara. "Remind me to tell you the story about the time my sweet little sister gate-crashed her ex-boyfriend's wedding."

"Don't you dare!" Jemmy smacks my arm. Hard.

The evening's entertainment is as unusual as the bride and groom: it's a famous American rock band Phoenix knows from her days on the road with her musician father. The bride and groom take their places in the centre of the dance floor, and the crowd forms a wide circle around them. The music starts, a chart-topping rock ballad from our youth, and Max and Phoenix start to move, eyes only for each other. Even a cynical heart like mine can't help but be moved.

When the song ends I hold my hand out to Khara. She places her hand in mine and I lead her out onto the dance floor to join the bride and groom. The next song is another of the band's most famous hits, but they've slowed the tempo into a romantic rumba. I turn Khara into my arms with a little spin and place one hand on her waist, holding her other. "Remember: keep looking at me. Don't look at your feet. I've got you."

I lead her into the steps, our thighs and hips brushing as we sway together through the dance. She keeps her gaze on my face, and I couldn't look away even if I wanted to.

I'll admit, I've seduced a lot of women, and I've been seduced. I've danced in far more romantic settings; I've practically made love to a woman on a dance floor. But no moment I've ever experienced is as sensual as this one, or as all-consuming. The slide of her silk dress beneath my fingers, her subtle rose perfume, her pupils so dilated they're like pools of ink, and the rise and fall of her breasts as we glide together. I'm barely aware of the other couples on the dance floor: Max and his mother, Phoenix and Max's grandfather.

I only realise the song is over when applause breaks through the bubble that seems to surround us.

We stop moving and I lean close to whisper in her ear. "I want you."

"Yes." Her breath is warm against my cheek.

Then she spins away with a soft laugh, holding her hands out to Max's grandfather. With a sigh, I remember my own duty and move to dance with Anna. This time as we dance, a more sedate foxtrot, I'm barely aware of my partner. I'm just going through the motions, my entire awareness focused on Khara, who looks so confident and so poised with the old man that I think she'd win the glitter ball if this were *Strictly*.

Other couples are joining us on the dance floor now. "Go claim your girl." Anna laughs, releasing me.

But it's not as easy as that.

This is a royal ball, after all, and there are people who want a piece of me. A piece of Khara too, it seems. Over the shoulder of the Crown Prince of Norway, I see her dancing with Mateo, and it takes every ounce of self-control I have not to be rude and cut short our conversation so I can interrupt their dance.

I manage to smile and make polite conversation to any number of dignitaries, before my mother rescues me and insists I dance with her. "Lajos tells me you're going to Erdély tomorrow," she says, not wasting time on small talk as we circle the dance floor. I merely nod, too busy searching the ballroom for Khara. I finally spot her by the bar with the lead singer of the rock band.

"I'm very proud of you," my mother says softly.

I flick my attention back to her.

"I know this isn't an easy decision, and I know what we're asking you to give up, but I'm proud of you for making the effort and for at least considering Lajos' offer. Whatever you decide, we'll support you."

"Dad too?"

"Him too." She sighs. "We just want you to be happy."

By midnight, I can safely say that I've done my bit as the

dutiful son and potential heir. I've talked to so many people that I haven't had much time to either dance or drink. This might be the first wedding I've attended since I turned eighteen at which I haven't been drunk by this time.

The DJ who replaced the band some time ago stops the music, the dancing ceases, and we all gather around the cake which is carried to the edge of the dance floor by two liveried footmen. Together, Max and Phoenix cut the towering croquembouche cake with a ceremonial sword, though it's more for show, since the creation of puff pastry balls is held together by nothing more than a delicate web of spun caramel threads.

They feed each other cake, then the footmen start to serve the guests. With this important ritual over, the ballroom gradually empties as many of the older guests leave, and I finally get a moment alone. I take a seat at an empty table, helping myself to the remnants of the bottle of Cristal, and watch Khara twirl around the dance floor with a famous American stock car racer, looking every bit as if she's having the time of her life. She's lost her shoes and dances barefoot, and that possessive feeling is back, holding me in its vice grip.

"I created a monster," I mutter as Max sinks into the chair beside me, though I say it with fondness.

"Your Galatea has done you proud." He's lost both his tie and his jacket at some point during the evening, and his shirt hangs loose beneath his waistcoat. "If you decide you don't want to be a prince, you can always take up a new career as a makeover artist."

I shake my head. Khara is no Galatea or Eliza Doolittle. "I

didn't give her a makeover. She's still the same person she always was. I just gave her some tools to boost her confidence. Besides, this was a one-time thing. There was only ever one Galatea for Pygmalion."

"Pygmalion also fell in love with his Galatea."

Ha. There's no chance of that. I don't fall in love. Can't. Won't. I'm not sure which verb fits best. Perhaps all of them. Instead, I say to Max, "You are such a nerd. You should have studied Classics instead of wine-making."

"Right back at you. But seriously, what's going on with you and Khara? You've been dancing around each other figuratively as well as literally all week."

"Nothing's going on with her. You're the one who told me Khara would have my balls and eat them for breakfast. You have no idea how right you were."

He chuckles. "Must be a novel feeling to be turned down."

I blow out my breath. "She hasn't turned me down. Quite the opposite. But she has made me want to be less of a bastard." It feels good to be honest for a change.

"Ouch. That's got to be a real challenge for you."

I cast a dark glance his way, only to see that he's laughing at me.

"I want her more than I've wanted any other woman, but if I act on it I'm just going to prove to her that I'm exactly the bastard she thinks I am." Was that Cristal laced with truth serum?

Max shrugs. "Or you could act on it and not be a bastard."

I don't answer, not wanting to admit I have no idea how to do that.

"You'll figure it out. Consider this an opportunity to try to be a better man." He slaps me on the shoulder and rises. "I'm going to find my gorgeous wife so I can dance with her."

The ballroom lights have dimmed, and the music changes from an upbeat tune to a slower song. Khara is still dancing with the racing driver, and no way am I going to sit here on the sidelines and watch him put his arms around her. I drain the last of the Cristal from the bottle and stride onto the dance floor.

"I believe this dance is mine." I hold out my hand in invitation to Khara. She glances at her dance partner, who shrugs and turns away to join the group gyrating behind us. I feel no qualms about interrupting. Any man who can walk away from her that easily doesn't deserve her.

She takes my hand and I pull her in close, wrapping my arms around her waist.

"Are you having fun?" I whisper against her ear.

Her breath hitches. "More fun than I've ever had in my life. I even danced with the same rock star whose posters decorated my teenaged bedroom."

I don't want to talk about the other men she's danced with. All that matters is this moment.

She presses closer against me, her breasts brushing against my chest, and this time it's *my* breathing that stutters. It takes all the willpower I possess to keep my hands where they are, rather than slide them over her curves the way they want to.

"You're not going to take this opportunity to hit on the bridesmaid?" Her voice is low and husky, filled with temptation. "This is your last chance."

I clear my throat. "Are you flirting with me?"

"What if I am?"

I can't resist. I'm not strong enough to resist. What can I say? I *am* a bastard. I slide my hand down to the curve of her ass, holding her so close that she can have no illusions about my state of arousal. With a laugh and a toss of her hair, which has tumbled loose around her shoulders some time during the evening, she spins away from me. But she doesn't slap my face, or pin me with that icy glare I've seen too many times, so I pull her back against me. Her back is pressed up against my front, and we sway together for a long moment, our bodies pressed together, my hands on her hips. Then I drop my head to trail my lips down the curve of her neck, not caring who sees.

Her skin tastes of roses and sweat and Champagne.

"You're not just the bridesmaid." I nibble on her earlobe and feel her shiver. "You're Khara Thomas, the most exasperating, desirable, intimidating woman I've ever met."

She turns to face me, eyes wide. "*I* intimidate *you*?"

"Yes. You don't fall for any of my lines. That's very intimidating."

She laughs, tipping her head back, and I take advantage of the move to trail kisses along her exposed collarbone.

"You don't need any lines to make me fall." Her voice is nothing more than a caress beside my ear.

"I wanted to prove to you that I'm not an entitled jerk who just wants to get into your pants, but it turns out you were right. I am that guy."

She pulls away to look me in the eye. "If that's your way

of telling me you're not going to stick around until morning, then I already know."

"And you don't mind?"

She presses her lips together as if thinking about it. "This is nothing more than chemistry," she says at last. "It doesn't mean anything."

My chest pulls tight, but I ignore the feeling. "Do you think anyone will notice if we leave the party early?"

"Probably."

"But we're going to do it anyway?"

"Of course."

Chapter 22

Khara

He doesn't lead me up to the guest wing as I expected. Adam snags a bottle of Champagne and two glasses from a passing waiter, and leads me out onto the terrace.

It's a balmy evening, the air thick and heavy with the scents of summer, fresh-mown grass and gently dying flowers. The air fills my lungs and clears my head, but I feel no less intoxicated, though I've stuck to virgin cocktails all night.

"I'm not having sex with you out here," I object, pulling him to a stop.

"No, you're not. But if I take you to bed right now, this night is going to be over way too soon."

That's almost romantic. Then he grins, that same arrogant smirk I used to want to slap off his face. "I want to make out with you for a while before I make love to you."

Make love. Not have sex.

But they're just words. They don't mean anything.

I let him pull me along, down the wide steps and onto the broad gravel path that leads through the water gardens. The gravel is rough beneath my bare feet, grounding me. But at least I'm not in two-inch heels.

The gardens are closed to the public now and there isn't another soul around. It's as if this magical fairyland has been lit up just for us. Fairy lights twinkle along the paths, and the blue fountain lights illuminate the jets of water surrounding the stone dragon. Adam doesn't need to tell me where we're going. We hurry down the avenue of fountains, which is dark and shadowy, the sound of splashing water loud in the still night air.

When we near the secret garden, the one with the grotto, we see the bobbing flashlight of a patrolling security guard up ahead. Adam pulls me back behind a tree, pressing me up against the rough bark until the light weaves away past us. Then we step back onto the path.

We climb the fence, Adam catching me just as he did the first time, then we dash through the waterfall and into the grotto. The cold water is refreshing after the oppressive heat of the warm night. We shake off the droplets, laughing breathlessly.

It's dark inside the cave, the only illumination a murky green light from the fountain beyond the curtain of water. I sit on the floor, my legs stretched out in front of me, and Adam sits beside me. I can't see much more of him than an outline. His body is like a beacon to me in the dark, radiating heat. Or maybe that heat is coming from inside me, pulling me toward him.

He opens the Champagne, the popping cork sounding like an explosion in the cave, then pours the frothing liquid into the glasses and hands me one.

I raise the glass to my lips and sip. The Champagne is dark, with a taste that's fruity and smoky. "What is this?"

"Bollinger. Made from black grapes."

I empty my glass and set it carefully aside, then, casting aside every last excuse I've ever come up with to convince myself that this shouldn't happen, I straddle his lap, cup his face, and lean forward to kiss him. I don't need to see to know where to find his mouth. It's as if his face is imprinted in my brain.

It's even better without light because I can concentrate on the glide of his lips over mine, the pressure of his hands against my lower back, the taste of the Bollinger, and his delicious, unique scent. His tongue licks over my lips, urging my mouth open to deepen the kiss.

My hands are on his chest, on those same pecs I first touched right here in this grotto. But this time they're hungry, roving, undoing the buttons on his waistcoat, pulling on his shirt to free it from his pants, then sliding up and under the soft fabric.

His skin is hot and smooth and solid. As my hands slide higher, they hit the roughness of a dusting of chest hair, and then a rigid nipple. I tweak it ever so slightly with my fingers, and he moans into my mouth.

"I feel like you're objectifying me," he whispers.

"Of course I am. It's only fair turnabout for all the times you've ogled my breasts."

"And don't forget your legs. And this gorgeous arse." His hands move lower, and I giggle.

He nibbles at the corner of my mouth and I sigh, opening up to him.

His hands rock me closer, his erection hard against the

apex of my thighs, and it's my turn to moan. The friction feels so unbelievably good, and I'm already wet and needy.

The kiss could last five minutes or it could last an hour. I lose all sense of time. I could do this forever, lose myself in him, because ... Oh. My. God. This is the best kiss I've ever experienced and I never want it to end. It's long and slow and passionate and teasing.

Our hands explore each other and he nuzzles my breasts through the silky fabric of my dress until I'm a writhing mess of desire. I rock against him until he stops me with his strong hands. "I'm going to come in my trousers like a horny teenager if you keep doing that," he groans. "And I don't want this to end just yet. I want to be inside you when I come."

We take the Bollinger and the Champagne glasses back with us into the palace, though I suspect it's going to be flat before we get around to drinking the rest of it. The party is still in full swing, with loud music pumping from the ballroom. There are at least two other couples in the gardens now, in the shadows, and they're just as careful to avoid being seen and recognized as we are. Adam leads me in through a side door and up a narrow flight of stairs I've never seen before.

"The servants' staircase," he explains. It opens into the corridor close to my room. I swear when we reach the door to my room. My key is in the tiny purse I left downstairs at the coat check. Adam reaches into the pocket of his pants. It's so unfair that his wedding suit has pockets.

"You have a key for my room?"

"No, I have a key for my room. But the locks in this palace are ancient, and one key pretty much opens all the doors in this wing."

I don't want to know how he found that out.

He unlocks the door and we slip inside, tearing off one another's clothes as we stumble toward the bed across the moonlit room. We leave a trail from the door to the bed: his shoes and socks, his waistcoat, his shirt.

It's only when he's pulling my dress over my head that I remember what I'm wearing underneath, and it's not pretty.

Do you know how to make a curvy figure look good in a clingy silk bridesmaid dress? Spanx.

I'm about to get naked with the hottest man I've ever been with, and I'm wearing Spanx.

It's Adam's turn to swear and I don't blame him. They're a bitch to get out of. We squirm and wriggle together on the bed in the most decidedly unsexy way to get the damn things off. We lie side by side; I'm breathless and Adam's chest is heaving.

"Don't you dare laugh!" I warn.

He presses his lips together, but doesn't manage to hold it in. His laughter is infectious, and I bury my face in his bare shoulder, trying to stop the laughter that bubbles up. He wipes my crazy hair away from my face and gently cups my cheek. My laughter dies, replaced by something else, something far more primal.

This time his kiss isn't slow. It's wild and furious. And while we kiss, his clever fingers unhook my bra and pull it off me. I'm completely naked to him now, and I wait for that moment of insecurity to kick in, but it doesn't come. My hands are on his belt, fumbling to get it undone, then the button on his pants.

"Screw this," he says, placing his hands over mine. He rips the button, yanks at the zipper, then I help him slide the pants down his thighs. My breath catches.

I've always been attracted to jocks, to athletic builds and broad shoulders, but Adam's body is by far the most heart-stoppingly gorgeous I've ever seen. All lean, solid muscle. I glide my palms down over his bare chest, his torso, over those washboard abs, taking my time to admire and explore, to commit every plane and angle of his body to memory.

His erection is tall and straight, flat against his stomach, the silky skin stretched, veins throbbing. Oh my word. I wrap my fingers around him and, slowly, I glide my hand up and down his length. He drops his head, his eyes closed.

Then he shakes his head. "Not now." His voice is rough. "Later."

He flips me onto my back, and moves to kneel between my legs. It's his turn to explore, his hands roving over my body, taking his time until I'm nothing more than molten need, wet and hungry and desperate for him.

His fingers trace taunting patterns across my skin, and I want to hurry him up, want to grab his hand and move it between my legs so I can have relief from this torment, but I don't. If all I have with him is this one night, then I want to make it last.

Finally his fingers dip between my thighs, circling excruciatingly slowly around my clit until I can't bear the torture another moment. I throw my head back, close my eyes, give myself over to the sensations coursing through me.

It's both a shock and a relief when he dips his head between my thighs and places his mouth on me. Every single part of my body is focused on that tiny spot where his tongue flicks over me. Then his fingers are inside me.

I have never known pleasure so exquisite. My entire body has become one massive erogenous zone, the scrape of his stubble against my inner thighs, his tongue, his expert fingers.

I come apart as spasms jerk through me, and I cry out his name, over and over.

He slides back up my body, feathering my skin with kisses, circling his tongue around my taut nipples, nibbling my neck. My body wants more, so much more. For someone as self-centered as I've always believed Adam to be, he's a very considerate lover. Every part of my body feels alive from his touch.

As the shockwaves ease, I open my eyes. His gaze holds mine. His pupils are so dilated his eyes seem to have no color. They're burning, fierce, alight with all the passion I've always sensed in him, those pent-up emotions he hides beneath that cool, detached exterior.

I draw in a shuddering breath. "I don't have a condom," I say apologetically, because without protection this can't go the way we both clearly want it to go. But he leans over toward his discarded pants and a moment later he raises his hand in triumph. Not just one condom, but four.

Pockets. Right.

"You come well prepared."

With a sideways grin he tears one open and stretches to lay the remaining three on the nightstand, while I unroll the precious latex over him until he's sheathed.

Then he rolls over me, his weight heavy between my legs, and he rocks against me. "Are you sure you want this?" he asks.

"Do you have to ask?"

"Yes, I do."

His gaze holds mine, his eyes so dark and intense that I can read nothing in them but need. "Tell me what you want."

"I want you inside me. Deep inside me. Now."

And he obliges. With his arms on either side of my head, holding his weight off me, he presses his erection against my entrance, still sensitive from my orgasm. He nudges tentatively against me and I raise my hips to meet him. He slides in, devastatingly slowly at first, a fraction of an inch at a time, filling me, waiting for me to accommodate his size, until he's buried deep. I close my eyes on a whimper.

"Look at me," he demands, and I force my eyes open.

He holds my gaze, unblinking, as he pulls out, then slides back in, moving harder and faster until we're both panting, both desperate. My hands claw at his shoulders, his back, trying to drag him closer, deeper. We rock together, sliding, slick, frantic, and all my inner muscles clench around him. His body stiffens, his back arches, and then he comes inside me and my own climax grabs hold and I can see nothing, feel nothing, but that place where our bodies are joined, the overwhelming sensation of pleasure that tears at me, turning me inside out.

When we're both spent, he rolls away off the bed to discard

the condom. I pull down the rumpled bedsheets and slide under them, stretching luxuriously, feeling every inch of my body as if for the first time.

So that's it. The best moment of my life and the worst. Because now he'll leave. This is all over.

But then the bed dips beside me and Adam slides under the covers too. He rolls up against me, his chest against my back, his hand slack on my naked breast.

For one long moment my body pulls tight with tension. This can't happen. It shouldn't happen. If he stays, I can't convince myself this is nothing more than sex. But the chemistry is overpowering. It dulls my brain, won't let me think. My body relaxes against his and my eyes drop closed.

These hormones are really good drugs. But what will I do when the high wears off?

Chapter 23
Adam

I roll over into a cold patch on the bed, and my eyes slowly open. This isn't my room. My room is wallpapered with thin blue stripes, not broad green ones. Then the night before – or, rather, the morning before – comes flooding back, and I grin and stretch.

It's hard to tell what time it is as the sky outside the tall windows is a leaden grey, heavy, dark and threatening a storm. Not unexpected after the last few days of oppressive heat. But it's definitely daylight outside the windows and I am still here, in a woman's bed, and I feel no desire to run.

The bathroom door opens and, probably still wearing the goofy grin, I turn to look at Khara. Her face is clear of make-up, her hair is pulled back into a bushy ponytail and she's wearing olive-green jeans and a loose beige pullover with a wide neck that leaves one shoulder bare. Is she aware she has a hickey on her neck?

"Oh, good, you're awake." She fetches a mug from the coffee station and brings it over to the bed. "I made you coffee. It's only instant, though, since I don't have a fancy coffee press."

I take the coffee she holds out and sip it gingerly. It's still scalding hot, but it manages to clear a little of the sleep fog in my brain.

Khara moves to the wardrobe and rummages around until she finds a plaid scarf to wrap around her neck. Clearly she does know.

Then she turns to me. "You need to leave now."

What?

"It's morning, and you don't stay until morning, remember?" she says pointedly.

Sure, that's the reason I led us to her room last night and not my own, so that I could make my usual quick exit rather than having to kick her out of my bed in the middle of the night. But instead, I'm the one being kicked out. That's a first for me, and I don't think I like it very much.

Even more of a revelation: I don't want this to end. Not by a long shot.

"Maybe I'm changing my mind about mornings." I lean back against the pillows and pat the bed beside me in invitation. "If I recall correctly, we still have one condom left."

She sets her hands on her hips. "The bridesmaid is no longer on the menu."

There's that stir of an echo again, but I still can't grab onto the memory. Probably because I'm too busy trying to process what's happening in the here and now. I run my hand through my hair. "So you've scratched an itch and now it's over?"

Is this how every woman I've ever walked out on in the middle of the night feels? No wonder everyone thinks I'm a bastard.

She smiles. I recognise it as her fake smile, an expression

she probably perfected on customers just like me. It may look sweet and innocent, but it doesn't reach her eyes. "Last night was fun, but it's over."

That's usually my line. How the hell did things get so turned around?

I fling back the sheets and slide off the bed, striding towards her. She holds her ground, keeps her chin high, but I know her 'tells' now: that slight hiccup in her breathing, the way her eyes dilate as I draw nearer, the intense way she focuses on my face so her eyes aren't tempted to drop to my naked body ...

"But that itch is still there, isn't it?" My voice comes out low and rough, because her nearness is having a similar effect on me.

She swallows and takes a half step back. Her eyes flicker unconsciously down to my chest then back up again. "I appreciate that you're trying to be a gentleman this morning to prove something to me, but you really don't have to."

"I'm not trying to prove anything, and I most certainly don't feel like a gentleman right now." I reach out to cup her face, and her lips part.

Then she shakes her head, as if trying to convince herself of something, and steps away, out of my reach. "I'm flattered, but we're due downstairs for the Champagne breakfast, and you're leaving in a few hours."

"I don't have to go. I don't want this to end yet, and I don't think you want it to either."

Her eyes narrow, and her tone is sarcastic. "Oh, look, there's your privilege showing again. Want, want, want ... That's what life is all about for you, isn't it? Do what you want, when you want – and who you want – without any thought for anyone else. Well, those of us who live out there in the real world don't have that privilege. We don't get to act on every whim because there are real life consequences. You're supposed to be leaving for Erdély in a few hours. If you break your promise to your family just so you can get laid one more time, you really are a first class douche."

For a moment she sounds just like my sister, and then a light bulb pops in my head. Jemmy said something ... My sister's right – I really can be dumb sometimes. "Why does it have to be either/or?" I pause, watching as Khara's indignation turns to hesitation. "Come with me."

She opens her mouth, then shuts it again. "I can't come with you. You're going there to work."

I shake my head. "My visit can't be an official one until the formal succession announcement is made." Uncle Lajos was crystal-clear about that. "I'll be going as just another tourist. Come play tourist with me."

"I'm supposed to be going with Max and Phoenix to Waldburg for the rest of the week."

"In its glory days, Erdély was a centre of culture and art. There'll be more frescoes and churches and history there than in Waldburg." I close the distance between us again. "Do you really want to be a third wheel on Max and Phoenix's honeymoon?"

"But—"

"Enough with the excuses. Look me in the eye and tell me you don't feel this attraction."

She meets my gaze. "Of course I feel it, but that doesn't mean I have to act on it. Chemistry doesn't last."

"Nothing lasts. But that doesn't mean we can't enjoy it while it's there."

She turns away. "I'll think about it. I'll let you know my decision after breakfast."

I make the walk of shame back to my room, not bothering to avoid the kitchen porter delivering breakfast trays to one of the rooms, or the housekeeping assistant polishing the gilt portrait frames. I don't care who sees me coming out of Khara's room half-dressed in last night's clothes. I want to shout it from the rooftops like a lovesick teenager. This feeling's new too, but at least this one I enjoy.

As soon as I've showered and dressed, I head downstairs to the breakfast room. It's already packed with people: the bride and groom, tired and smiling, Max's entire family, plus a handful of palace guests.

Khara is already seated beside Phoenix, with Claus and Rebekah on her other side. She barely acknowledges my entrance, though I know she's as hyper-aware of me as I am of her. Her back stiffens, as if she's trying to be on her best behaviour.

I grin. This is going to be fun.

There's a selection of Mimosas and Bellini cocktails on the sideboard, but I can't face alcohol just yet so I pour myself a cup of proper filter coffee.

Max joins me, reaching for one of the peach Bellinis. "You left the party early last night," he says, giving me the side-eye. Did he see me and Khara on the dance floor last night? Probably. He also probably noticed that we both left around the same time.

"It wasn't early. It was some time after midnight."

"Exactly. Are you all packed up and ready to leave?"

I haven't even started packing, and the charter plane János – my uncle's private secretary – has arranged for me is scheduled to leave in just a couple of hours. But even though I made a commitment to my uncle that I'd travel today, I can't think about leaving. Not without hearing Khara's decision. Not without Khara.

The thought of going anywhere without her, the thought of not seeing her again, of not touching her again, is a physical ache. Yes, I'm behaving like a spoiled brat with a new toy, but I can't seem to help myself.

So I simply shrug in answer. Max gives me another side-eye then moves away to take a seat at the table. I follow more slowly, pausing behind Khara's chair, and I lean forward to kiss her neck, right above where I left that hickey.

She goes still. So does everyone around us.

As if nothing just happened, I continue moving around the room to the empty seat beside Max.

"I make that two weeks and four days." Max looks at his new wife. "You owe me a hundred euros."

I splutter. "You took a bet how long it would take us to …?"

Phoenix grins cheekily. "I have to admit, I was sure Khara would cave much sooner."

Khara still hasn't moved. Then she chokes out a laugh, releasing all the tension in the room. "You were that confident in Adam's seduction abilities?"

"No, I just thought you two would be good together. But

I didn't realise you'd be so pig-headed you'd take this long to see it." Phoenix sighs. "Max called it."

Khara shakes her head, as if denying we're good together, though we both know that's a lie. We are absolutely bloody marvellous together, and I can't wait to do it again. Slowly, she raises her gaze to meet mine, and her eyes are hooded and hungry. Yes, we're good together, and we both want more.

The hum of conversation starts up again. We're no longer the centre of attention.

"Have you decided?" I mouth to Khara.

She nods, just once, and my heart leaps. *Yes!*

"Decided what?" Phoenix asks, and I curse her for reading my lips.

Khara clears her throat. "I won't be coming with you to Waldburg." She doesn't look at Phoenix. Her gaze is still focused on me. "I'm going to Erdély. With Adam."

"You're leaving us early?" Phoenix asks. Since she's still looking at me, Khara doesn't see the look of triumph in her friend's eyes. I reach under the table to kick Phoenix's shin, and she looks contrite. "I hear it's a great place for outdoor activities," she says conversationally. "Hiking, kayaking, camping." She glances at Max. "Perhaps we should plan a holiday there sometime."

Then she looks at me, her meaning clear. She expects to visit me there when I make it my new home. I shake my head. I'm not committing to anything.

A footman circles the table, offering fresh drinks, and I take a Mimosa, the sweet-tart taste refreshing. Khara sticks to plain orange juice, I note. Since this is a celebratory breakfast, there's cake.

"It's a Baumkuchen," Rebekah says as slices are offered around. "A multi-layered honey and almond cake that's a tradition at German weddings. It's a gift from my café in Waldburg."

The café where Phoenix was working when she met Max. Or at least that's the official story. But I remember something Khara let slip – she was there when they met. This is her first trip outside the US. Which means that Max and Phoenix met for the first time in the States. In Vegas. Why keep that a secret?

"Cake for breakfast! I could get used to this." Phoenix laughs and casts a coy look at her new husband. "Perhaps we should get married more often."

It's that coy look that slots everything into place. What's the one thing Vegas is best known for after gambling? I glance at Khara for confirmation, but she refuses to meet my eye.

Bingo! Max and Phoenix were married in Vegas. Which means they were already married before she arrived in Waldburg. Before he became archduke. I laugh out loud, earning a few odd looks.

They've been married for at least a year already.

I'm used to using my trust fund to seduce women. Expensive gifts, first class travel, the best Champagne ... But since all those things are more likely to remind Khara of the huge disparity between our lives, I can't pull any of my usual tricks. I cancel the charter plane and instead book us two seats on a regular scheduled flight into Graz, Austria's second largest city, which is the nearest airport to Erdély. It's a small plane, and there's no first class or even business class, so for more than an hour and a half I'm forced to fold myself into a cramped seat.

We left Neustadt amid a rain storm, but arrive to a Graz that's bathed in golden evening light. When we finally leave the small airport it's early evening already, and we've missed the last train of the day to Erdély, so we take a taxi to a hotel the taxi driver recommends – an art hotel with minimalist decor which overlooks the river. I'm not sure what I expected of the town, but it's charming, with cobbled streets and quaint Baroque mixed in with ultra-modern architecture. The hotel is a short walk from the historic city centre, so after we check in we wander hand-in-hand through the streets, taking in the sights on our way to dinner. This city is surprisingly hipster, full of trendy coffee shops and art galleries.

To reach our restaurant we take a glass-roofed funicular up the side of the Schlossberg, the hilltop fortress overlooking the city. We dine on a romantic cliff-edge terrace, above the rooftops, with the city lights spread out like a carpet beneath us. I only whip out my credit card to pay when Khara slips away to the ladies' room.

"That was certainly different from our first lunch together at the Landmark Café," she says as we walk down the two hundred and sixty steps carved out of the stone cliff to the square below.

"Yup. This time you didn't have your nose stuck in a book all the way through the meal."

"I was avoiding you," she admits ruefully.

I laugh. "I guessed."

"And you aren't trying to impress me with your wealth now."

"Nope. I've found a much better way to impress you." I pull her to a stop in the middle of the crowded square, tucking my hands into the back pockets of her jeans to pull her close. Then I kiss her, and the crowd of rowdy tourists and students parts around us, laughing and cheering. Loud music thumps from a nightclub and a distant siren cracks the night, but it's nothing more than a blur. My whole world is this woman who tastes of caramel and the local blue gin. When she sighs against my mouth I cannot get her back to the privacy of our hotel room soon enough.

The train journey between Graz and Erdély is only an hour and a half, winding through lush countryside – mountains and woodland and, once we cross the border into Erdély, a surprising number of vineyards. Khara spends most of the time glued to the view outside the windows while I catch up on work emails. I have to admit, though, that the scenery is stunning.

It's only when we reach the quaint station in the main town of Arenberg that I discover the flaw in my plan. By arriving unannounced, we have no transport to the palace. We can hardly hail a taxi and ask the driver to take us to the palace's front door. I'll have to phone the palace to send a car for us.

We step out onto the pavement, where tables from the station's café spill out into the sunshine, and I look around at the town which could one day be my home, if I say yes to Lajos. It's certainly picturesque. The buildings clustered around the square in front of us are multicoloured, some part timber-framed, and all painted with intricate folk patterns. It's also very provincial. There isn't a single building over three or four storeys high.

"It's beautiful," Khara murmurs, her voice awed.

I'm less impressed.

I glance towards the taxi rank, where a queue of cars waits, and notice an Uber pick-up sign. At least some modern-day conveniences have made it past the ring of mountains.

A car pulls up at the kerb and the driver jumps out, gesticulating towards us. He's middle-aged, tall and long-limbed, and he speaks in rapid Erdélian, too fast for me to understand, but I catch my name.

"Yes, I'm Adam Hatton," I answer. Though Uncle Lajos assured me this is an easygoing place, I have no idea what local sentiment is towards the royal family.

To my intense relief, he grins and switches into English. "You need a lift to the palace? I'm going that way."

I do not plan to jump into a stranger's car but, before I can politely decline, Khara gives the man a bright smile. "Thank you, that would be lovely."

"American?" He beams back at her. "We don't get many Americans here. I'm István. I run a bar in town, next to the court house."

"Khara." She shakes the man's outstretched hand, then I reluctantly help him load our bags into the boot. He insists we sit in the back as if this were a taxi, but since he then spends most of the drive weaving in and out between other cars and pointing out various landmarks, all the while looking over his shoulder to chat to Khara, I wish he hadn't.

"That way is the town of Veldes, which was a popular spa during Victorian times." István takes his hand off the wheel to indicate the way. "Visitors came from all across Europe. There's a new luxury spa resort. You should visit it while you're here."

We leave the town centre, passing office buildings, a school house and a small hospital. That's when the palace becomes visible. It stands on a hill overlooking the Arenberg valley, against a backdrop of forested hillside.

Khara gasps and leans forward in her seat. "Is that it? It's a real fairy tale castle!"

Unlike Neustadt's elegant Baroque palace, this is a nineteenth century Neo-Gothic castle, complete with steep roofs and at least half a dozen turrets. The lower floors are made of stone, the upper floors are timber-framed.

The road becomes a single lane winding through a residential neighbourhood, with chalet-like houses on one side and meadows of grazing sheep on the other. We pass through tall iron gates that stir a vague memory from my childhood, and sweep up the driveway. István drops us at the foot of the grand stone steps that lead up to the front door and unloads our suitcases. Then he shakes our hands, invites us to stop by his bar and is off down the drive, tooting his horn in farewell. I head up the steps to ring the doorbell. This is so far from Westerwald's formal dignity that I can't quite wrap my head around it.

At least the door is opened by a butler dressed in a formal black suit, who looks like he'd belong just as easily in Hartham Manor. He ushers us into a drawing room, a bright sunny room with French doors that open onto the wide terrace overlooking the meadows separating the palace from the town. When he leaves us alone, I blow out a breath. This was a seriously bad idea. What the hell was I thinking dragging Khara off to this backwater?

We wander around the room, pausing to look at the display of photographs on the carved stone mantel. They're almost all of Nick. There's one of us, taken years ago at a polo match. "My cousin," I tell her.

"And the other man in the picture?"

"My friend Charlie." I set the frame back down and turn away. She looks at me strangely, as if I'm a puzzle that needs to be solved.

When the door reopens I expect to see János, but it's my aunt Sonja. She hurries across the room, arms open in welcome. "Adam, thank you so much for coming!"

I give her a hug.

"I'm sorry we missed you at the wedding," she says. "We didn't stay for dinner, for obvious reasons. But I'm sure you were busy anyway." She spots Khara, who is hanging back shyly. "You brought a friend – how lovely!" Sonja crosses the room to Khara, who stands awkwardly as if wondering whether she should curtsey. I give a subtle shake of my head. Our family have never stood on ceremony.

"This is Khara Thomas. Khara, my aunt Sonja."

They shake hands and Sonja invites us to sit, then rings

for refreshments. "Your uncle will be with us shortly. He's in a meeting with the trade commission."

She pats the seat beside her for Khara to sit, and Khara throws me a nervous glance as she moves to perch on the edge of the antique gilt-edged sofa.

"I am so sorry for your loss," she says.

Sonja nods, then her smile brightens. "You looked gorgeous at the wedding. Just as beautiful as the bride. I can see why my nephew is smitten."

Khara coughs, and I realise it's to hide a laugh. "I don't think smitten is the right word, and I hope he sees more in me than my looks."

Sonja casts me an amused glance. "I would hope so too, but Adam hasn't shown much depth in his taste in girlfriends in the past." This time Khara doesn't even bother to hide her laugh. I'm starting to regret inviting her. I did not intend for all the women in my life to gang up against me. On the plus side, Sonja is looking happier and more composed than the last time I saw her. It's good to see her smile.

The women chat about our journey until a servant arrives with a tray. It's not tea, as I expected, but juice. "Apfelschorle," Sonja explains. "Apple juice mixed with sparkling water."

Soon after, Uncle Lajos joins us. It's as if a tornado has arrived as three dogs erupt into the room with him, tails wagging, barking their excitement. They're tall and slender, with long bodies and sturdy frames, their fur brown and white. With a curt command, Lajos sends them to lie in front of the unlit fireplace. His bearing is still straight and proud, but his eyes betray strain. I rise to greet him.

"When you cancelled the plane we were worried you were no longer coming," he says, and I immediately feel remorse for having added to his stress. I also hope Khara didn't catch that reference to the private plane.

"We came via the scenic route, by train from Graz."

We make polite small talk as we sip our Apfelschorle. Khara holds her poise, conversing as easily as if she'd been born to this. That's my girl.

"I've never seen dogs like these," she says when one comes to sniff around her feet. "What are they?"

"Magyar Agár hunting dogs." Lajos looks as proud as if he were talking about his own children. "They're sighthounds bred long ago to be good long-distance runners, to run alongside horses for many miles." He scratches the head of the dog that has now come pushing its nose into his hand, smiling indulgently at it. "Loyal and very affectionate, but they need daily exercise so I take them out with me every day when I go riding. At least they keep me active." He glances up at Khara. "Do you have dogs?"

Khara shakes her head, her body suddenly tense. "Where I live, we're only allowed one small pet, so we have a cat."

Uncle Lajos asks about the wedding and as the conversation swings away Khara's posture eases. If anyone notices that talking about her home makes her defensive, they don't betray it.

Sonja shows us to the suite where our suitcases have already been brought up. *Our* suite. János assumed we'd be sleeping together and put us in the same room, but Khara sends me a doubtful glance as if trying to gauge my reaction. I picture waking up beside her every day for the next week, not having my own bed to run away to. The image is strangely appealing.

As soon as Sonja leaves us alone, I sweep Khara up and deposit her on the bed, to show her just how much I *don't* mind sharing this bed with her. She stretches out, looking up into the canopy of the four-poster and letting out a deep sigh, as if she's just survived an ordeal.

"It's not that bad, is it?" I ask. This isn't London or Paris – or Vegas – by any stretch of the imagination, but it's not as rustic as Nick always made it out to be.

She rolls onto her side to face me. "Not so bad. Actually, I like your family. Your uncle was a little intimidating at first, but your aunt is so ... motherly. I was expecting to be greeted by one of those matriarchs you see in all those made-for-TV movies – you know, the regal, manipulative queen who's determined to get rid of the new girl because she's not good enough for the precious heir."

I can't help myself. I burst out laughing. "My family clearly doesn't watch enough television. But I'll suggest to Sonja that she needs to up her game in that department."

She smacks my arm and I roll on top of her, pinning her to the bed. Then I kiss down her collarbone and she moans, pressing her body up against me. "I've always wanted to sleep in a four-poster bed."

"Sleeping isn't what I plan to do with you in this bed." I slide my hands under her tank top and for the next hour show her just what I *do* intend to do with her in this bed for the next week.

Chapter 24

Khara

Erdély's magic is very different from Westerwald's. Max's Archduchy felt like a fairy tale version of Vegas, with its traffic, commuter hustle and skyline of high-rise offices contrasted against the ancient churches and quaint, tree-lined squares. But Erdély is like climbing through the looking glass into an entirely new world.

It is utterly quiet in the palace at night. The thick stone walls absorb all sound, and when I step out onto the ornately carved wooden balcony that links our suite to the next I breathe in fresh mountain air which is rich with the dark aroma of wet earth. High above the silhouettes of the mountain tops, the Milky Way glitters against the velvety sky, breathtakingly clear. There is no constant rumble of traffic, no sirens to break up the night, just the night song of crickets. An honest-to-goodness owl hoots, and Adam laughs when I jump at the sound.

When I wake in the morning, Adam is still asleep. I watch him, tempted to lean forward and kiss his eyelids, rub his stubble across my cheeks, but I hold myself back. I don't want to wake him just yet, don't want this moment to end, as if I can somehow freeze time.

In six days, I'll be on a plane back to Vegas. In six days, the fairy tale will be over.

To avoid temptation, I slide out of bed, pull on my pyjama shorts and favorite sleep shirt, and let myself out onto the balcony. This side of the palace overlooks the forest, and the peace and stillness is absolute. After the craziness of the last few weeks, this quiet moment to do nothing but stop and breathe, to smell the lush vegetation, feels glorious. But it can't last.

I need to start thinking about the life waiting for me back home, about my final semester and finding a new job, about my mother and her no doubt ill-fated romance with her latest boss, about my new niece, who is due any day now. Yet that life seems more like a dream than where I am right now. Vegas feels like a mirage on the horizon.

A maid brings a tray of coffee and pastries to our sitting room, her knock waking Adam. Since I know all too well that he's still naked beneath the sheets, I hurry to get the door. She greets me in what I can only assume is the local dialect, and doesn't even bat an eyelid at my skimpy pyjamas. If I made the bed here, I suspect *she* wouldn't turn up her nose at me.

Last night's dinner was a quiet family affair, and when we go downstairs for breakfast we find Sonja alone at the breakfast table, staring unseeing into her coffee cup. Her face brightens as we enter. There is no entourage, no uniformed footmen, and Lajos has already gone to work at his office in the parliament building in town. Unlike the palace in Neustadt, which always seemed to be teeming with people, this palace feels too big and too quiet. How lonely must it be without kids and grandkids to make it feel more like a home?

After breakfast, Sonja gives us a tour of the castle. With its massive stone hearths, high beamed ceilings and suits of armor, it looks more like a movie set than a home. The main part of the palace seems to have been designed for entertainment. There's a great hall, drawing rooms, a music room, a billiard room, and even a small theater, but everything is under dust covers, closed-up and silent. It's a place where there should be parties and people, where kids should play hide-and-seek. Instead, it's the dogs that chase around us in circles. My initial nervousness around them quickly eases. They're very eager to roll over on their backs to let me scratch their tummies.

"You'll never get them to stop now," Adam says with a laugh. "They clearly know a sucker when they see one."

That's me – the sucker who's let herself be sweet-talked into the playboy's bed, and into believing that maybe fairy tales really do exist. I'm an idiot, right? But a strangely happy idiot.

In the portrait gallery which connects two wings, Adam pauses for a moment. "I remember this room. Nick and I played here together. We turned it into a bowling alley until my mother found us and made us go play outside instead."

It's such a normal memory, the kind of memory any kid could have.

Sonja smiles sadly. "Yes, there are good memories too."

The formal rooms have wood-panelled walls decorated with

portraits and tapestries, and the library is barely half the size of the one in Max's palace, but there's a private family wing which is far more modern, complete with a den with a big flat screen TV ("Lajos is addicted to European football," Sonja says) and a private gym. The way Adam's face lights up at the sight of the gym tells me how he manages to maintain that gorgeous physique.

I've never been a gym bunny. I prefer the outdoors to air-conditioning and piped music. But a few hours later I'm regretting that thought, because the one form of outdoor exercise I never in a million years pictured myself doing was horse-riding. It's like dance lessons all over again, except that in place of stepping on Adam's toes and bumping into him, I'm bouncing up and down on the back of a big, scary horse, going around in circles. Thank heavens the only two people there to witness my awkward attempt are Adam and the groom.

The other thing that dancing and horse-riding have in common is that when I wake the next morning I ache all over from using muscles I didn't even know existed. "You are so lucky that sex with you is pretty good," I groan. "Because I can't think of any other reason why I'd let you sweet-talk me into doing that."

"Only pretty good?" He nudges his morning erection against me. "Perhaps I need to give you another chance to re-evaluate that opinion."

As he reaches to pull me closer, I slip away with a giggle. "Not now, you won't. At the moment I feel like I was kicked by the horse instead of riding it." And if I'm suffering, he can suffer too.

I stand in the shower, resting my forehead against the cool tiles as the water beats down on my back.

Only five days left.

There are bicycles in the royal garage, alongside a handful of discreet luxury vehicles. There isn't a flashy sports car or Rolls Royce in sight, so Lajos and Sonja clearly don't do ostentatious displays of wealth. As we follow the cycle path along the river into Arenberg, we're joined by more and more cyclists, schoolkids and commuters on their way to work. Cycling seems to be a major form of transportation here.

The town is small enough that it can be explored end-to-end in just a few hours. The historic centre of town is pedestrian only, with quaint storefronts, cobbled streets and little squares. Apart from a few high-end stores, there are no big name brands here – not even a McDonald's.

On either side of the main square are the town's two most impressive buildings, the parliament building and the main church, surrounded by street cafés, bars and souvenir shops.

"This is where the parliament meets?" I ask, incredulous. It's only three stories high and, though the windows have fancy pediments and there's a coat of arms painted beneath the high gabled roof, it looks like any other building. The flag hanging at half-mast reminds me that this is a country in mourning for its crown prince.

"The senate only consists of twenty people. They don't need a whole lot of space."

"But where are the soldiers to guard it?"

Adam laughs. "Erdély doesn't have an army. It has always relied on diplomacy to keep it safe."

The church of St József's is a medieval building, its domed interior decorated with colorful frescoes that surpass those I saw in Westerwald. The church has a vaguely eastern look to it, with a bulb-shaped bell tower that reminds me that this area was once the borderland between Europe and the Ottoman Empire.

We wander the streets and pop into the art museum, housing the amazing collection gathered by a former *Fürstin*, an Austrian princess who was a great patroness of the most famous artists and musicians of her time. Adam tries valiantly to hide his boredom, and after an hour I show mercy on him and let him take me to lunch in one of the local inns.

Four days left.

The castle's gardens are a fraction of the size of those at the palace in Neustadt. There is only one formal garden, with neat paths, trimmed hedges and color-co-ordinated flower beds and a couple of lawned terraces.

"Is this where we have the obligatory archery scene?" I ask as we wander across a stretch of lawn mown in neat patterns.

Adam looks at me as if I've asked where they keep the elephants. "What?"

"You know, bows and arrows – like in the movies? There's always a scene where the heroine accidentally shoots someone in the ass."

"In which case, I'm not letting you anywhere near any bows. I don't fancy an arrow in my arse."

I giggle. "I'm flattered that you think I'm the heroine of this story."

"Aren't you?" He pulls me up against him and kisses me so thoroughly that I'm breathless and panting. "For the record," he says as we resume our walk, "I don't think I've fired an arrow in my life."

Pre-dinner drinks are served on the fountain terrace each evening. "Or in the library, when the weather's not so good," Sonja says. The sun sets behind the mountains, turning the sky blue-gray as it darkens.

This evening we're joined by guests, a dynamic, dark-haired man with sharp eyes and his young wife, a pixie-haired woman not much older than me. They're both wearing jeans, so I relax and chat easily with them until Adam whispers in my ear: this is Erdély's prime minister, Yannik, and his wife.

He laughs at my shock. "You expect all government ministers to be old men with white hair?"

They stay for dinner and the conversation flits from hobbies and favorite foods, to skirt the forbidden topics of politics and money. Seems the etiquette rules can be broken. The men dance around the more contentious subjects, keeping the conversation light but feeling each other out, no one wanting to give away too much, or come out and directly ask the question that hovers, unspoken: will Adam step up and be this nation's next leader?

It's exhausting, and a tension headache builds in the base

of my neck. Maybe this is why everyone avoids stressful topics – because it's stressful.

But then I discover that the prime minister's wife, Lena, is an art history professor at the university in Arenberg and a local history buff and, like me, she too waitressed her way through her college years. We swap funny stories, and I'm able to relax again. She tells me some of the more outrageous exploits from their nation's history until we remember that the same spoilt royal whose shocking behavior we're laughing over is an ancestor to two of the people at the table.

"Oops," she mouths at me, and we burst out laughing.

I like her. If we'd been together in school, we might have been friends.

"Our department runs a part-time history course in English you might find interesting," she suggests. "How long are you here for?"

"I leave on the weekend."

"Maybe when you come back, then."

I don't bother to tell her I won't be back. I can barely bear to think about it, let alone say it out loud.

After dinner, when the men head off to catch the end of a football match on TV, Sonja gives Lena and me a tour of her personal passion: her antique porcelain figurine collection.

Westerwald may have its fancy jewelry vault, but I think I prefer this display. The figurines are delicate and intricately detailed, and vary from early eighteenth century Meissen figures to art deco ballerinas.

Sonja picks up one of a mother with a child in her lap, both dressed in white, and cradles it lovingly. "This one isn't very valuable. It's a nineteen-eighties soft paste piece in the Capodimonte style. Nick gave it to me one Mother's Day."

She sets it down and turns to us, her face composed but her eyes haunted. "Would you please excuse me from joining you for coffee?"

I recognize her smile. It's the same one I use on customers when I'm not really in the mood, but have to maintain appearances. "Of course."

Lena and I head back downstairs to the drawing room where after-dinner coffee is always served.

"I know one shouldn't speak ill of the dead," Lena says softly as we head downstairs, "but now that I've met Adam, I think Prince Nicholas's death might have been a good thing for this country."

What can I possibly say to that? Secretly, I agree. Nick's death wasn't just a blessing in disguise for Erdély, but for Adam too, if only he'd open his eyes and see it.

Three days left.

Borrowing one of those not-too-ostentatious sedans, we explore the rest of Erdély, driving through a landscape of farmland, vineyards, traditional farmhouses and tiny hamlets, finally arriving in the spa town of Veldes with its public, Georgian-era hot and cold mineral baths. The complex has an indoor heated pool, steam rooms and a splash pool full of kids outside, but the buildings look sad and tired, a vivid contrast to the brand spanking new luxury resort next door which is so classy it makes the casino hotel I worked for look like a Best Western.

The true gem is our discovery of a brewery close by. As we sample the local beers, the owner stops to chat. "You enjoying your holiday?" he asks, making friendly conversation. Friendliness is definitely a local trait.

I smile up at him. "What gave us away as tourists?"

"Aside from your accents? Locals don't stop to sample the tasters. They stock up on their favorite brew and leave. And since the day-trippers who come across the border for a few hours never come this far south, you must be visiting a while. You staying at the spa resort or one of the *gasthofs* in Arenberg?"

Adam catches my eye. "On a farm. Of sorts."

"Ah, a farm stay! Well, I hope you enjoy the rest of your trip."

"More people should know about this place," I tell Adam when the owner moves away. "Not just this brewery, but Erdély itself. Do you know this country doesn't even have a Frommer's tour guide? I think that's something you should get right onto."

"I haven't agreed to take the job yet."

"You should. This place has so much potential for tourism. And I don't mean in a kitschy Vegas way."

He shrugs. "I'd have to live here for at least part of the year."

"And how is that a problem? Look around you. This is as close to paradise as any country can get."

He stares into the distance, not looking at me. "I like my freedom. If I accept, I'd be tied to this place and its people for the rest of my life."

This isn't news, but a sharp, sudden pain twists inside my

chest. He doesn't do commitment, to places or to people. It's not like he has ever led me on or promised anything more than this week. But I *do* do commitment.

I want commitment. The realization hits me like a sledgehammer: I'm falling for him. The way I always feared I would, from that very first time I laid eyes on him. I'm falling for my very own kryptonite, a man who will never commit to me, who is going to leave me as soon as he's had enough.

Chapter 25

Khara

Two days left.

I can't sleep. Adam lies sprawled across the bed, the covers thrown back. I listen to his deep breathing, and the steady sound of rain on the roof. The sky through the tall sash windows is utterly dark, with none of the reflected city light I'm used to, just wan moonlight illuminating the distant mountain peaks.

He hasn't once mentioned what happens after we leave here. It's all I can think about.

Adam has a job in London he needs to get back to. Next week I need to be in Vegas to register for my final semester. But my mind cannot wrap itself around the idea of a life without Adam in it. Without his smile, his touch, his laugh.

I love him.

How stupid is that?

After the overnight rain, the air is crisp and clean and smells of fresh pine, and the sky is a brilliant, cloudless blue. The cooler air blowing down the valley is almost a relief from the late summer heat of the past few days.

I wake tired, restless and on edge.

We cycle into Arenberg, but since we've already seen all the sights, there isn't much to do.

"We haven't been to István's bar," I remind Adam.

The bar is easy to find. It's on a tree-lined square, with the modern glass and steel courthouse on one side. The building is a traditional, two-story timber-framed inn, with a beer garden at the back. Though it's not yet noon on a Friday, it's still holiday season in this part of the world and the beer garden is filled with the lunchtime crowd.

Since word has filtered out that Adam is in town, he's no longer anonymous, so we avoid the busy beer garden and choose a quiet booth inside the bar. István welcomes us like long-lost friends but, as he's alone behind the bar and the servers working the beer garden are constantly in and out with orders, he's too busy to say more than a few words to us.

The bar gets busier as people arrive, flowing through to the garden at the back, some pausing at the bar to chat to István or to place an order, and we get a lot of curious stares. It's not just Adam they're looking at. I get my fair share of inquisitive looks too.

Nothing to see here, people. I'm just this week's novelty toy. Next week it'll be someone else.

My chest hurts at the thought.

Soon it's not just stares. This is a friendly place after all, and a steady trickle of people pass by our table to ask if we're enjoying our stay. Complete strangers come up to introduce themselves and welcome Adam to Erdély. He's in his element, oozing charm and shaking hands, just as he did at the palace parties in Westerwald, as I imagine he does in the boardroom too.

"Is it always this busy in here?" I ask István when he stops by briefly to check on us and re-fill our drinks, Apfelschorle for me and the local draught beer for Adam.

He grins. "Someone posted on Twitter that you were here, so I think half the town is dropping by to get a look at you. It's been years since we've had a member of the royal family in here, mingling with us common folk."

Adam looks surprised. "My cousin Nick visited Arenberg at least a couple of times a year, and he always loved a good bar. I'm surprised he didn't stop in sometimes."

István's grin falters, and Adam sighs. "You banned him, didn't you?"

"There was an incident with one of our waitresses. We don't tolerate that sort of behavior here."

I remember Nick's too-soft, wandering hands and give István a sympathetic smile. "You sound like a good boss to work for. But you're also clearly under-staffed."

"I don't want to be ungrateful, but it would have helped if you'd chosen another day to visit here," István replies. "My barman quit yesterday. He fell in love with a Norwegian tourist he met right here in this bar, and followed her back to Bergen." He shrugs, turning his palms up. "What kind of man would I be if I stood in the path of true love?"

He returns to the bar, where a queue of thirsty patrons is already building up.

I watch him wistfully. There's a certain dance that happens behind a bar, a rhythm you get into when you're serving a busy crowd. I can almost feel that rhythm in my blood as I watch him mix drinks, crush ice, pull draughts. It stirs something inside me that I haven't felt in weeks: a sense of belonging.

"Don't even think about it," Adam warns. "I didn't bring you here so you can wait tables or serve drinks."

No, he brought me here as his plaything. It's as if that memory of Nick's unwanted hands sliding up under my dress has opened a floodgate, bringing back other memories from that long ago night in Vegas.

I remember Adam's smirk when he offered me his room card. It might have taken a whole year, but I took him up on that invitation after all.

I raise my chin in defiance. "I'm free to do whatever I want."

"You don't need to work. Enjoy the break." He leans back, smiling, confident. Smirking.

It's that look that does it for me. "Is that a royal command, Your Serene Highness?"

His eyes narrow, as if he senses that something is shifting between us, but can't figure out what. "I'm not a prince."

"Yet."

A middle-aged couple approach us, shaking hands with Adam, and he switches on that charm which comes to him as easily as breathing. I quietly excuse myself and head behind the bar.

"You look like you need help," I say to István.

His expression is scandalized. "You can't work here!"

"Why not?"

He opens his mouth to answer, then thinks better of it. "Thanks. You know how to mix drinks?"

"Yup."

"Then I need two Aperol spritzes, a G&T and three draught beers."

With my seat across from Adam now empty, more people stop by to talk to him. While I pour drinks, clean glasses and buss tables, I watch out the corner of my eye. It's not Adam I watch as much as the people he's talking to. They approach warily, not sure what to expect, and they leave smiling, charmed.

I send up a quick prayer to any deity who might be out there listening that he realizes what this means to the people of Erdély, that he realizes the impact he can have on all their lives.

It's late afternoon when István's late shift staff arrive – two university students – and Adam and I retrieve our bicycles and head back to the castle through the gathering dusk.

Though on the outside nothing has changed and he seems his usual easygoing, charming self, that evening it's as if he's a million miles away. In all the time I've known him, I've always felt that heated awareness connecting us. Even when we're in a crowded room, or when he was pretending to sleep in the back of Max's SUV on our road trip, I've felt his focus on me. But now it's gone.

"The plane will be at your disposal whenever you want it on Sunday," Lajos says at dinner. "János will have the helicopter standing by to take you to Graz Airport."

A helicopter? Under the table, I pinch myself. Nope, still

awake. I've never been in a helicopter before. Can't say I ever wanted to. That's more Phoenix's style than mine.

"Thank you." Adam sips from his wine glass, looking as if helicopters and private planes are an everyday thing. I suppose for him they are.

"Are you going back to Westerwald, or straight to London?" Lajos asks.

I try not to look as if I'm listening in, and focus on my plate.

"London. Khara has never been before, so I thought I'd show her the sights."

My heart leaps.

"And you'll be back again next week for the funeral?" The slight hitch in Lajos' voice is barely discernible.

I should think of him as His Serene Highness rather than by his first name, but it's impossible when I've seen him playing catch with his dogs and talking nonsense to them. He and Sonja insist there should be no formality with family. As if I'm family.

I press my eyes closed for a second and picture my own family. I didn't think it would be possible, but I miss my mother. I even miss our trailer, and all the little things that make it home.

I miss my stepdad, Isaiah. He's a lot like Lajos, a man of few words, reserved, but with a warm and generous heart.

Most of all I miss my brother. His baby is due next week, and I hope to be home in time for her arrival. Calvin texted me pictures of Aliya's tummy, and she's massive and can't wait for the pregnancy to be over.

That's my real world, I remind myself. Not this.

"Khara?"

I look up, startled, and realize Sonja has been speaking to me. I blush. "My apologies – I was thinking of my family."

"Of course. You must be eager to get home to them. Will you be back here for the funeral too?" She sounds almost hopeful. I have to swallow the lump in my throat before I can speak. "I'm sorry, but I can't. I have to register at college next week."

I sneak a look at Adam when he doesn't say anything. That feeling of distance is back again, even stronger now, and I can't tell what he's thinking.

It's like that first day in Westerwald when he took me sightseeing, and he was smooth and charming and insincere. I've seen enough of the sincere Adam – the one who wears glasses, and reads financial reports in bed before he goes to sleep, who throws his head back when he laughs, and who is grumpy in the mornings before he's had his first cup of coffee – to know when he's not being himself.

The Adam I've fallen in love with, the real self he so rarely shows to anyone, is withdrawing back behind that arrogant, amused façade. I'm losing him.

Our last day in Erdély dawns warm and sunny.

Since my ass no longer hurts after my daily riding lessons, and I no longer walk like a drunken sailor when I get out of bed in the morning, Adam decides I'm ready for the next level: an actual ride beyond the castle's grounds. We head through the forest at a gentle trot, the dogs chasing after us, up to an alpine pasture on the mountain that rises behind the palace.

Apparently it's not really a mountain, just one of the last foothills of the Alps, but I still find it pretty impressive.

We stumble across a wooden ski hut where we stop for a picnic, letting the horses graze in the fenced-in paddock behind the hut. It's like we're the only people in the world, just us and the beautiful, raw, wild, nature of the mountain.

In front of the hut is a table and benches where we spread out the picnic we brought with us, and Adam finds an unopened bottle of local wine inside.

"Doesn't that belong to someone?" I ask, scandalized, when he opens it and fills the glasses from our picnic hamper.

He shakes his head. "These alp huts are public property. Off-piste skiing is a popular winter sport here, where skiers move from hut to hut, kind of like hiking in the snow. Whoever left this here will probably never even remember it, let alone come back for it."

The wine and food and sunshine make me feel lazy, but after lunch we throw sticks for the dogs to fetch, until they're tired out and flop down in the shade of a giant spruce tree. I'm tired out too, but when Adam grabs my hand and suggests a swim, I don't resist. I need to make the most of every moment I have left with him.

We skinny-dip in the freezing cold of a mountain river, lying afterwards in the sun on the grassy river bank. I'm probably going to itch like hell tonight, but I can't bring myself to move away, to shatter this precious moment.

A light breeze wafts down off the mountain and I shiver.

"Cold?" Adam asks, rolling me into his arms to envelop me in his warmth.

I close my eyes and bury my face in his shoulder, breathing in the scent of his skin.

The breeze is a reminder that fall is around the corner, that summer is ending, and with it this fantasy I've been living. Not the fantasy of castles and princes, but the one where Adam and I are a couple. Though we lie skin against skin, his arms around me, so close I can feel his heartbeat, I sense him pulling away, the increasing distance between us. This is the beginning of the end. I've known all along that this was coming, but now that it's here the pain is a physical thing.

It's my own fault. I knew this would happen. I knew I would fall in love with this man who is incapable of loving me back. I am my mother's daughter after all.

"We need to talk." Adam's voice is low and intimate, his breath brushing my cheek. My body stiffens and I force myself to relax. "I want you to spend a few days in London with me before you go home."

"My ticket is booked for tomorrow." Neustadt to London to JFK, last stop Vegas.

"I'll change it."

His offer is so tempting. This doesn't have to end. I can have another few nights with him.

But I can't lie to myself. This last week we've been living in our own little bubble, but the moment we leave Erdély that bubble will pop. What we've had here this week won't survive out there in the real world.

And every extra day I spend with him will be a day spent waiting for that axe to drop, waiting for him to say, "Thanks, that was fun, but it's over now."

How many times have I watched my mother fall in love with men just like Adam, starting with the father I never met, who didn't even stick around long enough to find out if I was a boy or a girl? How many times have I watched her fall apart and put herself back together again when they say, "That was fun, but it's over now"?

I always swore I would never let any man say those words to me, that I would be the one saying them. I know what I have to do. Tomorrow, I'll pull the Band-Aid and I'll say goodbye and walk away, and I will never see Adam again.

He takes my silence as agreement, and I don't set him right. There'll be enough time for that later. For now, I want to enjoy these last moments we have together.

The idle stroke of his fingers down my back turns deliberate. No matter what mood I'm in, his touch has the power to ignite a never-ending high for my senses. My skin trembles where his fingers graze, and I sling my leg over his thigh, bringing our naked bodies even closer together, pressing up against his erection, which springs to life, ever ready.

He groans. "I didn't bring a condom."

This could be the last time we ever make love, the last time I feel him inside me. "I'm on the pill."

"I don't ever do this without protection." His voice is shaky, as if he's trying to convince himself.

Once, just once, I want to feel him skin on skin. I want one moment, one memory, where there are no barriers between us. In the back of my mind I know I'm deceiving myself. Those barriers aren't physical, they're emotional. But just this once I'm willing to lie to myself.

My hand slides down to stroke him, and he nuzzles my neck.

"Don't you dare leave another hickey!"

He laughs softly against my neck, his breath warm on my skin.

We take our time, enjoying the freedom of the fresh air and the sunlight and the chemistry that still sizzles between us. He works my body into a fever of anticipation, until I'm wet with need and can't wait a moment longer. I roll on top of him, taking control, desperate to have him inside me, desperate for that sense of completion I have only ever felt with one man. This man.

A man who is as impossible to hold as quicksilver, like a lightning bolt flashing through my life.

Chapter 26

Adam

My orgasm is so intense, so overwhelmingly powerful, that for a long moment afterwards I can't think, can't move. Khara's weight is warm and comforting on top of me, her breath still shaky from her own climax.

I have never experienced anything like this before. Never felt as if this act was more than mutual desire, more than physical pleasure.

What I feel for this passionate, outspoken, honest woman is something I never thought I could feel. Certainly more than I want to feel. I should end this right here. Walk away before it's too late, before I can't walk away any more.

But I can't. Maybe it's already too late.

I stroke my fingers through her wild hair, brush it back from her cheek. Her eyes flutter open and she looks at me in that way she has, as if she's looking deep inside me, and I pray she can't see what I'm feeling. She cannot know the power she has over me.

It's on the tip of my tongue to ask her to stay. Not just for a few days more, but forever. But then she stirs, moving off me, out of my arms, and my brain clears. Maybe it was just my dick doing the thinking for me. I pull those terrifying thoughts back deep inside, where they belong.

The moment will come when I will let her down, as I've let everyone I love down. That moment is inevitable. Better to do it sooner rather than later, before I can do too much damage. She doesn't deserve to be hurt. And she certainly doesn't deserve a 'douche' like me.

Just another few days. A few days more to drink my fill, to slake this near-constant thirst I have for her. That will have to be enough.

She pushes to her feet, and I follow more slowly. We swim again in the cold mountain water, washing off the sweat of our lovemaking, then dress in silence.

Back at the hut, I whistle for the dogs and they come bounding back, ready to play. Khara perches on the wooden fence to watch as I re-saddle the horses.

"I'm not staying in London with you."

I turn to look at her, unsure I heard her right. "What?"

"Tomorrow, when we get to London, I'll be using my ticket home to the States. This has been fun, but it's time for me to leave."

"But we discussed this—"

"No, we didn't. You told me what you wanted, but you never asked what *I* wanted."

It's as if I've been dunked back into the icy river. My chest is so tight I can't breathe. She doesn't want to stay with me.

The horse fidgets, reminding me to finish tightening the girth. I secure the cinch strap before I turn back to her, my expression and emotions now firmly back under control.

"I thought you wanted to see London." I keep my voice even.

"I do, and maybe one day I will. But I have my own life to get back to. I need to go back where I belong."

"You belong with me." I didn't intend to say that out loud, but now that it's said I'm glad. It's as if a tremendous weight has lifted off my chest. I can't let her go without at least giving this a shot.

She casts me a withering look. "You and I both know that's not true. You live in a castle and I live in a trailer park."

I drop the stirrup back into place and walk towards her. The sun is behind her, in my eyes, and her face is in shadow.

"Why does everything have to be 'us versus them' with you? You're American – why do you even buy into all this class crap? What about the American Dream, and how anyone can achieve anything? It doesn't have to be one or the other. There's always another option." I hear Jemmy's words as I hold Khara's gaze.

I shouldn't do this. I'm going to end up hurting her. But I find myself saying the words out loud anyway. "Stay with me. Please."

I can't read her expression. She's quiet for a long moment, then, "You believe anyone can be or do anything they want, because that's what you do. But you don't get to stand there in your lofty position, with all your white male privilege, your expensive education and your trust fund, and tell me I can have that life. The world isn't made like that, except for people like you. Girls like me don't get to live in fairy tales. We don't live in castles, or go to balls, or drink Champagne at polo matches. And that's okay. I don't need any of that to be happy. And, besides, the people of Erdély deserve better than a crown prince who is shacking up with a cocktail waitress."

"I'm not going to be crown prince. Come live with me in London. My life there isn't a fairy tale, and my flat isn't a castle."

She jumps down off the fence to face me, hands on her hips, eyes narrowed, anger rolling off her. "You can't do that. You can't walk away from your responsibilities."

"I was never going to say yes."

"Then what was this all about?" She waves her arm, indicating the valley before us. "Why even come here and get everyone's hopes up?"

"Because I promised my mother I would consider this offer, and I promised Lajos I would at least visit here. But that's all I ever promised."

She stares hard at me, as if she doesn't believe me.

"And because I thought you might like it, and I wanted to get in your pants." There. I've said it. I'm no better than that jock who did a number on her in high school. "I am not the person everyone wants me to be."

"You are exactly that person. You are the best person to lead this country. You know how to speak to people, how to win them over to your side. You understand the issues they face, and have the ability to fix them. So please explain to me why you won't do this, and don't give me that bullshit about it interfering with your self-indulgent lifestyle. You're bored as all get-out with that lifestyle."

I turn away to check that the picnic hamper is secured

onto my saddle. "We need to get back to the castle. They'll be wondering where we are."

"We are not leaving until you tell me what this is really about."

I release all the breath inside me, still not looking at her. "Because one day I will let them down. I won't be there when they need me, and this time it won't be one life, but many."

"We're not talking about Erdély any more, are we?" Her voice is soft, and I know now she really is seeing inside me, because I can feel her gaze scraping me raw.

I finally look at her. "I was so absorbed in myself that I had no idea what Charlie was going through. He called me that day, wanted to talk, and I blew him off. I don't even remember why. Probably for a party or a woman, or just because there was something else I wanted to do instead. But if I'd talked to him, if I'd listened, maybe I could have stopped him from killing himself." The words tumble out, things I've never told another living soul. "For a long time I blamed everyone else. His parents for their dysfunctional family. Kenzie for being in the house when he shot himself and for not stopping him. But the person I blame most is me. No one knew him better than I did. I knew that, underneath the cheerful face he showed the world, something was eating at him. I should have done something about it, and I didn't."

Khara is right there in my space, wrapping her arms around my waist, filling my cold and emptiness with her warmth. "That was a terrible thing that happened, but it's not your fault. You need to forgive yourself. You can't let that one thing determine who you are for the rest of your life."

"It's not just one thing. There was Nick too."

Her gaze burns into mine, steady, relentless. "Nick made his own choices. His death had nothing to do with you."

"We were both on the same path to self-destruction. I pulled myself out of it, and I should have done the same for him. But I didn't. I was selfish and I cut him out of my life, even though I knew where it would end. I should have been there for him too."

She cups my face with her hands so I can't look away. "You did what you had to do to save yourself. That's not selfish. You are a better person than you think you are. You once told me I should have more faith in myself, but you're the one who needs to have faith in yourself."

I pull away from her. That deep, dark fear I haven't wanted to name rears up and stares me in the face. It's the knowledge that behind the money and the family name, behind the destructive lifestyle, I am not worthy, and I do not deserve to be happy. I am certainly not worthy of a woman like Khara.

This is the reminder I need, the reminder that I have to cut these ties that bind us together before they get any more entangled. I need to set her free so she can be happy. She deserves her dream; that house with the yard and the white picket fence, with a husband and kids who adore her and treat her right. I can't give her any of that. I can't give anyone that.

I unwrap her arms from around me. "When are you going to accept that I'm not the man you think I am?"

Grabbing the horse's reins, I pull myself up into the saddle, leaving her standing, staring up at me. "You've made your position clear, so I guess we're done."

I turn the horse's head, dig in my heels, and head back down the mountain, whistling for the dogs to follow. I should have been a gentleman, should have helped her mount, but if I'd stayed another moment I might have lost the courage to do the right thing and walk away from her.

No matter how I try to make it appear that nothing has changed, Sonja and Lajos sense the tension between us. Dinner is awkward, filled with stilted conversation and long silences.

"We'll be leaving early," I announce. Khara doesn't even look at me.

When we get to our room, we don't say a word. She quietly packs her suitcase and I take a shower. Then, while she is in the bathroom, I pack my own bag and make myself up a bed on the sofa in the sitting room. When she emerges from the bathroom, I pretend to be asleep.

Yes, I'm a coward. I have never pretended to be anything else.

In the morning the maid brings our coffee and pastries and we eat in silence, then I ring for a servant to carry our bags down. The helicopter is already waiting in the meadow below the castle. There are no sheep today.

Lajos and Sonja are at the entrance to say goodbye to us. Khara hugs them both, and I shake Lajos' hand.

"I'll see you next week," he says, his face impassive.

Khara sends me a pointed look. *Tell him now*, that look says. *Don't keep him waiting. Be honest.*

But I can't. Not while I'm still feeling all these mixed-up emotions. I don't know what I might say.

János escorts us to the helicopter to see us off. It feels as if we've come full circle since that Friday morning when he came to summon me to my uncle.

The noise of the helicopter makes it impossible to talk. Arenberg falls away behind us and then we're up and over the mountains, crossing over the border into Austria. Airport officials are ready on the tarmac in Graz to transport us to the plane, and then we're up in the air again, the flight attendant offering us Champagne and snacks. With each mile we draw closer to London, the sense of dread inside me deepens. I drown it out with Champagne. By the time we land, I've finished most of the bottle on my own.

The car I requested is already waiting for us on the runway at Heathrow. While the flight attendant goes to supervise the transfer of our luggage, I turn to Khara. "This is your last chance. Are you sure you don't want to change your mind and stay?"

She shakes her head. "This has already lasted longer than it ever should have. You were never even supposed to know my name."

I have no idea what she means by that. "You were never going to give this a chance, were you? You had your mind made up long before Max and Phoenix tried to bring us together for their little bet. You were prejudiced about me before you even knew me. Who was it who put that chip on your shoulder, because it couldn't just have been some arsehole back in high school."

Her eyes blaze. "No. *You* did. The day we met."

I flash back through everything I said and did when we first met and frown, confused.

"Once upon a time, there was a girl who worked in a casino." Her voice is calm. Too calm. "One of the customers groped her inappropriately, and his cousin stepped in to stop it. She was very grateful, and she thought maybe this other man was different, that maybe he wasn't just another entitled jerk. She thought maybe he was one of the good guys. For about twenty seconds, until he offered her money and his room key card."

"Sounds like a douche." It also sounds like the kind of thing I would have done not so long ago. She looks at me intently, and something finally clicks in my brain. "*I* was that douche." The last time I was in Vegas was a year ago. But ... "I would have remembered you."

That was the night I decided I was done with being Nick's nanny and bailing him out of every scrape, the night I met a sparky waitress who looked at me with such disdain in her eyes that for the first time in my life I was ashamed of who I'd become. I would have remembered that woman.

It's not disdain in her eyes now. It's pain. "I don't think you would. If I'd served you food and drinks in a restaurant in London or Paris or Tahiti, or on board this plane, you still wouldn't have remembered me. You only truly noticed me, not as an easy conquest but as a person, when we were introduced inside a palace."

A slow anger starts to burn beneath my skin. "I am not that shallow. I don't care about class or money."

She shrugs. "Maybe not, but they've made you who you are. How many times have you flashed your smile and crooked your finger and expected everyone to do your bidding? And on the rare occasions when that air of entitlement isn't enough to get you what you want, you simply whip out that black card and buy it."

Her words are like bullets striking me. Because I know she's right.

She raises her chin, as proud as she was that night in Vegas. But the look in her eyes wasn't there the first time we met, of that I'm sure. Because I've put it there.

"But you can't buy me. I am not for sale."

She turns and heads towards the exit, disappearing out of the door and out of my life.

By the time I finally leave the plane and make the short walk to the waiting car, there is no sign of her. There is nothing left of her but the gaping hole where my heart should be. Once again, I've let down someone I love.

Chapter 27

Adam

Nick's funeral takes place in the Church of St József on the main square in Arenberg. The mood in the town is sombre, and everywhere the streets are decorated with black sashes and the flags fly at half mast, but there is no street procession and no crowded pavements as there were in Westerwald when Rik and Max's father died.

The service is conducted in a mix of Erdélian, German and English. The church is surprisingly full, considering how many people Nick pissed off before he died. There are school friends and polo friends, prominent local citizens, even a few of Nick's ex-girlfriends. The entire family is there, aunts and uncles, extended cousins, including those from other royal families, and including Sonja's Danish relatives. Max and Phoenix are here too, though I'm doing my best to avoid them. I don't think I can look Phoenix in the eyes.

But I've made peace with Kenzie, at least. She and Rik aren't here today. Their baby boy was born just a couple of days ago. They're calling him Nicholas Charles. Another Nick. Hopefully with a brighter future ahead of him than his namesakes. I realise now that I took my anger at myself out on her.

I never truly thought she could have done things any differently. It feels good to apologise. But the one person I need to apologise to most of all isn't here. She's on the other side of the world.

Lajos and Sonja sit alone in the front row, in the royal pew. His shoulders slump, and her eyes are glazed. Her calm seems brittle, and I expect she's taken another sedative to get through this ordeal.

My family sit in the row behind Lajos and Sonja. My parents, Jemima, me. Mátyás, with his mother and his new fiancée, a Belgian countess. They announced their engagement only a few days ago and I have no doubt the sudden betrothal was brought on by news of my visit to Erdély. He's hoping to outmanoeuvre me, hoping that if he appears to be settled and stable, with the right kind of wife, then Uncle Lajos will announce him as the heir.

The press conference is scheduled for tomorrow. I still haven't given Lajos my final decision. I believed my decision was made, but I can't seem to bring myself to say the words.

The priest instructs us to stand to pray. I rise with everyone else, but don't hear the words of the prayer. I hear Khara's voice in my head. '*Men like that don't marry women like us. They'll happily screw us, but when they marry they choose women from their own social circle, and they break our hearts …*'

Until I met Khara I assumed I would live and die alone. The thought of marriage never even crossed my mind. But in the week since I watched her walk away I've been thinking about it rather a lot. What would it be like to have a partnership like Max and Phoenix's? Or my parents'? Not a marriage to score points or to be dutiful, but because you simply cannot live without the other person.

I can live without Khara. I can get through the day. I can go to work. I can eat and sleep and breathe. But if I thought my life was empty and meaningless before I met her, it's even more so now. Because now I know what I'm missing. She put a face and a name to my dissatisfaction. I can live without her, because I have to. I've already hurt her enough for one lifetime, and I won't hurt her again.

In the pew in front of us, my uncle reaches out to take his wife's hand. For the first time since I heard the news of Nick's death, tears prick my eyes. They look so small, so alone, just the two of them. Glancing sideways at Jemmy, I see she's noticed too. She brushes the corner of her eye.

Around us, everyone's heads are bowed in prayer. Before I can reconsider, I slip past Jemmy, out of our pew. Her eyes go wide.

I step into the front pew, to stand beside my aunt. Lajos turns to look at me, and smiles.

The prayer ends, the organ starts to play and the priest waves for us all to sit.

I've sealed my fate. By moving to sit in the royal pew, I've announced my decision.

When the ceremony is over I stand beside my aunt and uncle on the church steps while everyone files past. Sonja is too distraught to speak, and Lajos' responses to the well-wishers are perfunctory, so it's left to me to shake hands and thank everyone for coming. My first duty as the new heir.

The royal mausoleum, where Nick's ashes are to be interred, is on the castle property. The procession of cars winds its way out of town and up to the castle, where a buffet has been laid out in the Great Hall. Mindful of the occasion, I avoid being drawn into questions of the succession, but when Yannik and Lena come to take their leave, he grasps my hand. "Thank you," is all he says.

It's good to know I have an ally in the Prime Minister, because I suspect that "shit is about to get real," as Khara would no doubt say. What the hell have I just committed myself to?

Hard as I try, I can't avoid Max and Phoenix forever. But I decide that offence is the best defence. "Did your bet also cover how long we'd last?"

Max looks contrite, but Phoenix is less easy to manipulate. "You're an idiot," she says.

"I think the preferred term is 'douche'."

She doesn't smile. "Do you have any idea how good you and Khara are together? She brings out the best in you."

"She's the one who left."

"And you don't have a passport, or the funds to travel anywhere in the world to go after her?"

"If I cross the ocean for a booty call, I'd only be proving to her yet again how selfish and entitled I am."

"Firstly, it's not a booty call if you're trying to win back the love of your life, and secondly, what have you got to lose?"

"Is she this mean to you too?" I ask Max.

He smiles. "All the time. Why do you think I married her?"

With a sigh, I answer Phoenix. "I am not such a dick that I'll force myself on someone who has already made it abundantly clear she doesn't want me. She has a plan for her life, and it doesn't include me."

She rolls her eyes in a very non-archduchessy way. "That's because she doesn't yet know what she really wants. If you'd been paying any attention, you'd have noticed that you bring out the best in her too. You were supposed to show her that her grand plan sucks. She's settling, when she deserves so much more."

I agree that Khara is capable of so much more than she realises. But I also think she deserves better.

The wake seems interminable, but at last it's only the immediate family left. We retire to the library, where the pre-dinner drinks have been set out. Mátyás is already there, and he's already clearly a drink ahead of us. The ice in his glass rattles as he rounds on me. "How dare you? Did you seriously think you could just force yourself into the succession like that?"

Lajos shuts the door with a snick, preventing our voices from reaching the servants cleaning up in the hall beyond. "I invited him."

Since Mátyás can hardly argue with that, he flings himself over to the drinks cabinet to refill his glass. His mother, dignified as always, her back ramrod-straight and her chin high, does not give up so easily. "I am the oldest. It should be *my* son."

"Our constitution enables me to choose the best successor from among my male relations, and I have done so."

"Mátyás speaks the language."

"And Adam will learn it. As he has already studied our laws and our finances."

"You don't mind him bringing his slapper into this castle?" Mátyás asks.

I'm not sure who moves quicker, Lajos or me. He's no longer a grieving father but the *Fürst* of Erdély, a respected statesman. He pulls himself up to his full height, and even I check when he stops me with a hand on my arm. He speaks calmly and quietly, but his words ring around the room. Or maybe they just ring for me. "Khara Thomas was my guest in this house, and will be accorded the same respect as any other guest. She will always be welcome in my home, whether or not Adam has the sense to bring her back here."

"But she's a *waitress,*" protests Mátyás' mother.

"So what? But if you really can't get past the outdated class divide, then consider this: less than five percent of the citizens of this country have aristocratic blood. The other ninety-five percent of the electorate, the ones with the power to turn this country into a republic if they feel we are obsolete, are people just like Khara. They respect her far more than they respect this family. Right now, I think I do too."

The tension in the air reverberates like a plucked guitar string. Then Jemmy speaks into the fraught silence. "Remember that time when my cat died and I was so devastated, and Nick spent the whole afternoon playing dolls with me so I wouldn't cry?"

My mother giggles. Clearly she remembers. I do too. I remember him playing dolls and then threatening to break my arm if I told anyone at school.

"And remember the time he dressed as Santa's elf to sing carols to us all on Christmas Eve?"

I laugh at the memory. Admittedly, we were both pretty drunk at the time.

The tension dissipates.

Just as Aunt Sonja said, we have a lot of good memories of Nick. Half an hour later, we're still sharing "remember when" stories, and I haven't laughed this hard in a long time. Even Mátyás is laughing, though I know it's going to take a long time before he'll be civil to me again.

My father moves to sit beside me on the couch. "As usual, your mother was right," he says quietly.

I cock a questioning eyebrow at him.

"She told me you were bored in your job and needed a bigger challenge. I have to admit, I didn't think you'd want the responsibility, but I'm very proud of you for stepping up today."

Though we're not a family that hugs, I put my arm around him and squeeze his shoulders. "Thanks, Dad."

"So when do we get to meet this paragon you're seeing?"

"You don't. She broke up with me."

This time it's his eyebrow that rises. "There's a first time for everything. What happened?"

"She thinks I'm arrogant, entitled and self-centred."

"Then don't be that guy."

I laugh. He makes it sound so simple. But later that night, trying to fall asleep in the same bed I shared with Khara, I start to wonder what it would take to change her mind.

Chapter 28

Adam

One month later …

"Will wonders never cease?" Jemmy leans up against the frame of my office door. "It's not even noon yet and you're at your desk."

"Ha ha. I might skive off from work occasionally, but I do actually earn my pay. Speaking of which, I have to leave soon for a meeting with a potential corporate investor and I need to prepare." I make a shooing gesture for her to leave.

Instead, she slips inside and shuts the door. "You'll be fine. You'll just switch on the charm and win them over, like always."

"I'm hurt that you think that's all I'm good for." I bend forward over the printed spreadsheets and reports on my desk, hoping she'll take the hint.

"You look like shit."

"Thanks, sis. I love you too."

"Are you getting any sleep?"

"Enough."

She knows I'm lying, but for once she doesn't call me on it. "As much as I love your newfound dedication to your desk, when do I need to start looking for a replacement for you?"

"And now you're trying to get rid of me. Your sisterly love knows no bounds." I push myself back from my desk to look at her. "As long as I can get to Erdély a couple of times a month for meetings or official events, you're stuck with me a while longer." Eventually, I'll need to move to Arenberg full-time, when Lajos is older and I need to take over more of his duties, but for now he's happy for me to carry on living and working in London. That's already more than Nick did.

"I'm not worried about whether Erdély needs more of your time. I'm worried about *you*. With everything you've got going on, all you do is work. You need to have a life outside of work."

I work because as long as I keep busy I don't have time to think. How is it possible to miss someone so much when you only knew them a few short weeks?

"I never thought I'd see the day you lecture me about working too hard. Since when do you have a life outside this office?"

Jemmy looks smug. "Actually, I have a date tonight."

"Who's the unlucky guy?"

"Your new language tutor."

I groan. "Please don't scare him off. I need him."

"I don't *try* to scare guys off. It's just so hard to find a man who isn't intimidated by a confident, successful trust fund baby. Well, unless they're after the trust fund, of course. Then you can't get rid of them."

"Are you just trying to annoy me, or is there a reason you're preventing me from getting any work done?"

"Mum asked me to speak to you. She was in Westerwald yesterday for a meeting of the ballet trustees, and she had lunch with Phoenix."

"Oh?" I try not to sound too interested.

"Apparently Khara is seeing someone."

The hum of the laptop fan is loud in the sudden silence. I loosen the tie constricting my neck and remind myself to breathe. "I'm happy for her." My mouth is dry. I reach for the half cup of cold coffee on my desk and gulp it down. It tastes awful.

"Liar," Jemmy says.

It's possible to be happy for someone and utterly devastated for yourself at the time, I discover.

Jemmy leans forward. "So are you going after her?"

I assemble the papers in front of me into a neat pile. "You've just told me she's dating someone else."

"Exactly. If you don't hurry, you're going to lose her forever."

It's on the tip of my tongue to say that I've already lost her, but I don't say the words. Is there a chance I could still win her back? And who *is* this guy she's dating – is he good enough for her?

"Was that the whole message from Mum, or was there more?"

"She also said she wants you to come for Sunday lunch, if you can squeeze us into your hectic schedule." Jemmy rises to leave, but pauses with her hand on the doorknob. "I'm proud of you. I think you're finally doing something that truly challenges you, something that's worthwhile. But you're still living a half-life. It still feels as if you're just going through the motions. You need to figure out what makes you feel whole and happy, and you need to go after it. And if that thing is Khara, then you need to do it soon, before it's too late."

For a long while after she leaves, I sit and stare out of the floor-to-ceiling window at the constant motion on the street below.

I can remember very clearly the first time I ever felt truly whole and happy. When I felt a sense of completion I'd never known before. It was that moment in the crowded drawing room of the palace in Neustadt, before the paediatric hospital dinner, when I wrapped my arms around Khara to make Elena go away.

The first time I pulled her close against me, and didn't want to let her go.

Rubbing the back of my neck where yet another tension headache is forming, I rise and gather the papers off my desk. I'm going to be late for the meeting and I haven't read through all the statistics, which means I'm going to have to do what I always do: switch on the charm and hope for the best.

Chapter 29

Khara

I park the car and switch off the engine. Since the doctor's Lexus is parked beside the trailer, he and Mom clearly haven't left for their date yet. They'll be late for their dinner reservation if they don't leave soon, and it's not a reservation they want to miss. Gavin let slip to me that he's booked a table at the Eiffel Tower Restaurant. There's only one reason for a big splurge like that – their dinner proposal package.

I pray that this time Mom doesn't let a good thing go. Not only does Dr Gavin Chen have a solid job and a house in the suburbs, but he's a widower who was married to his late wife for twenty-five years, which suggests he's not her usual love-em-and-leave-em type. He also has two daughters a few years younger than me. I always wanted a sister and if I get lucky I might soon have two. Three if Calvin ever gets around to marrying his baby mama.

But I've bought both Champagne and Ben & Jerry's, so we're covered whatever answer she gives him. Though if she turns him down she'll probably be unemployed again too.

Thank heavens I have a job at least. The construction

company where Isaiah works had an opening, so I finally have a desk job in an office with windows and natural light. I also only see the same three people all day every day. Who knew I'd miss the hustle and variety of the casino floor?

I can't sit out here much longer. I need to put my game face on and go inside or Mom will come out to check on me. I know she's worried about me, but if she asks, "Are you sure you're okay?" one more time, I'm going to scream.

Of course I'm okay. I've got everything I ever wanted. Just a few credits away from graduating, a job with a regular paycheck and benefits, a safe and steady boyfriend. What more could a girl want?

A lot, it turns out.

None of those things feel the way I thought they'd feel. Maybe because I'm not the person I was when I dreamed them. Maybe because, if I'm honest with myself, I'm hopelessly in love with a prince.

I've been having this recurring dream where I'm standing in the church in Arenberg, the one with the frescoed walls. I'm walking down the aisle and I feel so happy it's like I'm floating on air. But when I reach the altar and turn around, I realize the church is empty and I'm all alone. Every time I wake, I feel like I'm missing something vital.

That's completely stupid, isn't it – to feel as if a person can be so vital to you that when they're gone you feel like ... like I feel in that moment after waking?

The way I feel right now.

Suck it up, cupcake. You need to get in there before the ice cream melts.

I open the car door, swing my gym bag off the passenger seat and climb out. But even as I head up the steps to the front door, taking out my door key, I indulge in a moment's fantasy.

Imagine if Prince Charming were real. Imagine if he were waiting inside Mom's double wide for me, drinking beer out of a can instead of Champagne out of vintage crystal. Imagine if a girl like me could get over herself long enough to actually believe in love at first sight, could believe that the tremor she feels when she meets someone's gaze and thinks 'This is it', that it really could be something more than hormones.

I slide my key into the latch and turn it. Then I push the door open and step across the threshold.

And this *is* it. But it's not a tremor. It's a whammy that robs me of breath as our gazes meet.

"You have a visitor," my mother says.

I swallow, pull myself together and step into the living room, slowly shutting the door behind me. "So I see." Not just a mirage, but scrambling up off the polyester-fabric sofa. And there's an honest-to-goodness can of beer on the table beside him. I pinch myself. *Ouch*.

I clear my throat. "Shouldn't the two of you be leaving for your date?"

I glance pointedly at Gavin, who is leaning up against the kitchen counter with a big fat, all-too-knowing grin on his face.

"I think that's a hint for us to leave them alone," Mom says with a laugh. She picks up her purse, and she and Gavin head to the door I just closed. As she passes, impossibly smooth and steady in her two-inch heels, she bends to kiss my cheek. "Listen to what he has to say, okay?"

I nod.

Then they're gone, and we're alone. Though he's still across the room, Adam's presence fills the space, making my pulse flutter in my throat. It's all I can do to stop myself from jumping him, but somehow I manage to hold myself back. Damn hormones!

"Your mom is nice. So she and the doctor are still going strong?" He's making small talk and looks uncomfortable, which is hardly surprising. This trailer park has to be as far from his comfort zone as a palace was for me.

"Congratulations. I read online that your uncle has officially made you crown prince." I move to the kitchenette, unpacking the ice cream and Champagne from among the wet swimming things in my gym bag and stowing them in the freezer. Then I face him, hands on my hips. "What are you doing here?"

"I realized I owe you an apology."

"You could have called. Or texted. Or emailed."

"No. This is the kind of apology that needs to be done in person."

He gets down on his knees on the outdated carpet. "I am so sorry that I didn't recognize you from last year, and that I treated you like you were nothing more than an object for my personal gratification. I like to think I've grown a bit since then. I'm also sorry that I didn't talk to you or consider what you wanted, and that I tried to railroad you into staying with me in London just because it's what I wanted."

As apologies go, that's a pretty good one. "Apology accepted. You can get up now."

"There's more."

I nod for him to continue. My heart is thudding, the rapid pulse making me feel light-headed. This is surreal.

"I thought I had it all, and that I didn't need anyone. But meeting you showed me that I'd closed my heart to what I needed. I'm trying to be a better man, and that's all because of you. No matter what happens, you'll be with me every minute of every day, part of everything I do." He sucks in a breath, holding me trapped in his gaze. "But I'm begging you to please give me another chance."

Wow. Oh wow.

"Um … I'm dating someone." Raúl and I just got back together. Remember what I said about sparks starting fires? Well, things went up in flames for him and the woman he had a whole lot of chemistry with, so, like me, he's decided that safe and steady is better than fireworks.

The man still on his knees in the middle of the living room definitely falls into the fireworks category.

"I'm not asking to date you, or to be your boyfriend. I'm asking to be your husband." He reaches into the pocket of his jeans and pulls out a ring. No fancy box, just a ring.

Against my will, I move closer to take a look. It's a large square-cut diamond set on a double band, with smaller diamond chips inset in the bands. At least, I assume they're real diamonds. I wouldn't know the difference between real and paste.

"What happened to the Adam who said he didn't want to commit to anyone or anything?"

"I discovered that making a commitment isn't the worst thing that can happen. Watching the woman you love walk away from you is the worst thing that can happen."

Love. Whoa. I have to sit down because suddenly the room seems to be spinning around me.

I perch on the edge of the nearest chair and in an instant Adam is in front of me, taking my hands in one of his. "Are you okay?"

"Is this one of those plot twists where it turns out you have to be married to inherit?"

He laughs, though I can tell he's trying hard not to. "No, just a man in his mid-thirties who has fallen in love for the first time, and experienced his first heartbreak. A little late, I know. But I'm a wreck without you."

Oh-kay.

He's back on his knees in front of me, still holding my hand. And still holding the ring out to me in his other hand. "I know I come with baggage, a small nation's worth of baggage, but I hope you'll look at me as a partner, not a prince." He sucks in a nervous breath. "And if me being a prince is something you can't get over, then, much as I'd hate to do it, I'll step down. I'll look like an idiot, and Erdély will hate me, but I'd rather lose the whole country than lose you. Whether we live in Arenberg or London or Vegas, as long as we're together, I know we'll be okay."

"You can't do that! They need you. But I'm just a—"

"You're not 'just' anything. This is the twenty-first century, and ordinary people from all walks of life have married into the royal families of Europe – speech therapists, translators, software engineers, even academics. Waitressing is just as necessary and worthwhile as any of those professions." He grins, a cheeky grin that still has a touch of cockiness to it, but oh, how I love it. "In the interests of full disclosure, if you say 'yes' to being a princess, then I should probably tell you that you'll need to manage your expectations. It isn't anything like movies would have you believe. I plan to keep my flat in London for a good few years, so you won't be living in a castle. You'll be expected to learn the Erdélian dialect and attend charity events. Also, there are none of the trappings other royal families have. Erdély doesn't own any horse-drawn carriages, there's no royal guard in fancy uniforms, and our collection of crown jewels is nowhere near as impressive as Westerwald's."

He sits back, waiting for my answer.

Slowly, very slowly, I let out the breath I've been holding. It's really a no-brainer, isn't it? I've been miserable without him. Just having him here has already made me happier than I've felt any time this past month. I'd rather be completely out of my depth at dinner parties and polo matches than living here without him, and I was a fool to think I could.

I gaze deep into his eyes. "I'm a wreck without you too. I love you, Adam Hatton."

He laughs, but it has a nervous edge to it. "Is that a yes?" Who could have guessed that I'd be able to make that arrogant man I first met here in Vegas a year ago this anxious?

"Yes, I'll marry you. And yes, I'll be your princess."

He slides the ring onto my left hand, then pulls me down off the sofa and into his arms, but my weight topples him over and we collapse onto the floor in a breathless, laughing mess. He tilts my face up to his and kisses me, and there are those blinding fireworks.

Then he wraps me in his arms and I lean my cheek against his shoulder, my hand spread out on those glorious pecs. I'm not a saint – I can do some objectifying too. I close my eyes and breathe him in.

"You smell like chlorine." He pulls away, wrinkling his nose.

"I went to the pool to swim laps after work. After sitting at a desk for eight hours straight, I needed the exercise. I really hate having a desk job."

"Did I mention my apartment building in London has its own indoor swimming pool?"

"Okay, I'm sold!"

He leans over me, brushing my hair back from my face with gentle fingers. "I like the purple streaks."

"Don't get too attached to them, because it might be a different color next month. And in the interests of full disclosure, you should probably know that the family you'll be marrying into is as rainbow-colored as my hair."

"I know. There's this wonderful invention called Google that let me stalk you online every time I wanted to see your face this past month."

I guess that would be creepy if I hadn't done the same thing. I even went so far as to set a Google alert for his name. That's not stalkerish, is it?

He brushes his lips over mine and I shiver at the touch, my body growing needy and desperate for him.

"There's just one more thing," he whispers against my cheek. "We don't need to do the big white wedding if you don't want it. I don't care how or where we marry, as long as we get to say 'I do'. If you want a small and intimate Vegas wedding like Max and Phoenix's, then that's what we'll do."

My eyes go big and round. "How the hell did you ...?"

He places a finger over my lips. "I told you I could keep a secret. But I don't want any secrets with you." His expression falters. "I'm hoping you can handle my sordid past."

It's a question, and I kiss him first before answering. "I don't care about the past. Just our future."

We kiss, rolling around on the floor, hands exploring, tongues tangling, until the phone in the back pocket of my jeans vibrates with a message. I pull it out.

The text is from Gavin. *She said yes*.

And since this is, after all, the kind of fairy tale in which even trailer park Cinderellas can become princesses, I text back. *Me too.*

We marry in the frescoed Church of St József in Arenberg at Christmastime. Thankfully, it's nothing like in my dream. I'm not alone. Isaiah walks me down the aisle, and my entire family is there, including my new sisters. After today, I'll have four of them.

This wedding is nothing like the Vegas wedding I once dreamed of, and nothing like my best friend's big fairy tale wedding, but it's the perfect wedding for me: just the right amount of fanfare and magic for the girl from the trailer park who's about to become a princess. And in this sparkly eighteenth-century tiara I feel every bit like a princess.

The Arenberg school choir sings, and the winter sunshine falls through the high, leaded glass windows. It's a simple, private wedding rather than a public spectacle. No horse-drawn carriages, no soldiers, no cameras inside the church, and I have just one bridesmaid. She walks down the aisle ahead of me, with eyes only for her husband, who waits beside Adam in front of the altar.

My gaze meets his, and once again I'm lost in their gray-green depths. I sigh with happiness, and Isaiah squeezes my arm.

Love isn't a lie. It's real, and it's a whole lot more than a hormone-induced craving. It's finding that one person who brings out the best in you. The person you want to have holding your hand when you take the leap outside your comfort zone. The person you love in the way you want to be loved.

The way I love Adam. The way he loves me.

And yeah, there's chemistry too. Right now I'm looking at the groom and thinking 'I'd like to do him.'

THE END